FIC        Hedrich, Cleda
HED            Threat of a stranger

# Threat of a Stranger

# Threat of a Stranger

## by Cleda Hedrich

NewSouth Books, Inc.
Bonita Springs, Florida

This book is a work of fiction. Names, characters, places, and events are products of the author's imagination or are used fictitiously. Any resemblance to actual events, locations, or persons, living or deceased, is purely coincidental. We assume no responsibility for errors, inaccuracies, omissions, or any inconsistency herein.

First printing 2001
ISBN 0-9671680-0-7

Library of Congress Card Number: 00-112111

ATTENTION CORPORATIONS, UNIVERSITIES, COLLEGES, AND PROFESSIONAL ORGANIZATIONS: Quality discounts are available on bulk purchases of this book for educational purposes. Special books or book excerpts can also be created to fit specific needs. For information, please contact NewSouth Books, Inc., 10911 Bonita Beach Rd., #2073, Bonita Springs, Fl, 34135, ph 941-947-2372.

Printed in Canada

*To my husband, Norm,*
*who taught me love.*

*And my sons, Lee and Brad,*
*who taught me wonder.*

Also by Cleda Hedrich

*A Place to Go Someday*

*Children are the anchors that hold a mother to life.*
—Sophocles, *Phœdra*

# Table of Contents

## Part One

## Part Two

## Part Three

# Part Four

# Part Five

# Part One

# Drum of Silence

## Chapter 1

"Please, Mommy," Chris whined. "We just want to go fishing in the stream." The young boy was as persistent as a bumblebee on purple clover.

Diane lifted a strand of her long curly hair, reddish brown as cinnamon, twirled it with a pointed finger, then dropped the coil to dangle like a ball on a string against her tanned cheek. She searched the freckled face of her five-year-old cherub, his green eyes dancing with excitement, and, despite herself, ruffled his unruly blond hair. "Okay, kid," she said, shaking her head at the indulgence.

"We better go quick," Matthew whispered, flaunting his older-brother wisdom, "before she changes her mind." Matt grabbed Chris' hand and kicked the screened door open.

Diane slipped her slim body through the door before it slammed shut. "Daddy's getting the poles ready."

"Good," Matt called from the porch's shadow. He pushed his sun-bleached bangs back with a brush of his wrist, then knelt to the ground. She smiled at her sons' blue-jeaned buttocks, haunched on the heels of their boots as they dug for worms with their fingers, turning the damp black earth. They packed dirt into an old tin can, as dented and ashen as forsaken pewter. Blood-red worms writhed through the dirt, elastic tentacles flailing like an octopus trapped in coral.

Her husband Mel turned the corner, carrying two fishing poles, which clung together with twisted lines, and a shiny tackle box bought with good intentions, long ago. He knelt beside his sons and began to untangle the lines, then tie on tiny hooks.

"Boys like adventure, to challenge the wild—all that stuff, I guess." Diane tried to make sense of digging in muck for grubby worms.

Mel peered up from his tedious chore, as the sun pierced the trees. He shielded his forehead with a salute, squinting, and looked at her through narrow eyes. "Yes, boys like to fish. Matt's almost eleven now; he'll watch Chris. The stream's only ankle deep and a stone's throw away. They'll be fine."

Diane trusted those moss-green eyes, clear and cloudless as quartz. She still melted at their sight. But, as the only female in the family, she often felt outnumbered. Even their hound-dog was male. "I'll just go part of the way," she muttered defensively.

She followed them down a skinny trail into the woods, tramping behind them through the brush with Hounder underfoot. Matt held a prickly overhanging shoot at bay with his fishing pole, and Chris grumbled under his breath when the errant limb, cocked like a slingshot, slapped his face.

A blackberry branch scratched Diane's bare arm, and she wiped the bloody etch with her palm. "Hey, guys, maybe I'll head back. You're almost there," she called, watching her sons disappear into the brush ahead. As she turned back toward their tiny vacation cabin, dwarfed by tall trees, oak and elm and birch, she tossed a last caution over her shoulder. "Just be careful."

In a few minutes they reached the mountain stream, its shallow water rippling gently over glossy rocks. Matt knelt on the bank and stretched his hand out to test the water. "It's plenty cold. Dad said it should be just right for trout."

Chris pointed to some fallen branches beside a tree trunk, severed by beavers like a pencil in a sharpener. "Some of these are pretty strong. See!" He threw aside his pole and attempted to lift a thick branch, too heavy for his small frame. He crouched down and selected a thinner candidate, which he held at each end and, testing for strength, tried to crack over his thigh.

Matt flung himself to the ground to kneel beside his brother, his feet back with boot-tips buried in the mud. "Hey, you wanna build a bench? We could sit on it to fish." He began to sift through the branches, tossing aside the rotten ones and stacking the strong and straight ones in a neat pile.

"Okay," Chris agreed. "Go ask Daddy for a hammer and some nails."

"No, you. I'll start to put the bench together."

"That's not fair. You always do the fun stuff." Chris ambled over to the stream, pouting, then turned in defiance. "Just because I'm littler."

"All right, calm down," Matt said, exasperated. "I'll go back. Keep out of trouble. Don't go in the water or any-thing." He walked briskly down the trail, as Chris plopped down on a large branch and planted his elbows on his knees, surveying the job to be done. Matt looked back and laughed when the branch rolled backwards, dumping his brother on his backside.

Chris lay there with his legs propped over the branch, feet pointed to the sky. "Don't you laugh," he yelled. He jut-ted out his chin, stretching the baby fat on his neck, and crossed his arms defiantly. "I meant to fall down."

"Right, little brother," Matt called, chasing after Hounder, who flitted off through the brush in pursuit of a chipmunk, scurrying helter-skelter. He stopped to sample a few blackberries, dribbling juice, his lips curling into a pur-ple smile at the sound of his brother, still shouting in the distance.

The cabin porch—shaded by tall trees, cooled by the soft summer breezes, and blessed with the magic music of birds—invited relaxation. Diane lounged, reading, in an old rocker, shaky to its rungs, with her feet propped against the porch railing. When she heard a rustle through the woods, she folded her book into her lap, raising her arms distract-edly, elbows bent and fists clenched in a yawning stretch.

"Wanna come help us, Mom? We're going to build a bench."

"A bench? Why?"

"To sit on to fish," Matt said, holding out his arms, palms up, as if logic had totally escaped her.

"Of course," she said, nodding. "Where's Chris?"

"He's okay. Waiting at the stream."

At first Mel couldn't find the hammer, which was hidden among spider webs behind some discarded lawn chairs at the back of the toolshed. Then he searched for the right nails, picking through an odd assortment in a blue Mason jar.

Diane peered in the shed and scratched her head at his progress. "A building contractor without tools, huh?"

"Hurry, Dad," Matt called from outside the shed. He grabbed a stick off the ground and threw it, watching it spiral end to end down the driveway, then motioned for the dog to retrieve. "Get it, boy." Hounder rushed past his prey and pounced instead on a mound of dirt, rolling over to scratch his back, his ears flopping as he writhed. "Great, Hounder," Matt groaned, kicking up a cloud of dust.

Mel emerged from the toolshed, swinging a machete against the air, and handed Diane the hammer and nails. "Here, you carry these." He hacked at the underbrush as they headed back down the trail. Bright sunlight penetrated the thick foliage in thin brilliant beams. "Nowhere on God's earth is it greener than North Carolina," he said.

"You're right. North Carolina *is* green." Matt often echoed his father, as if training to become a man. "Florida's not so green, is it?"

"No, but it's just as beautiful," Diane said. "Especially the beach."

"Florida *is* beautiful," Matt confirmed with an exaggerated nod.

"And it's home," Mel said.

Matt pranced behind his father, jumping to land in his footprints, taking long leaps in the damp, matted undergrowth. He called ahead, "Hey, Chris, we've got the hammer!"

They reached the clearing by the bank where the fallen branches lay, toy logs for a boy's imagination, still in sorted piles, undisturbed. Diane walked to the shallow stream and, cupping her mouth, shouted for Chris in both directions.

"Where do you want the bench, Matt?" Mel asked.

"I'm not sure. I think here. No, here." Matt paced, frenetic as a divining rod honing in on water. "I don't know."

"Chris!" Diane yelled, her voice strained in a high pitch.

"Chris, come on!" Mel added, even louder. "We don't have all day."

But there was no answer.

Diane left the clearing and rushed toward the stream, lifting her legs like a high-stepping soldier marching over the brush. "Chris, are you hiding?" She walked up and down the stream, searching the water, her eyes beginning to glaze. "Where could he be?"

They walked the trail, looking off the path for a hint of trodden brush or broken branches. Diane opened the foliage with her hands, and the brambles scratched her face and bare arms.

Catching no sight of Chris, they waded the stream, calling out loudly. Mel forged ahead, his boots splashing torrents of water. Diane fought to keep up, her sneakers heavy as they took on water. She felt helpless, floundering blindly, as if in darkness. "It's my fault. I let him go."

"For God's sake, Diane. We'll find him," Mel said.

"The dog will find him," Matt assured them. "Go, Hounder! Go find Chris." Hounder took off, running frantically to and fro.

They traced the embankment hunting for clues—a shirt tatter on a thorny bush or a stray boot print. Diane stumbled over the root of an oak tree, clawing the ground like a falcon's talon. She screamed till her throat was raw, with no answer, no sign of Chris.

Her heart skipped at a scurrying sound in the underbrush. Hounder ran past her to the stream, panting, lapping up water. He scratched a bed in the muddy bank, then circled head to tail, in search of the perfect plop. Finally, he settled his rump into the mud.

"Maybe Chris went home," Matt said, his voice unsteady and his eyes brimming. Mel turned and ran in a fast break to the cabin, now suddenly distant. Matt tried to keep up, but stopped to catch his breath. He flattened his palm against his expanded chest, heaving in rhythm, and bent his head to the ground.

Diane approached Matt from behind and put her hand on his shoulder. She felt his trembling and knelt to hold him, patting his back softly. "Let's go. He's probably at the cabin." She gently grasped Matt's hand and held it behind her, as they walked Indian style, focused on the path ahead, silent.

She broke into a run as they reached the cabin's clearing, calling to Mel. "Did Chris come back?"

Mel walked slowly toward her, his feet dragging as if to delay bad news. "Haven't seen him." He stared down at his hands, weaving his fingers nervously, then looked up to face her. She felt his eyes, like magnets, desperately searching hers, as he spoke.

"He's gone."

The words—*he's gone*—reverberated through her mind like an echo in a deep cavern. Two simple words, spoken softly, bouncing in her head.

She began to comfort herself with all feasible scenarios. Chris could have gone exploring on the other side of the creek. He did wander off sometimes. Maybe he walked up to the road to look for blackberries. Or followed a neighbor's dog home.

"I'll try the neighbors. Stay here in case he shows up." She jumped into their Toyota 4-Runner, hoisting herself up by the grab bar, and tore down the long driveway, a tunnel of tall trees with emerald shadows and lacy edges of wild fern. She rose and fell with the truck as it fought the bumps.

Diane stopped at the nearest home and bolted up the front steps. She knocked on the screened door and glanced with nervous eyes at the rounded hydrangea bushes lining the porch, their huge blossoms of the palest pink and blue, as if covered with pastel dust. Mrs. Clemons, in a red and black flannel shirt, came to the door, wiping her hands on her jeans.

"Oh, Mrs. Clemons, have you seen Chris? We can't find him, and we've looked all along the stream and, well, have you seen him, maybe coming through your yard?" Diane stopped and took a deliberate breath.

Mrs. Clemons propped open the screened door. "No, I haven't seen no child in the woods or on the road."

"Please," Diane begged, "check with other neighbors, especially any children who might be playing in the woods. And do you mind if I use your phone? We don't have one at our cabin. It's only for vacations, you know, and in the mountains my cell phone never comes in. Just roams and roams."

Mrs. Clemons turned, appearing disinterested. Diane stepped into an abandoned living room—dark, with no risk of light through the heavy drawn curtains—and followed her neighbor, tracing her steps across the oak-planked floor to the kitchen. Mrs. Clemons gestured toward a wall phone over the counter, and Diane lifted the receiver with a shaking hand.

"Should I dial 911?" she asked, searching her neighbor's face for guidance.

"Nope. You have to call the sheriff."

"Oh," Diane said, her eyes diverting in disbelief. "Do you know the number?"

Mrs. Clemons opened a cabinet door and produced a skinny telephone book. "Here," she said, as she thumbed the book open and scanned the inside cover with a long forefinger, yellowed by nicotine, tipped with a jagged, untended nail.

Diane fumbled with the phone, punching wrong numbers, glancing back and forth from the dial to the telephone book, apologizing. "Must be nervous, I guess." Mrs. Clemons set some aspirin and a glass of water on the kitchen counter.

Diane listened to the dull and unhurried ringing at the other end of the line. Her heart throbbed loudly, as her chest rose and fell. They'll hear the beat of my heart, she thought, and grasped her breast, as if to quell it. Please answer, just answer. Finally . . . "Sheriff's substation, Collins speaking."

Diane told her story in a calm and deliberate voice, surprising herself. She felt as if she were outside her body, watching herself act in slow motion. Every move, every word, every sound was isolated . . . plodding, remote. She was surrounded by an utter stillness, a heavy hush—a drum of silence pounding her ears.

She drove back to the cabin, slower now, honking her horn and leaning out the window, calling frantically for Chris. He couldn't be far.

The sheriff's deputies arrived in force, mustering the strength of their rural operation. They saw no signs of an accident. The boy's body would be easily detected, if he had drowned in the shallow stream, and they discounted the old well behind the cabin. "That lid is too heavy for three of us men to lift. No chance your son could have," the sheriff said.

They found no early leads to suggest foul play. "No strangers around, I don't reckon?" the sheriff asked Diane, who shook her head. "Well, there're no suspects over the wire, either. No convicts just released, as far as we can tell." Between his lips he wedged a fresh cigarette, which bounced as he spoke. "On the other side of the creek there's a path that leads up-mountain to an access road. Traced it myself, but I didn't see any sign of recent use.

"Ma'am, does your son mess around on the Internet? Think he has a buddy on line who might take advantage of a young child? Sometimes adult male predators present themselves as kids, or even as girls."

"Sheriff, Chris is only five years old. Granted, he plays games on the computer, but—"

"I understand, ma'am, but I've got to ask these things. How about your other son?"

"Yes, Matt's on the Internet all the time. I try to over-see, but I guess he does have E-mail buddies who send instant messages back and forth. He's not supposed to go into chat rooms. And we don't have a computer here, at the cabin. That's only for home. We come up here to get away from the world, not invite it in."

"I'll have to talk to him. Maybe bring him down to the station, if that's all right. I need to know where he's been on the Internet. Might give us some leads."

"I'll come with him."

"Of course." He placed a firm hand on her shoulder. "We'll round up all the volunteers we can, to comb the immediate area. Try not to worry, ma'am. We'll find the lost boy."

Over the next days, the canvassed territory expanded, engulfing more communities and towns and states, running rampant with no trace of Chris to narrow the search.

# Treading Water

## Chapter 2

The days grew into weeks, and weeks into months. Chris became a face on a mail flyer, and Diane burst into tears at the strange, foreign sight of her younger child, only five, all alone, gracing an advertisement for mortgage loans. She hurt to think how many images of her son would be tossed indifferently into the trash. She glanced at family photographs, an array of memories above the fireplace. Chris with tousled hair, kicking a soccerball in the wind. Mel, the boys, and she, posed rigidly for a Christmas portrait, dressed up, slick and shining in holiday clothes. Chris and Matt, arms locked, grinning, a covert brotherly bond exposed in an unguarded moment. Her memory clicked with the shutter. Chris belonged there on the mantel, she thought, poised in a silver frame, surrounded by his family, safe, protected—his face, the face of an angel, smiling out at the world, unfettered, without fear.

So the days passed, and the pain deepened. Cramped and stunned, they treaded water in the tiny cabin for a time. Mel and Diane had bought the mountain retreat as a home-spun refuge, a vacation lair where the telephone, television, VCR were all banned, newspapers taboo . . . where life had a different pace, with time to read, talk, paint, rock on the porch, listen to the rain . . . to play cards, loaf, and smell the fresh mown grass. A place for Matt and Chris to run free in the woods, to dam the trout stream, with the muddy bottom oozing between their toes and the cold current lapping their knees as they piled rock on rock. A place to be together, where they had instead been torn apart.

Now the cabin and the acreage around it, the stream and the overgrown trails, were their closest links to Chris.

Diane hoped to heal there, to cleanse her tender wound at its source. One day she wandered down the trail to the stream and took off her shoes to stand barefoot in the slow current. The sun hit her face through the trees. She heard a small voice, "Mommy," and blinked her eyes at the bank of the stream. In a flash she saw a rustic bench of crooked branches, a small boy sitting there, jeans tucked into his boots, holding a fishing pole over the water, contented, smiling.

She spent many solitary hours, dredging up her guilt, while Mel clocked time between North Carolina and Florida, trying to keep their construction company—and himself—alive by immersing himself in the business. Diane had always worked with him, side by side, till now. She couldn't desert Chris, leave the cabin and lose him again—his smell, the haunt of his ghost at the creek, the memory of his laughter in the woods.

Mel had driven in the afternoon before to spend the weekend, exhausted from the trip, and, she knew, from facing his grief alone. Nevertheless, he went to work on the grounds—trimming and weed-whacking and sickling, cutting logs for firewood, cleaning out the stream—losing himself in work, even at the cabin.

Their bed at the cabin was a foldout sofa, creased from the toss and turns of many sleepers before them. Despite a few errant bedsprings, it was cozy with flannel sheets and three blankets piled high. The cabin's only heat was a Franklin stove and, until the fire was lit, even summer mornings were cold in the mountains.

The coffee smelled rich, its scent bouncing off the knotty pine walls. Matt slept late, in the deep coma of a healthy child who earned his night's peace with hard play in the fresh mountain air. The clock, hidden from view by a colorful skyscraper of jigsaw puzzle boxes, was all but ignored. With the luxury of time, Mel and Diane read in bed, sipping their coffee.

"Mmm, coffee's good," Diane said. She pointed her knees to the ceiling, slanting them for a book rest, and stretched her arms tautly forward. "Remember how Chris was always the first one up and tried to drag the rest of us out of bed?"

"Yeah, we'd beg for a few more minutes' sleep. Now I'd give my life for that bother." Mel stopped abruptly and buried his eyes in his book.

"Little Chris," she said, staring at the fire, as if mesmerized by its erratic embers. "He couldn't wait to get to those woods. He was always ahead of himself, thinking about the next thing to do." Her eyes fell to her book and she slipped a soft afterthought. "It's a shame you didn't get to spend more time with him."

"What do you mean?"

"Well, I have so many moments to treasure. I'm sorry you don't have more."

"I was working." He jerked back the covers, a difficult dramatic move because of the layers of blankets, their folds softening his intended sharpness. "So I could spend more time with him, and you and Matt." He got up and walked a crooked path toward the bathroom, as his inner ear tried to catch up with his feet.

"I worked with you every day. Remember me, your partner?"

"I have plenty of memories of Chris," he mumbled defensively.

She gazed at the fire, which was blazing now, and her eyes reflected the hot flames of yellow and red. She whispered softly, regretting the words as she spoke them. "Sometimes, I wish he'd never been born."

"How can you say that?" Mel grabbed a flannel shirt off the foot of the bed, looking at her in disbelief.

Diane rubbed her eyes, not recognizing her thoughts. "Sometimes I don't think I can take it anymore." She threw words at him, tears flirting with her crusty early-morning eyes. "I'd just like to go away and be by myself. Not see anything that reminds me of Chris. Just to be alone, and only have me to worry about."

"Yeah, I know. Believe me, I know that feeling." He shoved his arms into the flannel shirt, its red plaids crushed in wrinkles, and tore at the sleeves in a peevish attempt to roll them as he walked into the bathroom, slamming the door behind him.

Diane slinked back under the blankets, taking refuge in the darkness. She closed her eyes, ashamed. She was wrong to take it out on Mel, especially now when he was defenseless, emotionally unarmed. Not able to face the day, she drifted into merciful sleep, starved of oxygen by the heavy covers, free floating in the past, where Chris was safe, and their family, whole.

⁓

The cabin's acute memories had sparked angry words, turning the silky morning coarse. Mel and Diane attempted a friendly game of gin rummy, playing the cards by rote in aggressive silence. The cold slap of the cards on the table made Diane sad. She remembered the silly, giggly games of War that she had played with Chris, the frenzied slam of their palms as they fought to land first on a card, and Chris' delight when he won, as he often did.

A country singer whined a pathetic story of unrequited love on the radio, in perfect tune with her low mood. She tried to soften the hard edges of the morning. "This isn't much fun. Let's get some fresh air, maybe walk over to the pine forest."

Mel grunted something under his breath and rose, dragging his feet toward the door. He hesitated beside the hat rack, camouflaged with baseball caps of many colors, and chose a corduroy favorite with a trout emblem above the brim.

He always looks like a model for an outdoors magazine, she thought, perfectly attired to hike or fish, with rugged olive-drab outfits that would fade into a forest. As if to confirm her thought, Mel grabbed his binoculars—the perfect accessory—and circled the leather strap over his head.

"Hold on," she said, admiring his broad back. "I'll leave a note for Matt." She stopped at the counter to jot a few words on a pad.

They walked down the long driveway lined with giant ferns, each frond perfect, shaped like a Christmas tree in a child's drawing. She reached for Mel's hand, but he broke loose and rubbed his shoulder, groaning. "Ahh, my muscles still ache from sickling the tall grass on the road."

"Yeah," she kidded, "you really know how to relax." She didn't try to touch him again, but made light conversation as they walked, rambling on about safe topics—the movie playing in town, Matt's grades, the flop she'd made of a cherry pie last week.

He mumbled an occasional "uh-huh," but held his head down, concentrating on the cadence of his steps.

Neither spoke of Chris.

The pine forest was a garden of trees, planted long ago. These woods had none of a forest's wildness—no gnarly branches flung low or runaway underbrush. Stubborn tree trunks reached high, then burst into forks of fir, giant umbrellas of shade. The woods—dark and serene and safe—felt magical to Diane, who viewed the mammoth trees as great protectors. She often sought their refuge.

Mel and Diane weaved across the straight and perfect rows, touching only inadvertently. Winded, they fell to rest on a cushion of pine needles. Diane leaned back on a rigid arm and tossed her curly hair toward the ground. She regretted the morning, the hurtful words, blurted in anger and impossible to retrieve.

Apologies never came easily to Diane. She tried to warm the coolness between them, to soothe from a distance, and hoped that he would reach out to her and grasp her regret, unspoken. "Mel, I know you have special memories of Chris, of all you shared together."

She toyed with a fallen branch and dug among the pine needles, uncovering the damp mulch beneath. "God knows, you're doing all you can. Since Chris disappeared, you've spent every waking moment sick with guilt. I know it. I feel the same guilt." She threw the branch to the wind. "Why can't you talk about it?"

Mel and Diane generally danced around an argument. He had scarring memories of his parents' fights and refused to join in a verbal battle. Without an opponent, she could only flail in an empty ring. Silence reigned between them, and she watched as a squirrel ran up a tree and, looking about wildly, leapt into a dark hole in the trunk.

Finally he spoke. "Don't, Diane. We'll talk later." He offered a conciliatory hug, and, this time, she withdrew, instinctively jerking her shoulder away. His expression turned hard as stone.

She searched his face, with its hint of wrinkles, the lines dotted, like a puzzle, ready for life to trace. His eyes were gentle and unafraid, but tired, framed in black. "We're both going to go crazy with this," she said.

Ignoring her, he turned his head to the treetops, cocking his ear to a mockingbird. He echoed its staccato chirrup, retreating into a reverie. In duet, the bird warbled and Mel mimicked the melody with near perfection. The woods were still, as if poised to listen, and the sweet music brought peace to the moment.

She stared at him, this strong stranger who spoke with birds, but found human talk more difficult. Her resolve softened. I'm a rollercoaster of emotions, she thought.

She fell backward and cradled her head in her upturned, folded arms, staring at the tall trees that huddled over her, blocking the sun, caressing her with shade. "We'll get through this," she said softly.

And high above, the mockingbird chirped reassurance.

⟋

It was not the isolation, but the ache of memory that pushed them to rent an old farmhouse close by. Diane had admired it often for the serenity of its setting in a pastured valley, the home symmetrically shaded by two tall spreading oaks hovering protectively, like two parents holding the hands of their small child in a crowd of tall strangers. The home's clapboards were washed white, splotched by the strokes of a careless painter, the walls punctuated by dark shutters, green as grass, and pristine windows with white mullions. Half-wrapped by a one-story open porch with thin round posts, delicately carved, the old farmhouse had three bedrooms upstairs, with privacy for Matt and a bedroom fitted for Chris. His stuffed animal friends, shipped from Florida—a weary tiger, his beaded eyes chipped away, a huge St. Bernard with floppy ears, and a worn and tattered brown teddybear with a stitched smile—were poised on his bed to greet him when he came home.

Matt had spurted up and lost the pudginess around his middle. His frame was thick-boned, and Mel said he was going to be a big man. "Hunky, like you, I hope," she had teased.

Once transplanted to the North Carolina mountains, Matt began to speak in a strange new accent, drawling like the kids he met at Blue Ridge, a small middle school named for the nearby mountain range. He did well there, scholastically, as he had done in Florida, always the smartest kid in the class. He made new friends and particularly liked Kat, a neighborhood girl that he and Chris had played with on summer vacations at the cabin. Kat seemed to understand how rotten Matt felt about losing his brother, and she made him laugh. Diane relished the days Kat came to visit, when, somehow, a light shone through the ubiquitous dreariness that surrounded her.

But she worried that Matt spent too much time alone, that he felt vulnerable, unprotected. After all, he knew firsthand that a child could be snatched from his family, spirited away without a trace, without a warning. One evening she knocked on his door and offered to help him clean his room, hoping to share her concern. She always watched for an opening, a crack in his early adolescent armor, a time to strike a balance between his need for independence and her need to be heard.

Matt was pawing his chest of drawers for a sock, and, in frustration, he yanked the drawer, pulling it out too far, crashing it to the floor. Everything spilled out—soccer shorts and Dungeon and Dragon figures and coins and matted tee shirts, letters from his best friend in Florida, and rocks from his collection.

"Life's like that, isn't it, Mom?" he said softly. "One day, everything's going along okay, and then everything's jumbled upside down. You really didn't do anything. It just turned upside down, all by itself."

"Of course, you didn't do anything. That drawer had a mind of its own." She gestured to Matt, to sit with her on the side of the bed. She locked her eyes into his, hazel jewels inherited from his father, moist now with tears. She had not noticed that his pug nose no longer dotted the center of his face, which must have lengthened.

She reached out to hold him, but he brushed her aside and directed his red eyes toward the bathroom. "Gotta go."

She slumped to the floor, settling on her knees, and began to pick up the mess. Her tears fell, spotting the rocks and figures like early rainfall, hinting at the downpour to follow. Her shoulders rose, unrestrained, as she sniffled, then wiped her eyes with the palm of her hand. She didn't hear Matt slip up behind her.

"Mom, don't cry. I know how you feel."

She turned and hugged him, ever so gently, fighting her desire to squeeze him tightly until he felt safe, to prove that she could protect him. "I'd never let anything happen to you."

He pulled away, but held tightly to her arms. His eyes pierced hers, and a tear began to meander down his round cheek, which was pale now, with no touch of the Florida sun. "I know I shouldn't have left Chris. I know it's my fault."

"No, Matt, it's not your fault. You had no control over what happened to Chris. I know you'd never hurt your brother. And you know that, too."

"But I left him alone, and I shouldn't have."

"You only left him for a few minutes. He should have been fine."

"But what if some weirdo came along?"

"You're not responsible for the actions of a weirdo. Besides, we don't know what happened to Chris. You're feeling the same thing that Dad and I face every day. We blame ourselves. We all feel guilty, and we'll never heal until we deal with it."

Matt lowered his head and stared at the floor. "But what can we do to feel better?"

"You can talk to the doctor again, whenever you feel you want to. And we have to help each other. Chris wouldn't want us to be mad at ourselves." She raised his chin with the cup of her palm and looked him squarely in the eyes. "Matt, you're my life now. Our family survives because of you. I have a strong feeling—I can't really explain it—but I just know that you will play again with Chris someday."

"I think so, too," Matt said, nodding, his eyes following his thoughts around the room. "He'll like it here. I'll show him the great hiding places in our yard. We can make some radical BMX trails, maybe play some football."

"We'll get through this, son. We won't stop looking till we've found Chris. Trust me."

Matt put his hands on her shoulders and patted them, as if he, suddenly, were the adult, she the child. "Thanks, Mom. I feel better." He glanced abruptly at the ceiling. "Now," he said, grinning, "would you leave me alone? A guy needs a little privacy."

Diane walked to the door, burdened with Matt's pain. He, too, blamed himself for Chris' disappearance. Guilt is an insidious infection, she thought, and it's running through this family like an epidemic. "Well, good night," she said, shutting the door softly as her tears broke loose again.

# *Swan Song*

## Chapter 3

Detective Steve Williams raked arthritic fingers through his shock of shaggy hair, with unruly strands turned coarse from graying. Diane must not be home, he thought, after a few rings, and he mentally prepared a message for her answering machine. But then she answered.

"Hello, Rath residence."

"You sound breathless."

"Hi, Steve," Diane said with instant recognition. "Yes, I was just coming in and ran to catch the phone. Any news?"

"Nothing really to report—"

"Oh." Diane's voice fell an octave.

"Like always, I'm afraid, but I want to talk to you."

"Shoot."

"In person. I'm heading down your way tomorrow and wondered if we could get together."

"Want to come by the house? I'll make an apple crisp and give you some decent coffee—better than that diner stuff you guys drink."

"How do you know about the diner?"

"You're a cop, aren't you?"

"Okay, smartie. See you tomorrow morning, around ten."

Williams hung up the phone, smiling. Somehow Diane always made him smile. He admired her resilience, how she was able to pick threads of joy from a life entangled by disappointment. Maybe she faked it. That was probably it.

Detective Steve Williams was nearing the end of a frustrating career. For years he had been on the fly, pursuing a long line of elusive lowlifes, who always seemed to stay a step ahead. Although known to be a birddog, who refused to give up the scent of a suspect, once he'd sniffed it, somewhere along the way Williams had lost the thrill of the hunt. His eyes were steely, callused by defeat.

He fit the detective stereotype perfectly, with his burly build and pockmarked face. His physique was impressive for a sixty-year-old guy, tough enough to turn the heads of the creeps he pursued, although he was always popping a pill for one arthritic ache or another. His voice was gruff, but could give him away. It was gravelly yet gentle, like the touch of a grandfather's hands.

Detective Williams, as head of the missing persons division in Asheville, North Carolina, had been assigned Chris' case. He took an aggressive investigative approach, true to his compulsive nature, and put his experience to task, following up every lead, cross-filing kidnapping crimes as to date, location, age of child, suspect description, and *modus operandi*. He compiled notes with prodigious detail.

As the months passed, Diane's disappointment became his disappointment. He became obsessed with the search for Chris. I want this case to be my swan song, he told himself—the payoff for a long, plodding career. All those years, and so little to be proud of.

I'll apprehend the bastard who took young Chris, if I have to chase him in a wheelchair. I want this story to tell my grandchildren. They'll be spellbound, sitting on the floor by the sofa, looking up to me as I spin the web of pretty Diane, earnest Diane, distraught, destroyed by the loss of her son. I'll be the hero. I'll seek out the evil abductor and reunite the broken family.

He shook his head sadly. My children never understood my work, why I stayed away from home. I missed too many ballgames, too many recitals. But it's not too late to make the grandchildren proud.

He kept Diane informed of the latest news, or, more often, lack of news. Once the police unearthed the bodies of fourteen children in the backyard of a convicted kidnapper, a heinous child abuser, and she suffered as the autopsies were released, one by one. In South Carolina a young barren woman was apprehended in the company of three unidentified children, but Chris was not among them. Lead after lead stretched farther into darkness, cracking the door to hope, only to slam shut, time after time, in despair.

Detective Williams had been to the farmhouse before. Sometimes he would follow a lead down from Asheville, and he always called on Diane, never sure if he stopped by for her benefit or his own.

Diane answered the door at the first knock and reached to shake his hand. "Come in," she said casually and led him down a long hall, then detoured to the kitchen. She paused at the table to adjust the combs in her hair, intertwined among the curls.

"Okay," he said, pulling back a chair, "time to produce that coffee you were bragging about."

"Coming right up," she said, grinning, and quickly poured two cups.

The table was set with cream and sugar, and Williams loaded his coffee with two heaping teaspoonfuls of sugar. "This coffee might not need doctoring, like that off-brand stuff you're used to," Diane said.

He ignored her, pouring in a healthy dose of cream. "Guess you're wondering what's up."

"As usual, you're a master of understatement." Her eyes dug into his, searching for the meaning of his visit.

Williams concentrated on his cup, stirring his coffee, then looked up at Diane. Her face intrigued him. Long brown brows gently arched her luminous gray-green eyes, which always darted about, as if searching for a hidden truth. They seemed to sparkle with surplus moisture, to be brimming over with eyedrops, or perhaps tears. Her nose had a graceful slope, but extended farther than it should, then crimped with a perky tilt at the end. She had generous lips—too large for her triangular face—that could stretch into a greedy, contagious smile or fall into the most sullen pout. Her skin, seemingly indifferent to the sun, was porcelain, and her reddish hair curled out of control. Yes, Diane had a face that invited you in.

But he knew that it was time to set her free. He feared that, if he continued to douse her hope, he might also douse her spirit. And he could not bear to disappoint her any longer.

"You know, Diane, there's really no reason for you to stay in North Carolina. Our search mechanisms are set in motion, and we're going to carry on until we find Chris, whether you're here or in Florida. So much of my work, now, is over the Internet, communicating with detectives across the country. We've got the advantage over the criminals, and those bastards who snatch children are going down. Don't you worry about that."

His lips curved into a smile, but his sad eyes refused to join in. "Your life has been on hold too long. Mel needs you, and Matt, most of all."

Diane brushed a few rebellious curls off her face and squinted her eyes, as if to block out his words. Slowly, she nodded. "You're right, I guess, but I feel close to Chris here. I don't want to leave him."

Williams touched her cheek, his knobby thumb rough against her delicate skin. "We're going to find Chris. Leave that to us. You go on with your life."

A tear touched his knuckle, and then another. Diane seldom broke down, but he could feel it coming. And he knew he couldn't bear it. "Guess I better get out of here," he said, withdrawing his hand.

Diane wiped her eyes, rising. "Trying to escape, huh? You always were a softie."

He scratched at a thick mat of hair, sprouting below the hairline on the back of his neck. Poor Diane, he thought. I've thrown disappointment after disappointment her way. She's resilient all right, always bouncing back. But she must be getting tired by now, like I am. "Guess I might as well admit it. I do have a soft spot when it comes to you. And I'm going to find that boy of yours."

He stood up and hugged her quickly, then held her shoulders away from him, capturing her eyes. "You remember how we talked in the beginning, about ways to cope— one step after another. You need to go home. It's the next step."

"I suppose it makes sense," she mumbled. "You'll keep in touch, won't you?"

"You can call me anytime, day or night. Believe me, we'll find Chris. And he'll come home to you in Florida."

"Somehow, I do believe you," she said, fighting back tears.

"Uh oh, you're starting to gush again. I'm out of here." He turned for the door with heavy feet, reluctant, sad to release Diane, to admit his failure. His mission to restore this woman's family was a powerful motivation. It elevated his crummy job to noble purpose. He lifted his shoulders with determination and quickened his steps, his limbs suddenly youthful.

Diane glanced around the circle of faces, rapt in attention—a support group for parents who had lost a child, whether through death, legal cause, or, in her singular case, abduction. They sat in a Sunday school room on children's straight-back chairs, their adult legs sprawled out, awkward as Gulliver in Lilliput.

"I'm the only one who is not allowed to grieve," Diane protested. "You tell me I'm lucky, that I can have hope, unlike you whose children have died. You're right, of course, but you don't know the emptiness, the fears I have that Chris may be bruised and beaten in the hands of his abductor, or buried under a forgotten tree. It's not knowing that hurts the worst."

Jack, a hefty policeman in his thirties, ran his hand across the top of his buzz haircut. "We know, Diane. But you've done everything in your power. Try not to beat yourself up."

"That's right," Agnes, the group leader, agreed, tucking her skirt neatly behind her knees. She cocked her head, and the loose skin of her chin flapped in protest. "You've gone to extraordinary lengths to recover Chris, everything we recommended." She held up the fingers of her left hand, marking them off with her right forefinger, in order, as she spoke, until she exhausted her supply of fingers. "You've launched a publicity campaign, and we've mailed out thousands of posters with Chris' photograph, descriptions of his habits. You've listed Chris on the Internet on the Missing Children Gallery, registered with the Polly Klaas Foundation. You check the state clearinghouse information centers and search the child abduction recovery sites daily, or should I say, by the hour. You even have your own website. You've called on women's clubs and service organizations, written them nationwide—"

Jack broke in, "I've pushed Chris' disappearance at the precinct, and you've got your own detective assigned to the case. Really, you've done all you can."

"I know, and I want to thank you all for your help with the correspondence—four hundred letters just last week. Especially you, Jack. I know that you have it tough, fighting your wife in the courts, just for the right to see your own baby. And, as a policeman, you've given me a perspective that I wouldn't otherwise have."

Jack winked in Diane's direction. "Well, princess, I've got some news tonight. There's word in the ranks about a child-abduction scam, about children who are being stolen, right here in the South, to sell as adoptees. Of course, they're mostly babies, but you never know. Could lead to something."

"I suppose I can pray that Chris' abductor sold him for adoption." Diane bounced a clenched fist on her thigh in defiance. "Then, at least, there's a chance that he's alive." Her fist fell to her lap, unfolding limply as she took a deep breath. "I just feel so helpless; guess I'm still in shock. I grasp for anything familiar, something routine that I can control. Just making lunch for Matt is soothing. I know he likes his peanut butter crunchy, spread thin, that he wants tart lemonade, not milk, in his thermos, prefers a pear to an apple. I can handle that."

"How about your husband?" asked Judith, whose husband and only child had drowned in a freak whitewater accident, only a few weeks before. "You two should be supporting each other."

"We can't walk in Diane's shoes, or her husband's," Agnes interrupted, heading off the attack. "I know you're feeling alone, Judith, but we are here to help each other, to share our experiences, not to judge or criticize."

"It's okay, Agnes," Diane said, as she turned toward Judith. "God, Mel's no help. He keeps his blinders on and holds his hurt inside. I've tried to get him to join the group."

"You know that each parent needs to find his own way, his own time," Jack reminded her.

"I know I shouldn't pressure Mel, but I get lonely. I don't recognize my family. My son speaks in this foreign tongue—Southern, I think you call it." The group members chuckled. Diane's lips curled with her rare attempt at humor, and her face tossed aside its usual veil of mourning.

"You have a pretty smile," Jack said. "You should use it more often."

Diane blushed at the compliment, although unable to comprehend it. She stared at Jack with glazed, vacant eyes, deep in their sockets. "Matt feels guilty about Chris, and I make things worse, putting all my hope in him, expecting too much. The other night I actually told him that our family survival depends on him. Such crap. Such a heavy load for a young boy."

"But, Diane," Agnes protested, "Matt has talked with a psychologist a few times. He's adjusting all right, isn't he?"

"Miraculously. No thanks to me. God must be working His therapy on Matt."

"You're a good mother to Matt," Agnes said, "just as you were to Chris."

Diane's voice broke as she looked bravely around the circle, her moist eyes holding each member captive for a fleeting moment. "I thank each of you for your words of comfort. You have kept me alive this last year. But I've decided to follow the advice of Detective Williams—remember, the officer assigned to Chris' case. He says there's nothing more I can do here, that I'd be better off to go back to Florida and carry on with my life. He says that if . . . uh, when . . . Chris is found, he can join us there. At home in Florida.

"I suppose he's right. It's time for me to go back to work, to help Mel. The company's booming, despite my absence. Guess it's just the runaway growth in Southwest

Florida. Judith is right. Mel needs me, too, to be his wife. We need to heal together, with Matt, as a family." Diane paused, glancing down at her fidgeting fingers. "But I feel that I'm deserting Chris. Like I'm just leaving him behind." She shushed herself, bouncing a pointed index finger to her lips.

Diane fought back tears, but one determined escapee rolled slowly, sadly, down her cheek. The group surrounded her, embracing her in turn, and, as they touched, she felt alone.

# Threat of a Stranger

## Chapter 4

As promised, Detective Williams kept the search for Chris alive. He listed his office for updates on kidnappings and for all releases on abandoned or abused children. On a daily basis, by rote, he checked the new information and studiously cross-referenced it, as routinely as he opened the mail or drank his morning coffee. The search stayed fresh in his mind and in his dreams, and he was ever alert for the breaking clue that would crack the case and consummate his career. He could scarcely imagine retiring otherwise, with the bitter taste of failure forever in his throat.

One day, three years after Diane had returned to Florida, a strange bulletin came in from a small Georgia town, Peaceton, just south of Macon. They had received a 911 call from an unidentified person, a young voice—muffled, the report said, as if the caller held his hand over the phone to cover the sound or disguise his voice. The caller appeared to ask for help, but did not give his location. Williams knew it was a stab in the dark, but, numb to the odds, he dialed the contact number.

"Peaceton Substation, Miller speaking."

"I'm Detective Williams, out of the missing persons division in Asheville."

"Better let you talk to the sarge."

Williams heard the phone bang down, quick steps, then a long pause, and heavier steps returning. "Yeah?" The sergeant spoke with a thick Southern accent.

"Oh, hello, sergeant. This is Detective Williams, from Asheville missing persons. Heard about your 911 call."

"God, don't you have 'nuff folks to hunt up there? Now, you gotta come search our territory."

Guess the sergeant's not too practiced in the highly touted social graces of the South, Williams thought, ignoring the remark. "Got anything yet?"

"Nope."

"What'd the caller say?"

"Not much; spoke a coupl'a seconds. Said, 'I'm here . . . by the water.' Then the phone clicked, just that."

"What do you make of it? Think it's a lost child, runaway kid? Or just a hoax? Maybe someone on drugs?"

"Got no clue."

"Boy or girl, could you tell?"

"Hard to say. Young high-pitched voice, and all."

Maybe this guy just isn't big on sharing. Williams decided to try a different tack, to ask only for facts rather than opinion. "When was the call made?"

"Only about an hour ago."

"Do you have Caller I.D.?"

"Nope."

"Don't guess you were able to put a trace on it."

"Afraid not."

"No leads?"

"Nah."

"Well, are you guys going to pursue this? Or just let it drop."

"Don't reckon we'll be able to lose it, with the likes of you. Am I right?"

Damn straight, Williams thought. "Well, I might just head down to see if I can help."

"Great," the sergeant said, his voice oozing sarcasm. "See ya."

"You can count on it." Williams slammed down the phone. That aloof bastard doesn't belong in law enforcement, he mumbled to himself.

Williams made a quick call home, leaving a message that he'd be gone for the night. No reason to explain, he thought. The family didn't care where he was going—only that he was gone. He picked up a small overnight bag that he kept packed in his office, for just such occasions, and walked to a parking lot of undercover police vehicles. He selected a beat-up Ford pickup that would blend into the small-town milieu, registered the truck at the gate, and began the drive to middle Georgia, silent with his thoughts.

It was almost dinnertime when he passed a sign in the middle of nowhere—*Peaceton, Population 1,720*. Choosing a motel was a small decision, with only two in town. The Sun Motel was on Main Street, where Williams could watch the primary traffic, sparse as it was. After settling in, he changed to a solid black tee shirt, which he tucked into faded Levi's. He tightened his belt around a stomach growling for attention, then stood at the window, gazing at another Southern town, the latest installment in the long search for Chris.

Main Street was dusty with age. An antique shop spilled out of an old warehouse, lining the sleepy street with chipped dishes and cast-iron pots, silver saws and wrenches, broken chairs with legs askew. A paralyzed plow rested beside an enamel stovetop with round cavities, the burners missing like gouged-out eyes. A mansion on the square, with white columns turned gray, appeared to have lost its dignity. A sign—*Philip Proctor, Esquire, Attorney at Law*—marked its lawn of dandelions. The town's best scrubbed building was the library, its imposing marble facade a tribute to Southern culture. The town depot, with streaks of peeling paint, resembled a child's train set prop, once loved but abandoned for newer toys.

"Looks like the end of the line," Williams thought, with a trace of a grin. He strapped on his shoulder holster, shoved his arms into a lightweight denim jacket, and headed for the door, coattail flapping.

He walked briskly the few blocks to the police station, entering the old building from a side door off the rear alley. He wound his way down a maze of halls to the front entry and held up his identification for the young officer at the desk. "I'd like to see the sergeant."

The officer—Deputy Miller, his badge read—hesitated. "Well, the sarge, now he's awful busy."

Williams leaned his muscled forearm on the counter. "Why don't I just go see for myself."

"Well, I'll check," Miller relented. He disappeared behind a partitioned cage, and Williams overheard whispering, which grew louder into a disgruntled reply. "Not another one."

When the sergeant curtly rounded the doorway, Williams beat him to the punch. "Yep, another smart-ass detective here to pick your brain."

The sergeant shook his head helplessly. "You got that right, but long as you're here," he said gesturing for Williams to follow him to his office, "want some coffee?" He called to Miller, who clicked his heels and returned with small steaming Styrofoam cups, a straw basket of sugar and sweetener packets, and a can of evaporated milk with punctured holes of crusty yellow. A veneer of paper covered the sergeant's desk, and Williams pushed aside a stack to set down his cup. On a side table, thick files with hand-written labels were in disarray, like magazines at a garage sale. Williams small-talked while the sergeant scanned a pile of mail and avoided looking in his direction.

"Sarge, I appreciate your cooperation, especially this fresh-brewed coffee."

"That's kind of you, detective, but I'm afraid not much is go'wing on."

Williams rubbed the stubble of unattended whiskers on his cheek. Despite his rugged tough-guy exterior, which appeared altogether unkempt and disagreeable, he could convey a certain charm when pressed, and he wasn't above groveling. "I've been after a certain child abductor a long time, without any luck—kidnapped a five-year-old boy in North Carolina—and I could really use your expertise. I heard about the 911 call, and I was just wondering, was there anything unusual about it?"

"One thang did stick out," the sergeant said, nodding. "When the 911 call came in, the operator answered—that's our Miss M'linda—and the caller was silent, quiet as a shy mouse, for a few seconds. That's not too usual."

"How so?"

"Well, usually the caller's champin' at the bit, can't wait to blurt out the emergency. This'un was slow to start, spoke real softlike, calm, and then didn't really have much to say, not who he was, or where. Definitely a kid though, early teens—thirteen, fourteen, I'd reckon."

Williams glanced around the room, as if looking for a translator to render the sergeant's thick accent into recognizable English. "Before you said you weren't sure it was a boy. With young voices, sometimes it's hard to tell."

"Yep, pretty darn sure it was a boy."

"Not my boy, though, unless you're wrong about the age. Can we play the tape?"

The sergeant bellowed again for Miller, who appeared in seconds. "Brang that blasted tape in, would you, son?" Miller belted for the door, like a wind-up doll freshly wound. He came back quickly, his feet sliding to a halt, and set the tape recorder on the table. He wiped his fingers across the top, checking for dust, and positioned the control buttons to face the sergeant.

Anything to please the boss, Williams thought.

The sergeant fumbled with the buttons, then ordered his underling to set the tape. "Can't you get this thang going, son?"

"Yes, sir," Miller obliged.

The room was silent except for the high screech of the scrolling tape. Miller tested several segments, breaking into routine 911 calls. A female operator (Miss M'linda, Williams thought) indifferently advised a hysterical woman to "call an exterminator, honey; 911 doesn't do snakes," then chastised some kid on summer vacation with nothing but mischief to fill his time. "I recognize your voice, Billy Thurman, and you're going to be in big trouble if you hold up my line. Wait till I tell your parents . . ."

"It's coming up next," Miller cued his audience. "Listen now."

*911 . . . Hello, this is 911.*

No reply.

*Yes, go ahead.*

A four- to five-second pause, followed by a soft, muffled,

*I'm here . . .*

Another pause, three more seconds or so, then a halting finish,

*. . . by the water.*

"Almost sounds foreign," Williams commented. "No, not foreign—stilted, like he's reciting, not just talking. No sound of anyone grabbing the phone or interfering, is there? Let's listen again for any noise before the click."

After Miller eagerly replayed the segment, the sergeant reflected the question. "Don't hear it m'self. You?"

"Nope," Williams agreed. "You say you don't have Caller I.D.?"

The sergeant shook his head, wobbling his cheeks.

"And no trace on the call?"

"M'linda didn't think of it."

Williams nodded, not surprised. "We should be able to get the phone records."

"Phone company's working on it now. They show the incoming call from an old number, disconnected years ago. Either their records are all screwed up, or someone tapped in illegally."

"Well, then, can we get this tape cleaned up? Got anyone who can do that, for background noise?"

"We can send it to Atlanta; be back by t'morrow."

"Good," Williams said with a determined nod and then, forgetting his place, began to bark orders. "I need to know all about Peaceton. Give me reports of recent arrests. Have there been any juvenile offenders? Child abusers?"

"Not so fast," the sergeant said, rolling his eyes as if he'd just taken another child to raise. "You can't just walk in and call the shots."

Williams had cast himself as director, his accustomed role, and his charm began to flake away. "Why not? You may have a missing kid here."

"'Cuss it ain't your station."

Williams slowed down, reaching deep. He was stepping on egos here, he told himself. Better just tiptoe around.

"I don't mean to impose, sarge, but I can't do this without your help. I'm sure you realize that any acts of domestic violence in town could hold a clue. I would like to see your arrest reports for the last few months. Maybe there have been problems at school, kids acting up. Maybe you have a new family in town, behaving kinda strange, or some reclusive or standoffish folks outside town, in a remote area."

The sergeant puckered his mouth and crossed his hairy arms in a most uncooperative stance, stiff as a statue. Williams ignored him and cast his eyes, instead, at Miller, who was still fresh at the game, more anxious to please. "I didn't see a river coming in, but maybe there is one, or even a creek. I want you to ride me to every body of water in these parts—lakes, streams, anything bigger than a bathtub. I need to see it all. Maybe this is just a prank; maybe it's not."

The search was short. The next day Miller took Williams on a systematic survey of the county's water spots, finding nothing unusual at Otter's Creek or the small cove of Lake Larson that touched the county line. "There's a dried-up branch off the Ocmulgee River, about fifteen miles out," he remembered, and headed in that direction.

The riverbank was overgrown, green with the fresh wrap of spring, and the forgotten river branch had become a muddy marsh, dank with standing water. As they walked along the bank, Williams spotted a path and pointed toward it.

"Oh, yeah," Miller remembered, "there's an old abandoned house in the woods. I should have thought of it."

The path led them to a swath through the brush, a clay driveway, compacted from recent use. The house at the end was broken down, with a roof in obvious need of repair and a couple of cracked windows, but it hardly looked abandoned. A few rose bushes beside the front stoop had been recently tended, girthed with a mound of dirt, and a lone rocking chair stood sentry on the screened porch. The house overlooked a lake of stagnant water, where the defeated river found rest. Pine needles flecked the surface, trapped in a blanket of crusty scum.

"Jesus," Miller said, "can't believe I forgot this place." He crouched and drew his gun.

"Son, I hardly think . . ." Williams said, staring at the kid in disbelief, then added,  ". . . whatever. Check around back."

Birds were everywhere, darting and twittering in the trees. A pair of cardinals flitted by, in a flirtatious pattern as if tied together by an invisible string, tugging, the flaming-red male taking the lead and then the female, flying ahead, her brownish red a humble reflection of her mate's brilliance. Miller returned, shaking his head. "Nothing. Back door's locked."

Williams climbed the front stoop and cringed at the groan of the screened door as he opened it. Miller flattened his back against the wall, peering through the front window.

"See anything?"

"Naw."

Williams stood to the side of the door and rapped, waited, then rapped again, louder. The house was silent.

"Guess we'll go in." He grasped the doorknob, stopping in his tracks. "Wait a minute. What's this?" A key protruded from the lock, inviting them in. Williams turned it easily.

The living room was orderly, sparsely furnished with bare essentials, like a motel room. A sofa and one armchair lined up facing a television set, focused forward like a row in a movie theater. Cobwebs hung from the corners of the ceiling, and a recent issue of *Sports Illustrated* lay on an end table.

A crackling noise came from down the hall. They moved in its direction, hugging the wall, past a kitchen, and then to a closed door. Williams knocked gently. "Anyone there?"

No answer. He opened the door, first a crack, and then slowly, back against the wall. The room was a pigsty, the floor strewn with crushed cereal boxes and snack wrappers. Beside the rumpled bed, a book lay on the nightstand—*The Catcher in the Rye*, opened, facedown to mark the reader's place. On top of an old, scarred chest of drawers, angled in the corner, were crumpled paper plates, dirty glasses with leftover liquids, scummy as the river, and a radio, scratching in search of a signal. A door led to a bathroom. Williams could see the toilet, seat up, and the edge of a basin with metal legs. A sheet of cut plywood boarded the room's only window, further shielded by a small refrigerator.

A bare foot, chalky white with long skinny toes, propped against the side of the refrigerator, unmoved by the sound of their entry. The foot extended from a spindly leg in faded cut-off jeans, the other leg flat on the floor. The lanky body, stone still, lay stretched out, its head and face covered by a pillow mottled with stains. Two tight fists crisscrossed the pillow, warding off the world.

Looks like a teenage boy, Williams thought. "Son, you all right?"

The body remained immobile, with not a flicker. Williams moved closer and shook the boy's shoulder gently. "You okay?" His voice was quiet, concerned. Miller stayed back, but replaced his gun in its holster.

"Son," Williams said, "we're policemen, and we won't hurt you. We've come to help, if you need us." The boy lay still. "Okay, now, I'm going to move the pillow off your face. Don't be afraid." Williams lifted the boy's hands, which were heavy, weighted with resistance, then he raised the pillow slowly, carefully.

The boy's face was long, angular, his skin still smooth, without a hint of whiskers around his chin or on his upper lip, which Williams predicted would stubble soon. Straight hair, dark with oil, fell to his shoulders. His deep brown eyes gazed out with the naiveté of innocence. He didn't look afraid, just confused.

Williams leaned closer and attempted a smile. "I'm Detective Williams. Are you here alone?"

The boy turned his head and writhed against the pillow. An ear protruded through the greasy strands of hair. He began to moan, his head thrashing from side to side. His wails had no words, but their message was clear. Leave me the hell alone, Williams thought. That's what this boy is saying.

"Okay, son, we're going to check out the rest of the

house. We'll be back." Williams headed for the door, his arm shoveling the air, motioning for Miller to follow. In the hall, he whispered, "Watch the kid. I'll be right back."

Another closed door led to a small bath with a shower, neat as a pin. Williams checked a towel, carefully folded over the stall, for dampness, but it was dry. He worked his way back down the hall to the kitchen. Standard fare, he thought, as he peeked in one cabinet—jar of mayonnaise, several cans of tunafish, salt, pepper, a box of oatmeal—then another—pots, pans, a colander. He opened the refrigerator, which was well stocked with food. He uncapped a half-gallon of milk and sniffed its rankness. A slice of watermelon in a bowl had dried up, with pink, shriveled pulp and sunken seeds, its rind turning yellow.

A wall telephone was labeled in large red print, *Emergency, Dial 911,* with a small piece of paper attached. Appeared to be a note, handwritten in block letters. Williams picked up the phone, not surprised that the line was dead. He read the note and rushed back down the hall. "Call the station," he directed Miller. "We need a crime scene crew to get fingerprints. And call whatever kind of psychiatrist you have or someone with psychological training. Looks like child abuse to me. The boy will need special handling."

Miller pulled a cellular phone from his pocket, and Williams went into the bedroom and knelt beside the kid. The boy lay still, as if he had fallen asleep. Williams leaned over to see, but the boy's eyes were open, staring at the wall. "Feel like talking?"

The boy sat up slowly and propped a bony elbow on the pillow. "Uh . . . no," he said, darting his eyes toward the ceiling.

"You don't have to. It's all right." Williams sat quietly until the silence felt uncomfortable. "Would you at least tell me your name?"

The boy kept his eyes away, staring into the distance, as he spoke. "John . . . or . . . Gene."

"Which name do you like?"

"John. That's the . . . name . . . Johnson gave me."

"Oh. Who's Johnson?"

"He's like . . . my dad."

"Where is he?"

"He's away a lot. Travels."

"You go to school?"

"No."

"Why not? Are you sick?"

The boy turned his face toward Williams. He plastered his hair back behind his ear, pulling it tight with a fist. "John . . . son didn't like me to go . . . outside."

"How long has your dad been gone?"

"He's not really my dad . . . just like a dad."

"How long?"

"I'm not sure." John's eyes popped wide, as if he had solved an unfathomable mystery. "Maybe a few days." The words began to flow, as if he were warmed up now, stretched and loose, ready to go at full pace. "Johnson didn't come home every night, sometimes not for days. So I didn't think much about him not showing up, until I ran out of food. I got hungry. At first I didn't even try the door, 'cause it was always locked." John's eyes narrowed. He covered his mouth with the back of his hand and began to gnaw on its loose flesh.

Williams waited.

"But this time, it wasn't. So I stepped outside the door, down the hall to the kitchen. I'd never seen the house before."

"Never? Why?"

"Because I was in my room." He chewed on a nubby fingernail, then continued. "I saw the note and the number to call. I didn't know what to say. Or where I was." He threw his head back to the pillow. "So . . . I just waited."

"It's okay, son. You don't have to talk." Williams patted him on the shoulder. "Somebody will be here soon to take you to another home, where you'll be safe."

Williams wanted to ask John more questions, but he knew better. The boy would talk in his own good time. In the meantime he needed to feel safe, secure. And so they remained in the room, each in his place, silent, waiting.

"Mom, it's Detective Williams." Matt laid down the phone and reversed his baseball cap, brim to the back. The strap flattened the hair to his forehead, and he separated thick bangs over his eyes, peering out as his mother rushed to the phone.

She picked up the phone, picturing the aging detective at the other end of the line. "Hello there."

Williams jumped right in. "Diane, yesterday we received a kinda strange release . . . from Georgia, small town south of Macon. A youngster called 911 and asked for help, but didn't give his name or location."

"What'd he say?"

"Just 'I'm here . . . by the water.'"

"Steve, that's just too cryptic. Not much to go on."

"Right, but that's past history now. I decided to pursue it and went to Georgia, undercover. Didn't want anyone to get suspicious," he added gruffly, "on the off-chance it was Chris."

"Oh?"

"Yeah. Anyway, the search led us to a thirteen-year-old kid in an abandoned house outside of town. Turns out, he'd been held captive in his room for three years."

"My God, the poor boy." She sighed, then added quickly, "Do you think there's a connection to Chris?" Diane was seasoned to fruitless new evidence.

"No real evidence. Just a hunch." He never catered to her hopes. "But the circumstances of this boy's abduction are darn similar to our case. Took place in a remote area in North Carolina, by a stream not far from your cabin."

"Do you think we should come up?"

"I was thinking that. But Peaceton's a small town. Everybody knows everybody, that sort of thing. Might not be good to have too many strange folks around."

"Are you sure? I'd like to be there."

Williams took an endless pause. "Well, young lady, it probably wouldn't hurt. You might see something I miss."

Mel and Diane rushed to board a plane that evening,

only to be stuck on the runway, frustrated, waiting for the weather to clear. The runway was stacked with jets, rumbling their engines as they inched forward in an orderly procession, lights twinkling rhythmically on their backs and bellies, like fireflies dotting the night. As their plane crept along the runway, waiting its turn, Mel donned earphones and opened a newspaper, spreading his arms wide. Diane released her seat and leaned back. Trying to relax, she closed her eyes, but her ears, like a band of illicit microphones, picked the pockets of conversations around her.

In the back of the cabin a small child quizzed his mother. "Who invented earrings, Mommy?" In the darkness of her closed eyes, Diane pictured the child fingering his mother's earlobe, examining the primitive custom.

"Don't know, hon," the mother answered, then had a second thought. "Probably natives in Africa, I guess."

"Oohhh," the child answered, as if the fact had simply escaped him momentarily.

A couple argued through clenched teeth, unashamed, perhaps thinking that the high seat backs afforded them privacy. The man sounded exasperated. "I *told* you that bag was too big to fit under your seat. It's huge."

"I didn't want to send it through with the luggage." Apparently trying to show just cause, she whispered, too loudly, "It's got my *valuables* in it."

"What valuables do you have that weigh a ton?"

"I packed them with other things."

"What things? Must be your rock collection."

She answered with a giggle, and the conversation ended.

Earlier Diane had noticed across the aisle a gathering of businessmen, apparently a familiar group, as they huddled their shoulders together when they talked. Now their voices were louder.

"When Harold's wife took off, she left him the house and bought a new one up north. He tricked her good, though, and kept all the new furniture. She took the old junk, antiques and stuff." The man's voice emitted an ugly snort. "Yeah, he got the furniture, nice leather and mahogany."

"Why'd she leave?"

"He'd been messing around."

"They didn't have kids, right?"

"Yep, no kids. Just furniture."

The captain interrupted to apologize for the delay, as if he commanded the weather. He spoke in a monotone, his voice flat. "I'm sorry for the inconvenience. We have reports that the storm has loosened up and is heading northeast toward Jacksonville. It should not interfere with our flight path to Macon, Georgia, and we should be cleared to take off soon. Thanks for your patience."

Diane must have dozed off, as it seemed like only seconds later when she felt the enormous power of the jet, racing down the runway. A plane in this maneuver always sounded rickety to her, a piece of tin hurling itself into the air, against the superior forces of nature. She closed her mind to the unsettling thought and drifted back to sleep.

She woke up, as the plane descended, feeling sick at her stomach. She pulled a saltine cracker packet from her purse and tried to open the plastic wrapper with her teeth. Mel reached over to pull the red tab and offered her one. "Hold on," he said. "We're almost there."

When the plane touched down, he stood up in the aisle to retrieve their carry-on bag, the only luggage they'd packed. "Sir, stay seated until we reach the terminal," a flight attendant barked.

Mel grabbed the bag and slammed the overhead door shut, mumbling to Diane as he sat back down. "If she only knew how insignificant her precious safety procedure is to me."

"Yeah, she could have saved her breath."

Outside the terminal they hailed a cab and tried to convince the driver that, yes, they really wanted to go to Peaceton. "Nobody takes a taxi to Peaceton. You know how far that is, fellow? Twenty miles, at least."

"We don't have time to rent a car. It's already late," Diane whispered to Mel.

"You know how much that's going to cost? About twenty-five bucks."

Mel nodded his head. "I'd probably get lost, anyway."

"You still want to go?" the taxi driver asked, incredulous that he'd lost the debate. "Where you going in Peaceton? It's just a hole in the wall."

"The police station. And we're running late."

"Oh, why didn't you say so? Probably important then."

The taxi driver was mercifully silent on the trip, and Diane munched crackers, nursing her stomach. Finally arriving at the Peaceton police station, she felt harried, exhausted. Brushing cracker crumbs off the cuffs of her sweater, Diane took Mel's hand, extended toward her at the taxi door. As he pulled her along, she tugged at her skirt, which hugged the back of her leg like a cape against the wind. They dashed in, breathless.

Detective Williams stopped them in the reception area, to give Diane a hug and shake Mel's hand. "Let's sit down and talk, before you go in," he said gravely. "The boy is quite a bit older than Chris. This kid's just turned thirteen, we believe, and Chris would be only eight. But there's something about his story that's similar. He's from North Carolina, out in the country. Lived with an elderly uncle who died shortly after his nephew was kidnapped. The boy has no family, really a sad case.

"We know that he disappeared one day about three years ago, out of the clear blue, just like Chris, and from an isolated area, too. His home—if you can call the dilapidated old sharecropper's shack a home—was in Jansen, about forty-five miles from your cabin. Way up a mountain, surrounded by woods and some cleared cabbage patches. That's the economy there; no tourists yet."

Diane grew impatient with his rambling. "Did the boy say anything about his abduction?"

"Funny, he remembers that day, but has blocked out a lot since. I believe he's been drugged pretty good. His speech is halting, like he hasn't been talking much. The therapist thinks he has been mute for long periods of time."

"But," Mel pressed, "what did he say about that day?"

"The kid was ten then, about a half-mile from home, going to a lake close by to swim. Taking his time walking, he met up with a man who seemed to come from nowhere. The boy had never seen him before. The man spoke friendly like, so he wasn't suspicious. The man asked him where he was headed, and he answered truthfully. The man asked where the lake was and, when the kid turned to point the direction, he blacked out. Didn't remember anything till he woke up in a strange room. Except he did smell something real strong, some chemical, which was probably chloroform."

"What did the man look like? Did the boy describe him?"

"He was younger, he said, than his uncle, who was about sixty-five then. Said he had a nasty scar under one cheekbone, a beard, gray on the edges, and real mean brown eyes. Kinda fat, specially round the belly."

Detective Williams fingered the belt loops of his jeans, sucking in his gut ever so slightly. Devotion to a daily workout was the detective's only vanity, and his hard, sturdy body belied his sixty years.

"The kid said his abductor was about as tall as me; that's five-eleven. And he apparently didn't have an accent—not Southern, I guess."

"Can't you trace this guy through his telephone number or his billing address?" Mel asked.

"We tried, but the phone company has no record for that location. Somehow he tapped in illegally to a line they thought was disconnected."

"How about the property owner of the house where he kept the kid?"

"We searched the public records. The owner lives in Canada, and the police are trying to get in touch with him. According to local folks, he never comes down to these parts."

"Surely, someone must have seen the guy in town."

"So far, we haven't had any luck. He must have shopped in other towns—he traveled, you know. And John said that he only came home at night. Strictly on the sly, I guess."

"Do you think John was abused?" Diane asked, lowering her eyes.

"The kid claims that the man wasn't bad to him, gave him plenty to eat and all that, but kept him locked up, every day. Caged like an animal, and probably drugged, too, from the sounds of it. We don't have our blood tests back yet."

"Is he in good health?" she asked softly, tucking her skirt into folds in her lap.

"Excellent, apparently, although skinny as a rail. This guy—called himself Johnson—really looked after the boy, had him run in place, do calisthenics, knee-bends. Also exercised his mind. Schooled him in math, gave him books to read, bought him clothes. Even equipped his room with a well-stocked refrigerator and a radio. That's how the kid kept track of time, and the world outside. Strange, this Johnson gave the child everything but a real life. Hoarded him to himself."

"Can I see him?" Diane asked. "What do you think?"

"Don't think it'd hurt. The boy has no family, so there's no one to object. Maybe it'd be good for him to have some feminine attention. Probably starved for it. He seemed to respond to the nurses."

"What's the boy's name?" Diane asked.

"His birth name is Gene, but his captor called him John and he's asked to keep it. Now, remember, the therapist isn't here to monitor. She told me to call her if the boy gets agitated, so go slow. Not too many questions. We need to make John feel secure, so that, down the line, he can tell us things as he remembers."

Williams led them down the hall to a conference office. The room was set up like a living room with a comfortable sofa, magazines on the coffee table, some side chairs, a television in the corner, and a few plants, turning brown from neglect.

The boy sat stiffly in the farthermost chair, set off by itself, with a leafy plant shielding part of his face. Diane moved slowly toward him and bent her upper body, offering him her hand, not in a handshake but with the palm down, like a mother to a child to hold on while crossing the street.

John raised his head slowly, stiffly, as if cranked by an outside force. He glanced at her furtively, his eyes grazing hers before darting away. Greasy black hair fell over his pale face, like a curtain drawn.

"Hello, John. I'm Diane." She held her hand steady.

John's hand rose, limp as a marionette tugged at the wrist by a string. His hand was larger than she expected and cold to the touch. "Hel . . . lo, ma . . .'am." His words were widely spaced syllables.

"May I sit down?"

He nodded. Diane looked over her shoulder, gently dropping John's hand, and Mel picked up a straight-back chair and headed for her. Diane whispered as she turned in his direction, "I'll get it. Thanks."

She placed the chair in front of John, leaving a comfortable distance for his wiry legs, and sat down, not speaking. John leaned close to the plant and rubbed a wide leaf between his fingers, as if examining the texture of cloth. She waited a few seconds in silence, trying to conquer her impatience and not to be formidable in any way. She wanted to comfort this young boy, not to burden him with a threat he knew only too well, the threat of a stranger.

"Did they tell you about me and my husband? That we lost our little boy? Pretty much like your uncle lost you."

"Yes, ma'am . . . but my uncle didn't . . . lose me," he said, sniffling as he wiped his nose on his sleeve.

"He didn't?"

"No . . . John . . . son . . . found me." A tear began its stream down his cheek, and John tossed his head away from her in an upward swirl, as if he were propelling a ball with the thrust of his neck.

"John," Diane started softly. His head jerked back like a boomerang. He stared steadily into her eyes for the first time, his jaw set defiantly, shoulders square, ready to take on the world. She sensed a grave seriousness, as if a light thought had never occurred to him. "Tell me about Johnson."

"Well, he . . . he's . . . gone," John stammered, dropping his head, examining his stubby nails, chewed to the quick. "Can't really tell about him. He said . . . not to, if anyone ever asked."

"Why not?"

"He said they'd come after him. And he really didn't do nothin' wrong. Just took care of me." The dam had broken, and his words were spilling over.

"Why do you think Johnson took you?"

"He was lonesome, all by hisself. Guess he needed a family, just like me."

"Then why did he leave you?"

"He had to go, I guess. Miss Diane, I'm sorry, I can't talk no more." His eyes shut down with his words, and he stared vacantly toward the wall, his lanky arms and legs limp.

Detective Williams had warned her not to push. She touched his shoulder gently as she pulled back reluctantly. "I'll see you again, if that's all right." He remained immobile as she backed up a few steps, then walked away.

Detective Williams ushered Diane and Mel down the hall to a side office, motioning for them to sit. He sat down on the opposite side of a desk and stared into Diane's eyes as he spoke.

"The boy had been abandoned in a small house outside town, on a marshy river branch. Fingerprints were abundant in the house, but no match yet. The front and back doors were locked, deadbolts keyed from the outside, but Johnson left the key in the front door. He obviously wanted the boy to be rescued. And he unlocked John's bedroom door before he left, probably while John was asleep.

"Normally, I guess, John's bedroom door stayed locked, and Johnson wasn't in the habit of coming home every night. The boy said he didn't even think to check the door until he ran out of food. By that time, Johnson could have been gone several days. Anyway, the kid crept outside his room, where he'd been locked up for three years. Found his way to the kitchen, where he saw a note taped to the telephone.

"Johnson didn't give the kid much notice," Williams said, as he opened the top drawer of the desk and took out a plastic bag. He pulled out a note in crude block letters, clasping it carefully on the edge, and flipped it toward them on the desk as he read aloud,

JOHN, GOOD-BYE AND GOOD LUCK

# Just Walk Away

## Chapter 5

With its white clapboards and picket fence, the home was a picture of Southern graciousness. Inside, there were soft chairs to soothe aching backs and home cooking to satisfy hungry stomachs. Most days, the kitchen table was laden with cornbread turned from a cast-iron skillet, and the aroma of fresh peach cobbler spilled out into the hall, which rambled through the house. In the foyer gladiolas stood court on a polished oak console, with doilies stained from age, but boasting of starch. The bedrooms were small, with oversized antique furniture and soft sinking mattresses piled high with crisp cotton sheets and thick comforters. Clean stiff towels draped the racks of the bathrooms, which smelled sweet with soap.

The home, in a small suburb of Atlanta, served as a sanctuary for unwed pregnant women. Abused children were also housed there, in separate quarters, until they could be placed in foster homes. Detective Williams suggested that Diane visit the shelter, because it had been around awhile and processed a lot of children.

Diane sat on a loveseat in the parlor, throwing a crossed leg nervously into the air. A frail young girl stood at the window, looking out. She spoke, turning her profile toward Diane. "Are you adopting a child?"

"No, I'm just waiting on the housemother, Miss Pleasance."

"Oh," the girl answered with disinterest.

"Are you visiting?" Diane asked.

"Nope, I'm one of the inmates," she said, laughing softly. "That's what we call ourselves. My name's Prissy."

"Glad to meet you. I'm Diane."

The girl looks emaciated, Diane thought. The flowers that patterned Prissy's cotton dress were translucent yellow, their blossoms faded from washing. Her rail-thin arms, white with a freckled glaze, rested lazily on a protuberant middle, swollen in shame. Prissy's hair was shiny, like corn-silk. Sliced straight, it cut her chin sharply and glowed with the sheen of polished copper, matching perfectly the freckles spotting her nose.

"Bet you think I look young," Prissy said with a flip of her head.

"Yes," Diane said. "How old are you?"

"Fourteen."

"Oh," Diane said, shaking her head.

Prissy duck-walked toward her. "Don't you think this is just the finest house you've ever seen?"

"It sure is."

"I'm going to have a baby girl, you know. They ran a test." Prissy groaned as she shifted her weight and moved back to the window, staring out through vacuous eyes.

"Hey, Priss." A stocky young man in khakis and a crisp collared shirt slipped up behind her, calling her nickname softly. "How ya feeling, girl?"

Prissy turned and, at the sight of him, put a hand on her slouched hip. "How'm I supposed to feel?"

"Can't answer that one," he said, chuckling, "I'm awfully glad to say."

"Guess I'm just sick to death of the whole thing. Went swimmin' yesterday. They made me! Said it was good for having the baby." With a small attempt at animation, Prissy shrugged her shoulders and lifted her skirt to reveal a patch of sun-baked skin ready to blister. A pale panty line striped the inflamed red of her delicate thigh. "Now I hurt. Miss Pleasance rubbed aloe on me—some houseplant she picked and smashed up. Supposed to help."

Suddenly, Prissy glanced over. "Oh, sorry. Almost forgot you were there, Miss Diane. This here's Donny. He's from the adoption service."

The young man acknowledged Diane with a quick nod. "Nice to meet you, ma'am. I represent the Sunrise Adoption Agency."

His neck is as thick as his head, Diane thought, so that he appears to have no neck at all. Not very tall, but broad as an ox in the shoulders. Probably steroids. Rather attractive, though, with those deep-set eyes.

Donny chose a cushiony armchair and plopped down, resting his legs on an ottoman. He reached for a magazine from a wicker basket on the floor, filled with ladies magazines standing on edge, and glanced at it indifferently.

"Come on, Prissy." He beckoned to her with an exaggerated stroke of his arm, one-half of a swimmer's crawl. "We gotta talk."

Prissy ambled over to an antique sidechair and assumed the pregnant woman's squat, backing up to the low cane seat, anchoring her palms front forward on the armrests and planting her feet apart. Knees bent, she lowered her buttocks carefully down and eased her body against the chair back, then repositioned her hands on their natural mound, her stomach a perfect pillow. "Talk about what? I'm not in a rush, you know, to go nowhere."

"I guess that, when this baby comes, you're all set to let her go." Donny looked down at his hands, disguising an emerging grin. "Hope you don't plan to see the baby. That could make it hard for you. Might not be wise." He clenched his fist tightly, rippling the well-cut muscles on his forearm.

"Listen, Donny, I can't handle no baby. You know that, and I know that, but I'd sure like to see her." Prissy's head confirmed the thought, nodding up and down. "Yep, I gotta see my baby."

Donny glanced over at Diane, but she looked down into her lap and fiddled with the strap of her purse, pretending not to listen. "Prissy," he continued, "wouldn't it be a lot easier to wake up and, after you rest a while and feel better, just walk away? You'd be free to do what you want. Go back to that boyfriend of yours. No cares, no worries. Just walk away." He sat forward, his elbows on his knees, cajoling, convincing, playing this young girl.

Prissy glared at him. "Nope, I gotta see my baby."

"Diane Rath," a heavy-set woman called from the doorway. She wore a gingham dress, belted at the waist like an overstuffed present tied tight with a ribbon.

"Yes, that's me," Diane said as she rose, walking toward the woman with her hand outstretched. "You must be Miss Pleasance."

"Yep, that's her," Prissy confirmed.

Diane looked over her shoulder. "I really enjoyed talking to you, Prissy. I hope everything goes well with the baby."

"Please follow me," Miss Pleasance said, leading Diane down the hall into a sitting room with a stone fireplace and a semi-circle of rocking chairs, edging an oval rag rug. "Here's where we meet nightly for educational sessions. Our government grant mandates it, but we'd school these girls anyway. So many are naive, ignorant even of their own bodies."

"I suppose that's part of the problem."

"Yes, and part of the solution." Miss Pleasance swept her hand toward a rocking chair, inviting Diane to have a seat, as she lowered her plump middle, squirming to squeeze past the armrests. "Some of the visiting teachers scoff at our fat-bellied girls, who fidget and snicker, trying to be cool. But they're just hiding their fear. They've heard awful things about childbirth. That the baby can bang his head, as if against a stone wall, with the mother crying out in pain and no one listening. That, if there's no room for the baby to come out, the mother gets ripped, like a busted-out seam. Or even worse, that the doctor cuts open her stomach, and the mother gets stitched up with an ugly scar across her belly."

"Unfortunately, some of those stories are true," Diane said.

"But I try to dispel the horror stories, or at least put them in perspective. I've been housemother here for twelve years and seen a lot of things. But the birth experience is still foreign to me personally. I've never had a child of my own. These girls are my only children."

As Miss Pleasance talked about her girls, her face beamed. She had a sweetness about her, and Diane was drawn to her soft voice and accepting ways. "Now, Mrs. Rath—"

"Please call me Diane."

"Of course. Diane, I understand that you are in search of a child. What can I do?"

"Detective Williams—you know him, I believe—thought that you might be able to help."

"Ah, Steve Williams. A bit gruff, but a real workhorse."

"He's tenacious all right." Diane's face lightened for a moment, then turned serious again. "He's been on the case of my missing son for three years. Does all he can, but so far we've had no leads that have panned out. Miss Pleasance, you see a lot of young faces, especially on the ward for abused children."

"Yes, and sometimes runaways, too."

"Do these photos ring any bells?" Diane pulled an envelope from the flap of her purse, reached inside and handed Miss Pleasance photographs, one at a time. "This is Chris the day before he disappeared, from an isolated area in the North Carolina mountains. He was five years old then, and the last time we saw him he was wearing jeans and a brown tee shirt. Here's a poster we had printed up. We plastered it around locally and sent it all over the country. The Missing Children Society used the same photo for their mail flyer campaign. Steve had an age-progression portrait done on the computer. See, this is what Chris would look like now, as an eight-year-old."

Miss Pleasance looked back at the earliest photo. "Adorable kid. Look at those big green eyes."

"Yeah, the women in the grocery store always got right in his face, gushing over them. He hated that, sometimes cried." Diane began to chew on the edge of the envelope, smearing it with lipstick. "Do any of the photos look familiar?"

"Sorry, Diane. I'd give anything to be able to help."

"Would you keep the computer sketch, anyway? You never know."

"I'll do better than that. I'll put it on our bulletin board and periodically introduce it during the night sessions. And we'll post it on the abused children's ward. Please leave me your address and phone number."

Diane rose to leave, then had a second thought. "I met Prissy in the parlor. She seems awfully fragile."

"She is. And she doesn't have a chance in hell at a decent life, not with that family. Prissy's mother dumped her when she began to show, well into her fifth month. Even rednecks have their standards, I guess. When I first saw Prissy, she was standing on our porch, picking at the thread-bare tapestry of her overnight bag, as a rusty pick-up truck pulled away. She looked so weary. Can't really say any more, without breaking a confidence." As if to hush herself, Miss Pleasance touched her lips with the flat of her palm, puck-ering her chubby cheeks.

"I understand. Thanks for your time."

On the way out Diane stopped to say good-bye to Prissy, but the parlor was deserted. Diane stared at the empty room, so inviting, with its cozy overstuffed furniture, a stage set for a happy family scene. But the playwright had forgotten the players, and the room was sad and still.

# Boot Prints from the Sea

## Chapter 6

The Gulf waters were lazy that morning. An occasional wave lapped onto the sand, depositing soap-bubble foam that quickly disappeared, skidding into nothing. Diane felt native to the land as she walked solitary on the untouched beach, where eagles perched at dawn and pelicans dive-bombed the water for their breakfast.

The tide was low, and Diane gazed downward as she walked, searching for shells. From time to time she assumed a hunchback's posture, examining a familiar shape or spark of color.

Shelling was spiritual to Diane. A perfect Chinese alphabet cone brought good fortune. A brilliant horse conch, orange as Little Orphan Annie's famous locks, stood for prosperity. And the serenity of the search, in the raw sand on a fresh morning, brought her peace.

But the waters could be moody. The summer storms often coughed away the gentle spirit of the Gulf. And in the winter, toxic microorganisms called red tide sometimes poisoned the waters, launching hidden, hideous attacks on the life of the sea.

One morning earlier that year, Diane had shelled on a beach far from serene. The Gulf had suffered a bad bout of red tide, and the beach was strewn with dead conchs, their dark snail bodies stretched out in grotesque poses, stiff and dry, perfect bait for armies of ants that attacked them in droves. Bloated fish, with eye sockets picked clean by seagulls, were thrown into smelly piles by the waves. But amidst the havoc of dead marine animals, the sad display of nature's selection, lay the leopard shell of a prize, deepwater Junonia, buried in the damp sand—a rare find, a treasure amidst the ruin. The Junonia became Diane's amulet against the ominous.

But today the Gulf held no threat. Diane closed her eyes and listened to the measured swish of the waves, a hushed murmur, lulling, drowning, if only for a moment, the incessant chanting in her brain. Two words, spoken quietly three years before, still pounded in her head like an overbearing clock in a schoolroom, always reminding how much time had passed, or how much time remained. Diane had no measure of time since Chris had gone. The days blended together, fading without beginning or end. Her head ached from the painful rhythm of those two words, pounding incessantly. Two relentless words that had changed her life forever. *He's gone.*

Calling from down the beach, Mel startled her. He hurried toward her with his ubiquitous fishing rod and daily change of lure—one day a green and silver Mirrolure, the next a Bomber finger mullet. They walked to the south, where Mel liked to cast for large fish coming into the bays through the pass, which narrowed into a deep trough. He constantly searched the shallow surf for schools of snook, their narrow body stripes propelling like lasers through the clear green water, only inches from shore. Mel and Diane fell into step together, holding hands.

Diane's mind drifted to a troubling conversation she'd had with Matt, just the day before. Matt had asked to meet John. Naturally he was curious. Diane had been struck with the boy—alone after his abduction, so vulnerable, without family or friends—and two times she'd flown to Atlanta to visit him at Bradford Hospital, where he had been admitted to a psychiatric ward for observation. Perhaps she'd mentioned him too often.

Diane wondered about Matt's motivation, and her own. She wanted to rescue John, to mother him. It didn't take a psychiatrist to see through that. She transferred her longing for Chris—her desire, her need to save her son—onto another child, who suffered his same fate. Matt, too, had deep feelings about losing his brother, jumbled feelings of guilt and even jealousy, which he might act out with John. Diane had no clue as to whether the meeting would be healthy or harmful for Matt. But he had been insistent, and Diane knew better than to treat the matter lightly. She asked Matt to give her time to think about it.

"Matt asked to meet John," she said softly, as they walked, as if thinking aloud. Her eyes continued to survey the sand. "We were talking about school—soccer actually—when he brought it up. Said he wished he had a brother again, to play sports with. He thought meeting John might be like seeing Chris. What do you think?"

Mel tightened his grip, as Diane spoke, then abruptly dropped her hand and turned to cast in the surf. They reached a treeline of Australian pines where the snook often gathered in the shade to feed. Frantic baitfish churned the water, leaping in rapid bursts to escape their efficient predators. A snook flirted with the artificial lure, but passed it by for the more appetizing natural bait.

Diane watched silently, recognizing Mel's retreat. After a few casts, he resumed their walk. "I'm afraid to think about it, what it might do to Matt. He's still so mixed up about Chris, so jealous of his memory." Mel's jaws locked in resolve. "But I don't think we can ignore what he wants."

They crossed a sea turtle's deep round tracks, a path of close-spaced boot prints from the sea to the edge of the sand dune, ending in a freshly dug nest three-foot square. The prints turned in mirror image back to sea. Diane knelt beside the burrowed tracks, precise and even, and wondered how nature could produce such exactitude.

The turtle's maternal prospects were grim. Hurricane winds had narrowed the beaches, the tempest's waters eroding the sand, devouring much of the turtle's nesting land. Hungry predators—raccoons, birds, and even ants—stalked the sea turtle's nest, to eat her eggs and to intercept the baby turtles on their innocent march to the Gulf waters. The eggs would hatch at night, two months after being deposited deep in the sand. Lights from the shore, visible over sand dunes cut low by the winds, could disorient the hatchlings. Rather than head for the bright reflections of the moon on the water, they might crawl hopelessly inland, pulling their tiny soft-shelled bodies through sea oats and railroad vines to die from dehydration, or to be eaten by their predators, standing by.

Diane's eyes lingered on the tracks. Her shoulders drooped as she pictured the huge mother turtle struggling in the sand, plodding to plant her eggs. The turtle's instinct drove her to that spot, however distant her travels, however fruitless her eggs. A mother's plight was unending; her optimism, eternal. Diane rose slowly, then ran to catch up with Mel.

"You're probably right," she said, panting. "We can't always know what's best for Matt. We may have to go with him on this one." She walked briskly, pushing the pace, suddenly anxious. "I know he feels personally responsible because he left his brother alone on the bank of that stream."

Mel walked faster to keep in step, his eyes downcast. "Right. And now he wants to meet John. Maybe to set things straight, to make up for leaving Chris. Matt's a survivor, but he keeps so much to himself. You never know what problems lurk inside."

"That's what worries me. Like father, like son, I guess." Mel flinched and looked out to sea. She reached for his hand. "Matt doesn't want to talk about Chris anymore, or about himself. And he doesn't want to be praised for anything, as if he's not worth it. He won't do his best because he's afraid he *will* succeed, or stand out. You see his grades. He's settling for B's, or even C's, just feeding his low self-esteem."

"I know. If he would just use that brain of his."

Diane nodded in agreement. "I think he's punishing himself. When he excels, it adds to his guilt over Chris. He thinks about his brother, who is no longer around to succeed. Matt may feel that he's robbed him of that chance."

Diane paused in thought. "But he *is* a teenager." Dropping Mel's hand, she pivoted in the sand, her sudden pirouette sending a seagull flying. She opened her arms after him, appealing to the sky. "Who knows what's normal for a teenager?"

"Diane, honey, it may be that Matt's just a tad lazy." Mel chuckled. "What could be more normal?" He put his hand around her waist, gripping the moist skin above her shorts. "Maybe seeing John will be good for him."

Later that evening, despite her apprehension, Diane began to lay the groundwork for Matt's meeting with John. She called Bradford Hospital and received permission and guidelines for the visit, then decided to explore Matt's motivation, one last time. "So, son, have you thought anymore about John, about why you want to meet him?"

"From what you say, Mom—" Matt's voice cracked, and he shook his head in a quick shudder, his blunt hair swishing like grass in the wind. He put his hand to his throat to explore the changes going on. Matt's voice had always been deep, even as a toddler, when he had spoken with a sweet softness, an angel's tongue, conveying the purity and innocence found only in a child. Now his voice was getting husky, even deeper, but an occasional squeak slipped out.

"Sorry," he continued. "From what you say, I think I'll like him. We're the same age. And he probably needs a friend." Matt's face was solemn as he shook Diane's arm to catch her full attention. "Mom, I really want to meet him."

"Okay," Diane said, smiling through her fears. "You're right; he probably needs a friend." She reached for Matt's hand and stared at his thick fingers, at the big bones pushing through, rounding out the joints and knuckles. "You need to know some things, though, about John. He's a patient on a psychiatric ward where they're trying to help him adjust. He is completely alone in the world, without a single family member."

"Must be awful."

"Yeah. And you may see some patients who act strange; some of them are really sick."

"You mean, like psycho?"

"Well, they're not raving mad. Or, if they are, they're usually controlled with medication. I've felt comfortable, on both my visits. The staff is nice, and everything's set up like a home. They have a TV room and even a kitchen."

"Sounds pretty nice."

"Well, you can see for yourself. I'll call to get us a flight."

The Bradford Hospital staff facetiously referred to the psychiatric ward on the sixth floor as the country club suite, because of its finer accommodations relative to the other floors. The furniture was homey—upholstered and comfortable, rather than the metallic and straight, sticklike furniture that pervaded most clinical settings. The rooms were ample, particularly the expansive solarium where visitors were greeted. Sunlight poured in through the tall floor-to-ceiling arched windows. Chairs huddled around a long Formica table where the staff held craft classes, encouraging the patients to create works of art—some stilted, some free-flowing, some wild and stormy—under the stringent direction of a physical therapist. Paint smears splotched the table, which was set up with clusters of supplies—boxes of pastel crayons and finger paints, jars of paintbrush teepees dipped in clouded water, stacks of construction paper, and twisted tubes of dried-up glue, squeezed erratically as if subjected to death by strangulation. Not too different from a kindergarten setting, Diane thought. The balcony beyond was a lonely refuge for those who smoked.

An attendant greeted them. She wore no uniform, but Diane knew from previous visits that she was a psychiatric assistant. "Oh, you've come to see John," she said, turning immediately to retrace her steps across the polished floor, clicking her progress against the square tiles.

Diane and Matt sank onto a rattan loveseat and conversed nervously in pat phrases about the view and the weather.

"City doesn't look bad from here," Matt muttered.

"Yes," Diane said, nodding as she looked out over the city. "The dirt and grime doesn't show." She was struck with how grand the sun room appeared, with its high ceiling and tall sliding doors to the terrace, although the building's exterior was unimaginative and sat like a bulbous carbuncle on the Atlanta skyline.

Diane patted Matt's knee playfully. "It'll go fine. Don't be upset if it takes John a while to warm up. Remember, he's been through a lot, and he's only just discovering who he really is. He may be on some medication, too."

Matt winked impishly. "Hey, Mom, just being a

teenager is tough enough."

"You're telling me?" Diane flattened her palm against her chest.

A door opened, catching Matt's attention. The sparkle in his eyes turned off in a flash as the attendant appeared, pulling John along by the hand, his shoulders hunched forward.

Diane rose. "Hello, John. It's good to see you again. I'd like you to meet Matt, my son." She swept her hand at Matt as he stood.

"Hey, man." Matt offered his arm, hand high, elbow bent, with palm inward as if to arm wrestle. John looked confused and returned a light slap on his hand.

Diane broke into the awkward silence, speaking to John. "Matt's your age—thirteen."

Both boys clasped their hands behind their backs, as in practiced unison, and grinned into each other's eyes. Matt shrugged his shoulders playfully, rocking on his feet.

"What do'ya do here?"

"Mostly just watch TV, eat, and talk to the shrinks. You know—the doctors. Everybody calls them that. They want you to 'ventilate' all the time."

"'Ventilate'?" Matt tilted his head, squinting his eyes on the distant concept. "You mean, as in 'open the window for fresh air'?"

Now John had the upper hand, and Diane detected a rise in his shoulders. "Naw, as in 'talk.'"

"Talk about what?"

"Talk about anything. The shrinks are happy when I just talk at all." John's voice lowered, as if confiding a grave secret. "They say it's ther'peutic."

"But what do ya say?" Matt asked earnestly, his curiosity piqued.

"I tell them about my life, what I did with Johnson." John glanced over at Diane with questioning eyes. "Did your mom tell you about Johnson?"

"She told me a little bit. I wanted to know if you went through the same stuff as Chris—you know, my brother, the one who got kidnapped." Matt sat down and leaned forward, resting his elbows on his knees.

John sat at the other end of the loveseat, shuffling against the side cushion to maintain distance, his arms stiffly folded. "Yeah, heard about your brother. Guess that was hard for you."

"Not so hard as getting taken, like you were."

John faced forward, not acknowledging Matt's comment, and the psychiatric assistant quickly broke in. "John, let's go to the kitchen to make a snack for Matt and his mother. We'll be back in a few minutes." She started for the door, and John rose to follow.

"Mom," Matt whispered as they left, "do ya think I upset him?"

"I don't think so, not really," Diane said. "But the staff here have to watch their patients, not let them get agitated. They're probably pacing John, just like in a basketball game when the coach rests a player, so he doesn't get tired." She sat down and put her arm around Matt's shoulder.

"I talked with the doctor in the beginning because I was worried about saying the wrong thing. I didn't want to be destructive to John; his condition is so fragile. But you know what the doctor told me? She insisted that I shouldn't worry unduly about what I say to John—even if I mention something sensitive that strikes a raw nerve. John must learn to deal with the outside world, she said. Even simple day-to-day interactions with people are difficult for him to handle, because he's been cut off, completely alone. That's why I try to let him offer things about himself, rather than dig them out of him. That's better left to the doctors."

Matt sighed. "Hope I didn't upset him."

"Didn't you hear me, Matt? It's okay. Really." Diane gave Matt a playful hug, tightening her grip around his shoulder. He cringed at the display of affection.

In about ten minutes, John returned to report that the snack was ready. "Made it myself," he said, then led them down a long sterile hall into a kitchen with glassfront cabinets, checkered green and white placemats, and a large basket of apples and bananas on the counter. Fresh flowers on an oak banquet table wafted a sweet aroma around the room. Chairs lined the long table and at the head, looking lonely, three places were set with plastic glasses of pink lemonade and paper plates with wheat bread sandwiches and potato chips.

"Had to spread the peanut butter and jelly with a spoon," John explained. "They won't let us have knives."

"Why not?" Matt asked, cocking his head to cast John a puzzled look.

"They think we might hurt ourselves—cut our wrists or something, I guess."

Matt glanced at the table and sat down enthusiastically. "Looks good." Diane knew that Matt's breakfast cereal had expended its energy long ago. Although he ate mountains of food, his appetite was insatiable.

"Come on," Diane said, pulling back her chair.

John seemed to move in slow motion, but finally settled his lanky legs under the table. He sat looking at his plate with his hands in his lap, while Diane and Matt waited for their host.

After a minute Diane asked, "Shall we begin, John?"

"I was goin' to watch you eat, then eat myself. All right?"

"Why not eat together, at the same time?" Matt suggested, eyeing the food.

"Guess I'm used to eating by myself. Johnson watched me sometimes. Most of the time he left a tray. Sometimes he'd leave stacks of stuff to last a few days—bags of popcorn, and in the refrigerator, sodas and sandwich meat. Times when he had to go away." John shrugged. "Can't get used to eating at the table with other folks."

"Well, we'll start," Diane said, accepting the premise. "You just join in when you're ready." She motioned to her hungry son. "Go ahead, Matt. Enjoy your food."

"Hey, John, not bad," Matt said, as he took a bite and gulped it down, jelly oozing from one side of his mouth. He wiped it with the back of his fist, a quick stroke that smeared grape onto his cheek. Diane shook her head disapprovingly, but said nothing.

John toyed with a chip, lifting it, putting it down, rubbing the tips of his fingers together to shed the salt. Matt was downing his last bite when John's chip finally made it into his mouth. "I'm not really hungry," he said. "Why don't

I show Matt around?"

While John took Matt on a tour of the unit, Diane met with his primary doctor, fulfilling a requisite for the visit. Dr. Bozeman, a petite woman in her sixties with gray-streaked hair, invited Diane into her office. Diane glanced around as she sat down, remembering the doctor's collection of blue and white Oriental porcelain, set off by brilliant yellow walls. Nothing impersonal here, she thought.

"I've brewed some hot tea," Dr. Bozeman said, gesturing toward her own steaming cup. "Would you like some?"

"No, thanks," Diane said, shaking her head, "just had lemonade. In fact, John prepared lunch for us. He seems to have made great strides."

"Oh, yes. We're quite pleased."

"But what will come next?" Diane asked, fidgeting in her lap with the strap of her purse. "What'll happen to John now? Will he be ready for school by the fall? Where will he live?"

Dr. Bozeman nodded, acknowledging Diane's concerns. "John has no family, as far as we know. And no family friends have stepped forward. It's eerie to have a person so solitary in the world. John became utterly dependent on Johnson, who in all respects served as his father figure. And a doting father he was, by John's description, although our staff deems otherwise. John was violently ripped from his early home by a man who became his savior. Then—just as devastating—his adoptive father deserted him. Now this staff is the only family John knows."

Dr. Bozeman stopped for a sip of tea before leaning back in her swivel desk chair, her short legs dangling like a ragdoll's. "Now to your questions. Yes, John should be ready for school. He needs reliable authority figures, as well as contact with his peers. School will be overwhelming for him; he's lived as a virtual recluse. We're surprised at his speech skills, in view of suspected long periods of silence. We believe John was mute for months at a time. We'll structure his schooling—small classes, informed teachers with special training, tutoring as necessary.

"But his home environment is more critical, and we do have time constraints. The ward is set up as a diagnostic clinic, limiting a patient's stay to a maximum of three months. In most cases the patient returns to his family, whether the environment is stable or not. We don't have many therapeutic options. Sometimes we can place a patient in a halfway house, and then, of course, there's the state mental hospital. John has been severely depressed, but we're optimistic that he can adjust to an outside milieu, a normal living situation."

Dr. Bozeman absentmindedly twirled a pen on her desk, until it banged against a marble paperweight, stilling its whirl. Without looking down, she stared gravely at Diane. "The problem is obvious. John has no family, and we have no interim placements for an adolescent. We're interviewing foster parents with counseling backgrounds. And we're hoping for at least one sibling. Nothing's passed muster yet."

Diane broke in, pulling her purse strap taut between her fists. "Perhaps our family would fill the bill. We've lost a son, and that's left a huge void in our lives." Diane paused and shook her head. "But those are the wrong reasons. I know that, Dr. Bozeman, before you tell me." She felt her face growing hot in embarrassment.

Dr. Bozeman smiled, leaning forward to pat Diane's hand. "Don't apologize for being honest. Of course, there are always selfish reasons for adoption or even foster care. The needs of the child should be paramount, it's true, but the adoptive families have needs as well."

"I suppose I might consult the rest of my family," Diane ventured. "This is the most serious decision anyone could make, and I blurted out my thoughts without a brain check. My heart was definitely leading. John is a sweet boy—his case, so sad. I'll go home and do some soul-searching, then talk to Mel and Matt." Diane fingered a heart-shaped ruby pendant around her neck, rolling it from side to side on its chain.

Dr. Bozeman's lips curled into a trace of a smile. "You just let me know your decision. I won't say a word to John." She rose and motioned her arm to the door, excusing Diane. "From all I can see, your family would be the perfect fit." She spoke softly, her eyes twinkling as she offered her hand.

"Please keep in touch."

Diane walked through the ward with jumbled thoughts. Why had she been so rash? Was she out of her mind? She remembered the sea turtle's tracks, the mother's oppressive struggle through sea and sand to plant her eggs, to fulfill her destiny. Diane felt empty inside. Was she plodding with a purpose or hopelessly floundering?

As she rounded the corner, Diane bumped into a misplaced wheelchair, with a teddy bear slouched in its seat. She grabbed for the stuffed animal as it began to slide, but it fell to the floor, landing on its head. She felt like crying. I'm such a klutz, she thought. Nothing's safe with me, not even a helpless teddy bear.

Just then, she spotted Matt and John playing Ping-Pong on a table set up in a wide hall. Diane suspected that this sports addition to the ward was targeted just for John. She picked up her pace, forcing her melancholy thoughts aside. Her lips curved reluctantly, venturing a smile. "Hi, guys. Ready to go, Matt?"

John looked up, and Matt's serve flew past him. "Miss Diane, can Matt come back sometime?"

"Sure, John."

Matt slapped his paddle against the flat of his palm. "How about tomorrow, Mom? You've got that meeting with Detective Williams."

"Well," Diane hesitated, "it'll mean some extra driving, but I guess so, if Dr. Bozeman agrees. We'll call her. But we've got to go now. It's pouring outside."

"Just a minute, Mom," Matt called, preparing to serve. "Can't leave in the middle of a game. Besides, I'm winning."

# Prissy's Baby

## Chapter 7

Rain pelted the Bradford Hospital overhang, marked EMERGENCY in huge red letters, as Diane struggled with her umbrella against the wind. "Mom, we didn't come in this way," Matt said, glancing up.

"Oh, God," Diane answered, looking over her shoulder at the automatic swinging doors. "This place is so confusing."

A station wagon sped into the covered entry and screeched to a stop. A hefty woman, apparently in a dither as she was talking to herself, jumped out of the driver's seat and rushed to the curb to open the back-seat door. "Oh, Prissy, let me help you out."

A uniformed attendant brushed Miss Pleasance aside and eased Prissy into a wheelchair. "Don't need that," Prissy said, pooh-poohing the precaution, but her face turned red with pain and she relinquished.

As Prissy was rolled in, Miss Pleasance walked beside her, clacking sympathetically. "It's a real good hospital. Don't worry, child; I'll take care of you."

"You won't believe this, Matt," Diane said, holding her hand catatonic, with a finger pointing toward the swinging doors. "I know them."

"Come on, Mom. How?"

"It's a long story, son, but I need to catch up with them. Do you mind waiting inside, just for a bit?"

"I could go back up to see John." Matt nodded his head up and down, suggesting that he'd hit upon a great idea.

"I won't be long. Wait inside—" Diane tossed instructions over her shoulder as she bolted for the doors, "by the check-in desk." She spotted Prissy's entourage, waiting for the elevator, and ran toward them, her chest heaving. "Miss Pleasance, remember me? Diane Rath."

"What in the world are you doing here?"

"Just here with my son, quite a coincidence." She saw that Prissy was gripping the arm of the wheelchair tightly. "How are you, Prissy?" she asked, reaching out to stroke her hand.

"Not so good," Prissy answered, grimacing as she clutched at the throbbing pain, plastering both hands behind her. "It's in my lower back; hurts right through to my stomach. And I feel like I'm sitting in a cold puddle."

A nurse passed by, and Miss Pleasance grabbed her arm. "Please help," she begged. "This child's in pain."

The nurse touched Prissy's forehead. "She'll be fine when they get her to delivery," she said curtly and walked off.

Miss Pleasance began literally to run in circles, like a hen, twittering. First, over to the nurses' station. "See that girl—by the elevator. She's in pain." Then, without hesitating for an answer, to the uniformed attendant, who had strolled down the hall. "Can't you help?" And back to Prissy. "Is it hurting, dear?"

The elevator finally arrived, and the attendant rolled Prissy in, with Miss Pleasance hovering over her.

"Good luck, Prissy. I'll come see you," Diane said.

Prissy waved good-bye weakly, as the elevator doors groaned shut.

⟋

The next afternoon Diane peeked in the door of Prissy's hospital room. "Okay to come in?" she asked, holding out a bouquet of fresh-cut flowers, like a peace offering.

"How nice," Miss Pleasance said. Prissy lay groggy in her bed as time passed outside her grasp. Miss Pleasance tried to awaken her from the fog, shaking her shoulder gently. "Wake up, child."

"My eyes won't open, Miss Pleasance," Prissy said, with sleep on her tongue. She reached to rub her heavy eyelids, but her hand dropped as if struck with palsy. "You sound like you're down a tunnel . . ." Prissy's words faded, as her eyes closed.

Diane whispered, "How'd the labor go? Is the baby okay?"

Miss Pleasance puffed up with pride. "Oh, the baby— a little girl—was born perfect, we're told. We haven't seen her yet. Prissy's been really out of it."

"What about Prissy's family?"

"Surprise, surprise," Miss Pleasance said in a droll voice, oozing sarcasm. "We haven't seen them either."

A doctor in a white lab coat walked in briskly and punched a few buttons on the rolling computer beside Prissy's bed. He glanced at the sleeping patient, shaking his head slowly, sadly, as if faced with a dreaded prognosis.

"Doctor," Miss Pleasance said breathlessly, "she's really under. Won't wake up."

The doctor touched Prissy's arm, like a concerned father. "Poor child, she's exhausted. Vital signs are fine. Let her sleep. She's giving up her baby; sleep is a blessing."

Diane and Miss Pleasance sat for half an hour, hardly speaking, while Prissy slept. Finally Prissy stirred, throwing back her covers. She sat up slowly and shook her head to clear it. "I'm so zonked," she said, touching her middle, miraculously flattened, and then her breasts, tight and swollen.

"Do your breasts hurt?" Diane asked.

"Yeah, they're too tender to touch."

"They'll give you some medicine to dry up the milk, when it comes in," Miss Pleasance said.

"I guess I'll walk out of here like nothing happened," Prissy said. Wincing, she moved her tired legs to the edge of the bed. She wiggled her toes into bedroom slippers, waiting in place on the floor, and rammed her arm into one sleeve of her robe, its sash trailing the floor. "Let's go see my little girl."

Except for the click of their shoes, and the soft shuffle of Prissy's slippers, the hall was quiet. Stopping at the nursery's picture window, Prissy leaned against the glass. They were the only audience for the new life ensconced in rows of hospital bassinets. The infants were bundled in blanket cocoons, but some had struggled loose. Stray fingers and toes flailed in the air. Some babies were crying, but most were asleep, their stomachs full from the last feeding, resting after their burst into the world.

Prissy's eyes, crinkled in the low light, flew from bassinet to bassinet. She held her heart as she scanned the nametags, then pointed a finger, bouncing it from one bassinet to another, as if counting. She started again at the beginning, looking confused, finally turning white. "She's not here."

They hurried back to the room, where Prissy tumbled onto her bed. Miss Pleasance placed a gentle hand on Prissy's shoulder, and Diane pushed the call button. Prissy grabbed a pencil and tapped it loudly on the bedside table, staring fiercely at a pastel curtain flouncing from a track on the ceiling, pulled across the room for privacy. During the night a nurse had awakened Prissy to breastfeed her roommate's baby, brought to her by mistake, and in her dreamlike state she had fondled the newborn, but only for a moment.

Sheila, an obstetrics nurse, rounded the doorway and spoke cheerfully, "How's everyone feeling?"

"Nurse, please help me," Prissy pled. "I went to the nursery to see my baby, but she's not there. She must be sick."

Sheila flattened her fingers on her chin, her eyes wide. "But, Prissy, you've spoken with your mother, haven't you, and the gentleman from the Sunrise Agency?"

"What do ya mean?"

The nurse sat down on the bed beside Prissy, patting her trembling hand. "Don't worry; your baby's healthy. You just wait right here." Sheila scurried out of the room, as if in escape, without checking on Prissy's roommate or glancing back.

Diane checked her watch. She hated to leave, although it was time to pick up Matt. "I'll just run upstairs to check on my son, Miss Pleasance. Then I'll come back, if that's all right. Maybe I can relieve you for a while, so you can go get something to eat."

"I can stay by myself," Prissy said softly.

"Of course you can," Miss Pleasance agreed, "but I want to be here with you."

Diane returned in only a few minutes and sat gingerly on the foot of the bed. "Well, my son's fine—delighted, in fact, that he can watch the Olympic trials with his friend, John. Anything happen down here?"

Just then an attractive woman in her mid-thirties ambled into the room. She wore a tawdry chartreuse dress that fought to contain her plump body. A size too small, the silky synthetic stretched tight across her hips, almost giving way. It bunched at her dense midsection and flattened her bosom, forcing her ample breasts to bulge above a heart-shaped neckline. The limp skirt hung unevenly against her fleshy legs, which were perched on ungainly three-inch heels of red patent leather, which almost matched gaudy dangling hoops at her ears. She walked to the bed and put a protective arm around Prissy.

Diane stepped back against the wall, and Miss Pleasance joined her. They stood stiffly, silent, as if invisible.

"Priss, honey, how're you feeling?" The woman held her palm to Prissy's forehead, pushing her bangs back to uncover strands darkened in sweat. She curled the baby-fine hair with her fingers.

"Fine, maw. Where have you been the last four months?" Prissy had no patience for her mother's act. "Where's my baby?"

"Why, honey, don't you remember? When Donny, that nice fellow from the adoption agency, talked to you about me signing over custody, since you're underaged? You know you can't keep no baby, sugar."

"Mama, I told Donny I had to see my baby. He knew that. I've got to see her face—to see what she looks like and to be sure that she's healthy." Prissy fought back the tears that filled her eyes. "So where's my baby?" She clenched her fists and jutted her chin forward. "Where, mama?"

"It's too late, sugar. Donny's already took her to a nice family, where she'll be safe and loved. They'll look after her. It's best for the baby."

"But she's my baby! I don't remember agreeing to

nothing. I've been asleep."

"Too late, child. Baby's gone. You're young. You can have another one."

Prissy ripped a tissue from a box on the bedside table and dotted her eyes. "I think I could take it better, if I could see Bud. Can he come to visit me?"

"You just forget about that hood. He smokes like a chimney and gets drunk on cheap beer—wouldn't have been a decent father for the baby, anyhow. Doesn't have a decent job—"

"Maw," Prissy broke in, "I carried that baby in my gut; she's part of me. Don't ya even care?"

"When you're older and you have other children, you'll be glad there's one less."

"Like you'd be, maw, if I dropped out of sight?"

"Don't be smart." She slapped her daughter's arm, too hard for a light dismissal, and a red welt merged with Prissy's freckles. "This whole ordeal is your doing. Ain't nothing to me." She stalked out of the room, silky dress flouncing, her head stiff with indignation.

Diane, in disbelief, followed her down the hall. Perhaps she could say something—anything—to get through to her, to puncture her selfish indifference. Prissy had hard times ahead. She needed her family.

Diane could see Prissy's mother talking with some-one—a short, stocky man, with his back turned. She walked closer and stopped at the water fountain, shielding her face as she pretended to drink. The man turned his head, and she could see his profile. It was Donny all right. He slipped an envelope into the woman's outstretched hand. Prissy's mother fingered the envelope and looked inside, smiling as she pulled out something green and crisp, a wad of one-hundred-dollar bills.

# The Fairy-Tale Village

Chapter 8

Verdant fields with purple mats of clover flashed by the car window. Crisp white fence posts, rolling hills and horses, orange trees in spinning rows, and huge billboards with jumbled pictures, like a meaningless cartoon. Diane stared, mesmerized, her eyes entertained, but her mind focused far away, down its usual tunnel. They were heading for a vacation at the North Carolina cabin, and, during the tedious hours traveling through central Florida, she found little distraction from her thoughts.

Internally Diane debated, over and over, the pros and cons of taking John as a foster son, but she had not found the courage to share her deliberations with Mel. The family dynamics were muddled enough. Matt struggled desperately with the memory of Chris—his sibling rival, a ghost—and Mel couldn't face the loss of his son. She questioned her own motives for a surrogate one. And what about Chris, if he were to return home alive, should that distant miracle occur? How would he view a new sibling? As a replacement? A kid sleeping in *his* bed, playing with *his* brother, encased in the cocoon of *his* family? Diane mumbled a few words, unaware that her thoughts had decamped.

"You say something, hon?" Mel had driven for hours now in a silent car, with Matt asleep in the back seat, gawky limbs sprawled in every direction. Diane glanced over her shoulder, hesitant, checking to see if Matt were still asleep.

"I was just thinking about John," she said, trying to sound nonchalant. "He needs a family, and he has no one."

Mel took off his sunglasses and rubbed one eye, really hard, with a bent forefinger, his hand in a ball. "You always were a sucker for a stray." Mel shook his head, barely perceptibly, and bit his lower lip. "He's a nice boy, really. But let's leave it at that."

Mel seemed to have an inroad into her mind. Sometimes in the middle of the night, when she lay sleepless—her mind restless, but her body still, so as not to wake him—he would turn to her and say, "Please, hon, quit thinking. You're keeping me awake." And now, he'd read her most private thought.

Diane sunk down and coiled onto her side, as far as her seat belt would allow. "I'm not talking about a stray dog," she mumbled, but she knew Mel would be intractable. His feelings were still raw. He couldn't accept another child—certainly not a boy—as his own. She must have been bats to even consider it.

Having botched one subject, she tried another. "It'll be fun to see Kat, won't it?"

"Yep, I like that girl. Reminds me of you." Mel reached over to give Diane a gentle pat on her knee. "Really, she's a lot like you. Pretty, and she's always positive. Looks for the 'up' side of things. Don't you think?"

"Uh-huh." Diane was relieved that some of her spirit still showed; she felt dead inside. "That's why she's good for Matt."

Mel glanced in her direction and frowned. "Diane, you look tired. Why don't you lean back and go to sleep. I'll wake you up when we get to the mountains."

Diane closed her eyes and listened to the whirl of the wheels on the pavement, the swish of the wind whipping by. Her mind sped down its familiar tunnel of doubt for miles and miles, until at last, mercifully, the tunnel darkened and she found sleep.

Kat had been Matt's first girlfriend. A North Carolina native, she had shared his summer vacations, guiding him through the fresh mountain air to her favorite sliding rocks, fishing holes, and buckberry patches. Diane remembered those happy days, wonderful memories of her boys—both her boys, for Chris had always tagged along—at play with a friend.

Kat had a flair for theatrics. She had taken dancing lessons and was as graceful as a cat. She would pirouette down the driveway at the cabin, like a willowy, light-footed nymph through the forest. For her grand finale, reaching the end, she would curtsy low to the ground with arms outstretched to the sky, ballerina style, her delicate carriage in sharp contrast to the budding brawny bearing of her sons. The boys' moves were athletic but anxious, blustery, headstrong, with arms and limbs whipping and slapping, while Kat moved cautiously, with perfect control, as if analyzing each step.

But Kat could be a tomboy, too. She had roamed the North Carolina mountains all her life and was equally at home, digging for worms in the mucky black dirt or climbing the side of a rock ledge to capture a spectacular view or trekking for miles through curtains of vegetation to search out a remote waterfall. When Chris disappeared, and the family stayed on at the cabin, Kat had proved a loyal comfort to Matt, a peer who understood.

Diane couldn't wait to see Kat that evening. To pass the time, she dolled up the tiny cabin for company. With its miniature dimensions, the cabin was like a playhouse, and Diane felt like a girl playing. She picked golden-petaled daisies for the kitchen counter, slicing their stems diagonally and arranging them in a Nippon vase she'd found at a local flea market. Hiding its tiny chip to the wall, Diane remembered how she'd uncovered the treasure, like an ancient discovery, in a dusty, crowded box. Next, she grabbed a straw broom from the hearth, grasping its gnarled tree branch handle with the vigor of a ballplayer gripping his bat, to dust baskets and brush down cobwebs. She polished the cozy familiar furniture and scrubbed the pine kitchen cabinets that she'd stenciled in green ivy.

Later that afternoon, when it was time to prepare dinner, Diane was seasoning chicken with garlic salt and lemon pepper when she heard a vehicle approach, rattling down the bumpy driveway, scraping gruffly against the overgrowth. She rinsed her hands quickly and wiped them on a dishtowel as she hurried out, kicking open the squeaky screened door on the porch.

She's beginning to look all grown up, Diane mused, as Kat stepped down from her father's pickup truck, in a short denim skirt with a starched white cotton shirt, curved by budding breasts and tied at the waist.

"I've been up since five o'clock. I was so-o-o excited," Kat squealed, as she twirled around with the same grace she'd had as a child. Diane admired her long French-braided hair, then hugged her in delight.

"How are you, Tom?" Diane called to Kat's father, who waved from the window of the truck.

"Doing fine. What time do you want me to pick up my young'un?"

"If it's okay, we'll bring her home," Diane suggested, walking toward him as she checked her watch. "Maybe, around nine."

"Sounds good to me," he said, grinning, crinkling his parched farmer's face. His hair was red, even his eyelashes, and freckles congregated on his nose and cheeks. His green eyes grew serious. "How are y'all doing? Any word from Chris?"

"Afraid we're still in the dark. Not a single word." Diane looked down and brushed an imaginary fleck off her sleeve. "We're okay, though." She lifted her head and clapped her hands together. "We're excited to see Kat—especially Matt. He's really missed her."

"Kat's missed y'all, too. Well, see ya later," he said, watching the mirror as he began to back down the driveway. "Take care."

As soon as Kat waved goodbye, Matt grabbed her by the hand, tugging, pulling her along into the cabin for a quick look and then back out the porch door down the driveway. Diane called behind them, "Dad is going to start up the grill; we have chicken to barbecue."

She could hear Matt's voice trailing. "Remember when you and Chris and me played Robin Hood and whittled arrows with a stone . . ."

Diane questioned her own memories, why some haunted her and others escaped. She thought of the early family years, back when Matt and Chris were little learning machines, absorbing the world around them. That time remained vivid. But the most poignant memories, of Chris as an infant—his squeaky clean smell at bedtime, his soft baby skin against her breast as he suckled, his cry of protest when she left his sight—were forever frozen, too painful to thaw. She struggled to retrieve them, to restore them fresh, but they lay hidden, deep, out of her reach.

She saw no rhyme or reason, why some images of Chris set her reeling, thunderstruck, and others, perhaps too tender, forced her away. Sometimes a memory would pique, spurred by a simple sight or sound or smell—a young boy running in the park toward his mother's open arms; the scent of bacon permeating the house on a Sunday morning; a red-faced boy fighting to control a soccer ball; a stick family holding hands in a child's crayon scribble, posted on a friend's refrigerator door; a whimper from a baby's soft bundle. A cartoon theme song—"Scooby-Doo, Where Are You?"—might bring a fleeting memory of Chris laughing, as he always had, with uproarious, giggly delight, falling back on a giant floor pillow, his perch for watching TV.

Unable to face Chris' favorite book, Diane had hidden *Brown Bear, Brown Bear, What Do You See?* on the back of a shelf, but one day, cleaning, she'd come across it. She thumbed through the pages, and, for just a moment, she remembered Chris' sweet child smell, his determined rump as he backed into her lap, signaling for her to read, his baby finger pointing in delight.

Such an image usually tapped her gently on the shoulder and, when she turned her mind toward it, quickly—mercifully—escaped. Occasionally, a memory dragged on a little longer, and a stab of guilt would strike her with the force of hurricane wind, knocking her guard to the ground. She had failed to protect her child. How could she let it happen?

Dr. Bozeman said that pain was a self-protective block and that she would slowly, progressively, get better. Her memories would become more acceptable, her emotional tolerance stronger. Diane reminded herself to be patient.

Matt and Kat returned to investigate the enticing aroma from the grill. Diane had set the picnic table al fresco with a flowered tablecloth and fresh-picked rhododendron in a salt glaze pitcher. They sat down to attack the chicken with their fingers, relishing the crisp, slightly burned skin and wiping the runny brown sauce from their hands with paper towels, passing around the roll. Diane had boiled fresh white corn, with kernels that burst in their mouths and melted without chewing. Matt and Kat threw the mangled corncobs into the woods, shouting *Geronimo* at the top of their lungs.

After dinner, Matt and Kat chased fireflies, counting their prey, until the mosquitoes drove them inside. Matt wanted to play bridge, although Kat complained that she hadn't played lately and couldn't keep track of the cards. He elbowed her and kidded, "You've got me as a partner. Matt and Kat can't lose."

Matt had a competitive nature, which he fought to contain. Kat struggled with the bidding, tricky for an unseasoned player, and Matt added extra pressure. "I should have seen it coming," Diane chastised herself later.

Kat was not able, or perhaps willing, to provide the perfect play that Matt demanded. Diane led with a low card; Kat was next to play. She looked at her hand, selected a five from a diamond doubleton, ace high, and Mel took an easy sweep with his king. Later, when he discovered that Kat had held the ace, Matt exploded, infuriated with his partner. "I've told you over and over, Kat; play your high card." To emphasize he took a card, looped it high above the table and slowly, deliberately, laid it down, drumming its edge on the table with his thumb. "Your high card," he said, spitting slightly as he spoke.

Diane broke in. "Matt, don't talk to her like that. We're just playing for fun."

"I know, Mom, but jeez, we've been over this before." He shook his head in frustration.

"But, Matt, the way you talk." Diane took a sip of wine and curved her lips downward into a pout. "Wherever did you get that attitude, dear? Not from your dad or me, and certainly not your brother."

Matt stared down at the table, the room heavy with silence. He picked up his glass of iced tea, lifting it slowly to his lips, then slammed it to the table. "Yeah, Mom, not like you or Dad—or Chris, the perfect one. No telling where I came from. Maybe I'm adopted." He rose defiantly, hesitated a split second at the table, eyeing his glass. "No, not adopted. You wouldn't choose me." He grabbed the glass, flung it at the Franklin stove, and stormed out. The screened door slammed shut.

"I was just kidding," Diane offered meekly. "I shouldn't have said that. I don't know why I did, just wasn't thinking." She came quickly to her own defense. "Although it's just fine for him to say whatever he wants, to whomever, whenever."

"Yeah, you're right," Kat whispered. "I better go after him." She rose distractedly and weaved toward the door, as if her mind were overriding her body, which didn't like the path she was taking.

After Kat was gone, Diane lowered her head and dropped her first tears in many months. The joy of the early day had turned sour. She was hurt by Matt's words and disappointed by her own, so careless. Burdened with heavy shoulders, her neck strained to lift her head.

Mel rose to pick up the pieces of glass that had shattered against the hearth. Stooping for shards in the surrounding carpet, damp with tea, he suggested a ride to the lake. "We'll drop off the garbage at the dumpster, and it'll be good to get out for a while." They passed Matt and Kat down the driveway and backed up. Mel lowered his window, with a conciliatory invitation. "Want to go to the lake, you guys?"

Matt looked down, shook his head and turned away, without speaking.

"Guess not," Kat said, shrugging.

Lake Glenville, surrounded by craggy rocks at the top of the broad mountain, glistened in the gloaming. Natives said that a whole village lay at the bottom. The power company had bought the valley, parcel by parcel, removed all the residents, and one day, topsy-turvy, flooded the land to produce electricity. A beautiful lake, peaceful this evening, was left in its wake.

Diane envisioned the fairy-tale village below—a murky stillness, deserted sidewalks green with algae, bass schooling in the dark corners of the decomposing houses, bubbles rising through broken windows. She started down the rugged slope to get close to the bank, holding onto the larger jutting rocks to steady her balance.

She thought of the many arguments she'd had with Matt over the years, the deep hurts they'd caused each other. She felt as if she had failed in so many ways. Maybe she should have taken more time off work, spent more time with Matt. Staring into the water, clear at the shallow edge, she could see layers of rock, little stones settled into the mossy crevices of their parent rocks.

A few days before, at that very spot, she had watched a young boy throwing rock after rock into the lake, trying to sink a tin can. When he landed a rock close, but inland to shore, the spiraling waves took the can farther out. Each attempt brought the risk of failure, that his target would float out of reach. The boy was diligent, his play purposeful, determined, and after each toss he made a fresh assessment. Stooping down for a new rock, he bobbed his head close to the ground, choosing carefully. Then he rose and bounced the rock in his hand, testing its weight. He fingered its edges and swung his arm with practice throws. If only Matt could pursue a goal so patiently.

Lost in thought, Diane didn't hear the music begin—a boys' choir of heavenly voices, filmy as the mist rising over the lake at sunset. Gray shadows set the early evening mood. A breeze blew, gentle as the ethereal sounds, brushing past a few lazy fishermen in small boats weaving through the fog. She felt the moisture on her skin and smelled the heavy dankness. From Mel's car radio the music wafted down to her hungry ears, and the sun fell slowly, cradled in the mist, until it finally touched the peaks around the lake.

# The Sophisticated Farmer

Chapter 9

Matt's disquieting mood disappeared with the break of dawn. He rose early in cheerful spirits, as if the night before had never happened. Diane, still in flannel pajamas, hugged him, joining in the lapse, happy to forget, eager to swallow the pain. She had found serenity at the lake, somehow conquering her troubling ambivalence. All families had rough spots. She and Mel and Matt had climbed mountains of problems and withstood the avalanche of doubt and fears. She shouldn't underestimate the strength of her family, she told herself, or the depth of their need. Perhaps today she would find the courage to share with Mel her secret thoughts about John and her hopes for his future.

Mornings at the cabin, like Sunday mornings at home, invited a leisurely breakfast, and Diane hummed as she cooked. She set the table with forest-green placemats, trimmed with ivy, and, to make room for the feast, she crowded together in the center a pitcher of dried flowers and three tall, tiered iron candlesticks that held in their clutches green bulbs of thick, coarse Mexican glass. Sunlight peeked through the window and flirted with mottled bubbles in the glass.

Heavenly scents beckoned them to the oak table, laden with eggs and bacon, pancakes and hashbrowns, steaming gourmet coffee, and hot biscuits. They ate with relish, yawning and chatting and laughing, and finished up with molasses and butter, which they smeared together with a knife until creamy, then spread on the biscuits.

After the huge breakfast, Matt went out to run with Hounder. Mel hadn't shaved yet, and Diane playfully scratched his beard with her finger.

"Whoops, I could injure myself."

Mel caught her at the waist, pulling her squarely down on his lap, which began to bulge. She wrapped her arms around him, hugging him hard, then touched her lips to his and closed her eyes. Their mouths lingered, tasting of coffee and hazelnut.

"How about it, hon?" Mel asked, his voice husky.

"Not now. What about Matt?"

"Tonight, then?"

"Just covering your bases?" she teased.

Making love had been difficult for Diane, after Chris disappeared, as if, in re-living the raw act of his creation, she was forced to re-live the nightmare that followed. For months she looked in the mirror with disinterest, at a woman she didn't know, or understand. She felt nothing— not hungry or thirsty, empty or full, not strong or frail, or clever or mindless, or brittle or whole, or alive. Not even female; she felt sexless. She had no body to offer Mel.

Gradually she had begun to breathe again, to feel. "Okay, tonight," she agreed. "I've been wanting to talk to you, though."

"Oh, God," Mel said, the twinkle in his eye fading. "That sounds ominous."

Diane held his chin for attention. "I've been thinking about John—a lot. He needs us, and maybe we need him."

"I don't know, Diane. All I can think about is Chris, how he'd feel. And what it might do to Matt." His eyes fell in resistance. "Or what it might do to you. Hon, you can't replace Chris, no matter how hard you try."

"I know. But why don't we drive down to Georgia?" she implored. "Not to make any kind of decision—just to see John, maybe ask if he's remembered anything that might help Detective Williams."

"Well . . ." Mel hesitated. "I suppose you could call Dr. Bozeman."

"Deal." Diane quickly offered her handshake. "I'll check with Matt. Maybe seeing John will perk him up."

In the car on the way to Atlanta, Diane tested the waters further. "What do you think, guys, about asking John to come back to North Carolina with us? Just for a short visit. We could go fishing, maybe ruby mining."

Mel gripped the steering wheel, gritting his teeth as he concentrated on the serpentine road. The car was silent. Diane's shoulders slouched in defeat.

"Mom, it's okay with me," Matt piped up, with a delayed reaction. "Please, Dad, can we ask John?"

"I guess so," Mel said, resignation in his voice. "Sounds like your mother's made up her mind."

A breakthrough, Diane thought. She smiled at a herd of cows, a jigsaw puzzle of black-and-white bodies dotting the fields. The pastoral scene matched her mood perfectly. She dared not utter another word, except for small talk, until they arrived in Atlanta.

John was out of the hospital on a morning field trip, so they met first with Dr. Bozeman. Diane confided that her family had considered asking John to visit them at the cabin. "We'd like to have him, if you don't think it will interfere with his therapy."

"I'll talk to John," Dr. Bozeman said. "In the meantime, I'll update you on his progress. After all, you're the closest thing to family he's got. The staff has determined that John probably won't be ready, after all, to face a normal classroom situation in the fall. Like many patients, he makes great strides, then slips back a bit.

"We're tutoring him in a small group of teenagers with special needs, and we're pleased with John's behavior in the group setting. He's interacting appropriately with the other students, and it turns out that he has a high IQ. His captor was no slouch, either, when it came to education. I suspect that Johnson is an intelligent man."

She perused John's file on the desk. "In a way, I hate to interrupt his classes." Dr. Bozeman paused to rub her chin with a forefinger. "But perhaps," she deliberated, "it's time to test how he handles separation."

Matt winked at Diane, grinning. "I'll keep him busy, doctor. He won't have time to mope." Matt could be brash, downright brazen at times, thought Diane, but, when he took a mind to it, he could charm a cobra.

Dr. Bozeman laughed softly. "You're probably right. He'll be comfortable with you, Matt."

She turned to Mel and Diane, her face stern. "I have to impose ground rules. You must guarantee that you'll return John if he begins to exhibit anxiety or signs of stress. John must call me or a unit staff member each day, and the visit must not exceed three days. How does that mesh with your vacation schedule?"

"We can handle that," Diane said, glancing toward Mel, who nodded in agreement.

John returned to the hospital and, after talking with Dr. Bozeman, gave them a perfunctory greeting, cold and controlled. "Hello, Miss Diane," he said, extending neither a hand nor a smile.

"Hello." Diane smiled reassuringly, but, respecting his apparent need for distance, did not reach out to him. "We've been really anxious to see you again. Especially Matt. He had fun here before, at the hospital." Matt crossed his arms, nodding.

John stood stiffly, appearing not to listen. He avoided their eyes, lowering his head. Finally he spoke softly, still staring at the floor. "The doctor said you wanted me to visit."

"Yes, for a few days." Diane stepped closer. "Would you like to come?"

His body remained rigid, eyes still downcast. "Guess so."

He must be a jumble of emotions, Diane thought, wondering how to unravel his fears. "Matt, why don't you give Dad a tour of the unit? Maybe I can help John pack."

In his room John bordered on frenetic, pacing about, hesitating beside a duffel bag on the bottom bunk bed where he slept, darting off to pace again, uncertain, returning to the bag, finally unzipping it slowly. Dr. Bozeman, stopping by to observe, overheard John spout his many concerns, as he walked back and forth between his bed and a chest of drawers, picking out clothes piecemeal—a shirt here, undershorts there.

"Where will I sleep, Miss Diane? Will you be there the

whole time? What should I take? How do we get there? Isn't the cabin where your son was kidnapped? I'll be safe, won't I?"

Diane answered the barrage of questions honestly and matter-of-factly, but Dr. Bozeman broke in. "John, maybe it's too soon for a visit. Would you rather go another time?"

"No, Dr. Bozeman, it'll be nice to see the mountains again. Just like going home."

"But you seem agitated," she countered. "Are you anxious about going?"

"Guess I'm just excited." He placed his palms against his buttocks, shoulders back, and rocked side to side, like an athlete warming up.

"Well then, let's get you packed," Dr. Bozeman said. She nodded her approval at Diane, who began to fold a tee shirt, smoothing the Atlanta Braves emblem with flattened palms, smiling.

~

Diane stacked blankets on the foot of the bed and fluffed two pillows with fresh, sweet-smelling cases against the headboard. John had hardly spoken in the car. He watched her with a dreamy, almost sad expression, but, suddenly, seemed to flip his mood as agilely as he threw his body on the twin bed.

"Hey, Matt," he said, "this cabin's more comfortable than where I grew up."

Diane patted his shoulder. "Hope you'll sleep well." She kissed Matt good night and, as she closed the door behind her, the boys began to chatter. Matt was probably right. He'd keep John from moping—probably from sleeping, as well.

She closed a window, shivering. Summer nights could get cool in the mountains. Mel started a fire in the Franklin stove, stoking it for the night with a log from a locust tree he had felled the day before with his chain saw. The noise from the bedroom grew muffled, then stopped. Mel and Diane pulled out the sleeper sofa and went to bed. The cabin was still and warm, and flames from the fire flickered on the knotty pine, turning it rosy. Diane closed her eyes, finding the darkness delicious. Mel wrapped his arms around her, and she slept like a baby.

The next morning, they donned jeans and traipsed through the woods around the cabin. Matt pointed out the trails that he and Chris had blazed, stopping at a clearing where the stream widened. Water rippled over a fallen tree trunk with its gray bark clinging, as if holding on for dear life. Although the sun was shining, a chill fell over Diane, and she hugged herself, rubbing her upper arms.

"Here's where it happened, where Chris was kidnapped," Matt stated simply. He knelt beside the bank on ground mushy from rain.

John joined him, looking uneasy. "Right here, huh? Funny, I was around water, too, going to the lake, when Johnson found me."

"Do you think about it much?"

"Not about that day. I miss Johnson, though. He was like a dad to me, the only dad I ever had."

Matt pushed John's shoulder, toppling his balance. "Guess you're ventilating now, right?"

John laughed for the first time in their presence. "Yeah. Ol' Doc Bozeman would pee in her pants."

"John, really," Diane said, sounding motherly.

Hounder barked in the distance, and they could hear scurrying through the brush. "Probably another chipmunk," Mel said. "We should get a move on, though, if we're going gem mining."

Back at the cabin Diane gathered their mining gear—rubber gloves, cut-off socks to protect their arms from rubbing raw on the rim of the sluice, and baby-food jars in which to store their gems. She warned John to wear his oldest clothes or to borrow a throwaway shirt from Matt. "The red mud never washes out."

Matt found an old tattered tee shirt, which barely reached John's waist. "Perfect," Diane proclaimed, glancing down at her own grungy jeans. "Now, you won't show up the rest of us."

They left Hounder in the cabin—barking after them, looking out with his front paws on the windowsill—and headed for Franklin, an old mining town on the other side of the mountain. In its heyday at the turn of the century, Cowee Valley had produced sapphires and rubies for Tiffany, but the veins had mostly gone dry. Today, the mines were open to tourists who paid money to pan for gems, dumping buckets of clay into long flumes. Diane told Matt and John about a young amateur prospector, just ten years old, who found a sapphire that weighed over one thousand carats. "Guys, that gem was worth about thirty-five thousand dollars," she said, whetting their enthusiasm.

They joked about their odds, then brainstormed about how they would spend their fortune, if they were lucky in the mud.

"Guess a Porsche wouldn't be bad," Matt said, rolling his eyes.

John was more practical. "Maybe I'd buy a small place—you know, like a cabin." He stared forlornly out the window and shrugged his shoulders. "'Course, I don't know who'd live there."

Diane felt like crying, but stayed upbeat. "I could use a huge sapphire ring," she said, holding her slender fingers up toward them.

Soon they turned off the main highway, and the view opened wide. Cowee Valley was a grand landscape of rolling green hills with cultivated patches of corn and cabbage and tired old homesteads wrapped with porches and crowned with rusty tin roofs. Cows grazed lazily among a sea of ox eye daisy. Some bent their front legs into a crook, to lie down together in clusters under the shade of a stray tree, spared by a generous pioneer. Others licked greedily at a salt box.

"Does any of this look familiar?" Diane asked.

"All of it, I guess," John answered, pursing his lips, then letting out a long sigh.

Diane couldn't interpret the sigh, whether it recalled good times, or bad. "The Selby mine is just ahead," she said, pointing at a ridge in the distance. Their Toyota 4-Runner rumbled in protest to the bumpy dirt road, but soon they rounded a sharp corner and saw the faded sign.

### The Original Selby Mine
### Unsalted

"Unsalted?" John read aloud.

Matt snickered. "Doesn't sound very tasty."

"Come on, boys," Diane said, pretending to be peeved. "It just means that this mine has real rubies and sapphires. It's not salted with cheap imported stones from India, or somewhere." She hopped out of the car and grabbed her gear from the trunk. "Get moving. I'll show you."

They stopped at the old Selby farmhouse, the original family homestead, which was no longer occupied except by a half-blind run-down beagle hound with long chestnut ears that dragged the ground. A gem display hung on the porch wall, with specimens behind glass. The label assured each prospector that these uncut gems had all been "Found at Selby Mine—Ruby, Sapphire, Rhodolite, Garnet, and Rutile."

"See, John," Matt said, tapping on the glass, "this is what we're after."

Diane pointed at a sapphire. "Once the mud's washed off it, a sapphire looks like this. See—it has six smooth sides. The ruby is shaped the same, but you can identify it by its brilliant red color."

"Okay, let's get going," Matt said, then took off running down a clay path, marked with a big arrow. *To Mine.*

They bought tin buckets full of dirt, fifty cents apiece, and joined other prospectors on a bench that ran alongside a long wooden sluice, built on a hill, then dumped dirt into wooden trays with bottoms of perforated metal. Ice-cold spring water rushed down the sluice, to mix with the rocks and dirt, splashing over onto the bench, wet and ruddy with mud.

Diane placed her tray into the running water and began to roll the lumpy dirt around, pushing it against the metal until the water rid the dirt from the rocks. "Come on, boys, get started." They set to work, with the sun beating down on their backs and the water overflow drenching their jeans.

After a few minutes Matt began to grumble. "Mom, I'm soaked, and I'm not finding anything. Maybe we should have gone to a salted mine." Just then, the water exposed the red sparkle of a ruby, favored by the rays of the mid-day sun.

"Look here, John, a ruby." Now Matt changed his tune, chanting, teasing. "I found a ruby. I found a ruby."

"Is it real?"

"Yeah, just like that one," Matt answered, pointing at a clear, red stone in John's tray.

John picked up the stone, washed it better in the sluice, and held it up to sparkle in the sun. "It sure is pretty. Doc Bozeman's not going to believe this."

"How do ya like playing in the mud, now?" Matt splashed a handful of muddy water John's way.

"Stop it," Diane intervened. "Here, John, let me show you how to spot the sapphires. First, you need to get the rocks really clean. See, let the water do the work." She tilted the tray, as the freezing water washed away the mud, letting loose the rocks. "The sapphires don't shine like the rubies, so look for a rock with a barrel shape, with slick sides." Diane held up a perfect hexagonal specimen she'd found. "See—a six-sided stone. That's the natural cut of a sapphire. And look, this one even has a triangle." She turned the sapphire at just the right angle against the sun, and a glossy triangle shone on the surface.

At the end of the day they admired their find—seven clear rubies, fine enough to cut, and sixteen sapphires for the lapidary to appraise. They dragged themselves back to the car, tired and wet and spattered with red mud from the sluice overflow.

On the trip back through town, Mel spotted their favorite steak house. "How about dinner, Diane? Are we decent enough for the Ranch House? Sure could take a steak."

Matt agreed, always enthusiastic about food. "Let's go, Mom. Please."

"Fine with me," Diane said. "I'm too exhausted to cook, anyway. If we clean up in the restrooms, we'll look fairly presentable."

As Mel turned the car into the curb to park, John

gasped. "Oh, no." His eyes followed a red Chevrolet pickup truck passing by.

"What is it, son?" Mel asked, but John looked stunned and didn't answer.

"What, John?" Matt grabbed John's shoulder and shook it back and forth.

"That man in the truck." John pointed ahead. "I think he's Johnson."

Mel tore the car out into the street, speeding to catch the truck at the stoplight. There were several cars between them. "Matt, see if you can read the numbers on his license plate. I'll try to get closer." John looked helpless, paralyzed in his seat.

Mel managed to pass two cars that were chugging slowly up the hill, and Matt called out the numbers for Diane to write down. "Now, John, careful," Mel said. "I'm going to pass him. We don't want him to spot you, but see if you can glance over. Put a paper or something in front of your face."

Matt threw John his jacket. "Here, this'll do."

Swallowing hard, John did as he was told and peered over Matt's jacket, which partially shielded his face. He deliberated aloud. "If it's Johnson, he's going to be in big trouble and really mad at me. This man doesn't have a beard, so it's hard to tell. But he's bald. Sure looks like Johnson."

"What do you think? Is it Johnson? Should I try to head off his truck?"

John cried out, "No, don't."

"It's not him?"

John cradled his head in his hands, covering his ears. "I don't know." He began to sob. "I just don't know."

Diane asked Mel to stop at a pay telephone booth and promised to be only a minute. She dialed the direct line to Detective Steve Williams at his office. "Thank God," she said, when he picked up the phone. "It's Diane. We're in Franklin, by the cabin, with John. He thinks he might have seen Johnson. There was a man in a red pickup, but John wasn't sure. He's really upset."

"Did you get anything on the man?"

"Yeah, he's bald like Johnson, but doesn't have a beard. We've got his license plate numbers."

"Great, Diane. Shoot."

Diane held a finger to her ear, to drown out the passing traffic. She read off the numbers quickly.

"If we pick him up, I'll need the boy," Williams said. "I can be there in an hour. I'll put out an APB on the truck and leave right away. Probably the locals'll have him by the time I get there."

Next Diane called Dr. Bozeman, true to their agreement, to report John's distress. Dr. Bozeman listened, without interrupting, then insisted that he be returned to the hospital. When Diane protested, due to the circumstances and Detective Williams' request, the doctor agreed to wait until morning. "Maybe John needs to face this issue. But take him back to the cabin, immediately. And don't let Williams at him without calling me first." She paused, then added softly, "Diane, I'll pray for your family, as well as for John."

Diane followed Dr. Bozeman's instructions and asked Mel to drive straight to the cabin, where he and Matt stayed to comfort John. She headed back to town, to meet Detective Williams at the small brick substation and to help identify the suspect, if he were caught.

Diane walked in, breathless, her heart skipping beats. She asked a young deputy manning the front desk if Detective Williams had arrived.

"Who's asking?" the deputy questioned, not in a suspicious tone, but not too friendly, either.

"Diane Rath. I'm supposed to meet him here."

"Oh, yeah, he mentioned that. Can't see him now, though." The deputy looked over his shoulder to a back room. "He's getting ready to interrogate the suspect."

Detective Williams' prediction had proved correct. Before his arrival, the suspect had been apprehended, but, in deference to Williams, the local police had delayed questioning.

"Can I watch?" Diane asked.

"Oh, like on TV?" the deputy said, his baby face smirking with superiority.

"Well, I guess so," Diane said meekly. "Do you have a two-way mirror?"

The deputy winked and rose. Diane was surprised that he stood no taller than she. "You bet your boots, we do. Follow me, ma'am." The room was a narrow closet with four metal folding chairs lined up, facing a picture window. "It's not exactly the Cobb Theater—no popcorn—but have a seat."

"I'm too nervous. Thanks, anyway."

"I'll leave you to it, then. The detective should be coming in with the suspect soon."

In a few minutes Detective Williams ushered a rotund man in his late fifties into the interrogation room, followed by the deputy. The suspect was cooperative, even cordial. "I hope I can help you clear this up, sir," he said to Williams, his hands fiddling with a Tar Heel baseball cap. Although he had the appearance of a local farmer—starched dungarees over a faded flannel shirt and worn black boots—he spoke differently. His diction was precise, with no Southern drawl, no accent at all. Diane noted the slant of a scar under his cheekbone.

Conversing easily, a cup of black coffee in his hand, the suspect said his name was Adam McGuire. "I live a few towns away and often shop in Franklin. I manage a bookstore and buy most of my office supplies here. Do a little farming, too. Nothing big.

"No, I haven't spent any time in central Georgia, just going through on trips to Florida. Nope, never heard of a kidnapped boy named John, or Gene. Why do you ask? Am I being held for a reason? Have I done something wrong? Run a red light?"

"We can't tell you much at this juncture," Williams hedged. "But, Mr. McGuire, we are going to have to ask you to stay in town at least till tomorrow. Will that be too much of an inconvenience?"

"And if it is?"

"Then, we'll have to provide lodging for you," Williams said, pointing toward a door that led to a small cellblock.

"Considering the options, I suppose I can manage to

stay overnight. Where do you suggest?"

The young deputy spoke up. "There's a mighty fine bed 'n breakfast just 'cross the street."

Williams added politely, as if he were inviting McGuire to tea, "Please drop by at ten o'clock tomorrow morning," then sternly dismissed him. "You can go now."

McGuire pushed his chair back, freeing his round stomach so that he could stand. "Good night, then," he said good-naturedly, as he turned for the door.

Detective Williams left the room immediately to brief Diane, who rose anxiously when he entered the room. "What do you think, Steve?"

"Nothing yet. Could you hear all right? I detained him till tomorrow, to give us time to run a background check. We might dig up something." Williams paced back and forth as he spoke. "This McGuire has a sophistication not acquired in these parts. He *is* the same guy from the truck, isn't he?"

"I think so. I didn't get a very good look at him." Diane thought of John's description of his abductor, and her voice lifted. "Did you notice the scar?"

"Sure. Lots of people have scars. Do you think John could be here tomorrow morning for identification?"

"Steve, it's more complicated than you can imagine. We have to get clearance from John's doctor, which should put our odds right up there with getting struck by lightning." Diane began to fiddle with a loose curl that fell across her cheek. "'Course, she may be right. John's pretty fragile."

"Would you try? If not this time—at least, soon. We can keep tabs on Adam McGuire until John's able to face him."

Diane asked the deputy if she could use the phone at his desk. She noticed that he was staring at her legs, and she instinctively looked down. "Oh, I'd forgotten about that. I'm a mess from ruby mining."

He followed the line of her body with his eyes, slowly, from her knees to her neck. "Looks okay to me."

"Well, thanks, but could I use the phone now?" She sat down and called Dr. Bozeman to plead her case. "The police need John badly, doctor, for identification, or they'll have to let the suspect go."

Dr. Bozeman commiserated, "Believe me, I know how important this is to the police, to your family, and to John. But I can't just throw him to the wolves, without supervision. John's in state care. We're responsible for his well being, and we wouldn't be doing our duty. I can't have it."

"But Dr. Bozeman, if John wants to do this—if it's vitally important to him—what then?"

"I suppose there's another solution. You're only three hours away, and I do drive, you know."

"Dr. Bozeman, you're the answer to our prayers." Diane slapped her hand against her throbbing chest. "I'm going to the cabin to talk to John. If he expresses a desire to go through with this, I'll get him to a phone to call you. Can I reach you at home?" Diane paused, listening, then nodded her head. "Oh yes, if I sense the slightest hesitation, you won't hear from us again today, and we'll bring John back to the hospital tomorrow. I promise."

Diane drove back to the cabin, hunched over the steering wheel, intent on the white lines along the winding road. With my night vision, she thought, I'm dangerous. Her back began to ache, and she crossed her chest to rub her shoulder, digging her fingers into the flesh.

She rushed into the cabin and asked John if she could speak to him alone on the porch. John's face was white, and he obliged without speaking. They sat on rocking chairs in the dim light. The night was electric with crickets.

"How do you feel about seeing Johnson again?" Diane asked.

"I've talked to Dr. Bozeman about this. I'm all mixed up. I want to see him, but I wonder if he'll give a hoot about me anymore. He'll probably be real mad that I ratted on him. I don't think I can look him in the eye. What if the police lock him up and throw away the key?"

Diane listened to his jumbled emotions and remembered Dr. Bozeman's warning. "John, perhaps it's best that you go back to the hospital tomorrow. You don't have to make this decision now."

"No, Miss Diane, I've got to find out if that man is Johnson."

"I guess, then, we'll need to call Dr. Bozeman. She said she'd drive over to be with you. And we'll be there." Diane placed her hand lightly on his knee. "Don't be afraid of him."

"Miss Diane, you don't understand. I'm not afraid *of* Johnson; I'm afraid *for* him."

Diane reached for John's hand and they rocked together, their chairs creaking in unison. The night was still except for a tree frog, which sounded its foghorn in the distance.

# Broken Bravado

## Chapter 10

Marble-sized hail pelted the streets the next morning, lining the gutters with frosty pockets of ice. Unshaven and rumpled with his tie askew, Detective Williams leaned against the reception desk, sipping coffee from a steaming Styrofoam cup as he talked with Diane.

"Hell of a storm," he said, shifting his tie.

"Yeah." Diane blew into her cup, to cool the coffee, and noticed that her hand was shaking. The detective's eyes looked hazy. Probably hadn't had a full night's sleep, she thought. He always seemed so intense, and she suspected that he was an insomniac.

At nine o'clock a squatty woman, almost dwarflike in dimension, entered the Franklin sheriff's substation. Drenched by the rain, she shook her umbrella wildly about, so that water spewed like a sprinkler gone awry.

A few drops splattered Detective Williams' back, and he turned, frowning at the sight. "Dr. Bozeman?"

"Right, a wet and harried Dr. Bozeman. I don't usually look like a drowned rat, believe me." She greeted Diane, then turned toward the detective with her hand outstretched. "And you must be Detective Steve Williams. I've heard many good things about you."

"Likewise, doctor."

"Do you work just with child abductions, detective?"

"Actually, our department deals with all disappearances—kidnappings, runaways, missing persons. Why do you ask?"

"We're having a problem with illegal baby adoptions in the Atlanta hospital where I work. More and more complaints are being filed. Babies are being placed for adoption without the mothers' permission, and even sold."

"Like Prissy's?" Diane asked. "Remember, Steve, the young girl I told you about."

"Well, in her case, I believe you said the legal guardian did sign over custody, didn't she?" Detective Williams swept his arm toward the next room. "Let's take a seat, ladies. Would you like coffee, Dr. Bozeman?"

"No, thanks, but that sofa over there looks mighty inviting."

As Dr. Bozeman removed her coat and shook the water out of it, Detective Williams asked, "Do you know if there's an investigation going on?"

"Pardon?"

"At your hospital? If so, I would like to touch base with the investigator."

"Sorry," Dr. Bozeman said. "I'm foggy after that drive. A hailstorm you wouldn't believe. Actually, an FBI agent got in touch with our unit. I have his card back at my office, but I'll have to dig it out. I'll call you."

"Thanks. I like to be aware of all sources. You never know."

"Right. Where's John? I came early, hoping to spend some time with him before the identification session."

Diane answered, "He's in a private office with Mel, filling out some paperwork. Come on, I'll show you."

John sat at a messy desk, hunched over a stack of papers. Dr. Bozeman walked up behind him and placed her hands on his shoulders. "Good morning, John. Doing your homework?" He jumped up, more spontaneous than Diane had ever seen him, and gave Dr. Bozeman a hug.

"Do you need help with these forms?" Diane asked. "I can finish up, if you'd like to speak with Dr. Bozeman."

"Maybe you could just look them over for me."

Diane sat down and began to read, twirling her hair absentmindedly.

"If you don't need me for a while, I'll go get a cup of coffee with Williams," Mel said, heading out the door.

Dr. Bozeman glanced around the room, pointing at two straight-back chairs against the wall. "How about over here, John." They sat down, splitting a small table between them, and spoke softly in confidential tones.

"Have you had breakfast? I don't want you to face Johnson on an empty stomach."

"Yes, ma'am, eggs and bacon. We all got up early at the cabin. Don't think anybody could sleep. I couldn't." He dropped his gaze and bit his lip.

Dr. Bozeman stared at him, waiting quietly, until he lifted his eyes. "How do you feel about today?"

"Nervous." John shrugged his shoulders. "That's about it."

"I suppose Detective Williams has told you about the meeting. You'll be sitting in a small room, looking through a two-way mirror. We'll be there, too. The detective will bring in the man you saw in the pickup—the man you thought was Johnson. He won't be able to see you. Then, Detective Williams will call a recess, in order to get your opinion." She paused to catch her breath. "How does that sound?"

"It don't bother me none," John said, rubbing his palms together in his lap. "Honest."

Diane glanced up and saw John's hands trembling. She tossed the papers aside and rolled the swivel desk chair over to join them. "And what if the man turns out to be Johnson?"

John lifted his eyes to the ceiling, cocking his head to one side. "I want to talk to him—not alone, but with someone there. I want to ask him how he's doing, if he misses me. And I want to tell him I'm sorry—" John's eyes glistened, threatening tears, "for getting him into this mess."

Detective Williams opened the door, talking over his shoulder to Mel, then stopped in his tracks when he saw John's face. "Okay to come in?"

"It's okay," John said, raising his arm and contorting his head to wipe his nose on his sleeve. Diane handed him a tissue from her purse.

"The background check hasn't turned up anything suspicious," Detective Williams began. "McGuire grew up in an urban area in the Midwest, but settled in North Carolina fifteen years ago. Moved frequently from town to town, but never left the state or, at least, never left a forwarding address outside the state. He lives alone, no family. Has no record, no arrests other than a DUI from ten years ago. All in all, he seems like a decent enough chap."

He turned to John, as if there were no one else in the room. "Nothing to be afraid of, son. The sheriff's deputy will be with you, and, of course, Dr. Bozeman, Diane, and Mel. Now, the suspect, McGuire—"

"You mean Johnson," John corrected.

Williams nodded his head. "Johnson won't be able to see you through the glass. If you're not sure it's him, if something doesn't look quite right, remember to listen to his voice." Williams grasped John's shoulder and gave it a manly squeeze. "Are you okay?"

"I'm okay," John said weakly. Then—as if to demonstrate his mastery of the situation, the routineness of it all—he opened his mouth wide in a mock yawn, stretching his arms with fists clenched, elbows bent, and puffed his chest forward.

"Okay, follow me." Williams walked briskly out, and they hurried to catch up. He stopped at the door to the observation room and turned the knob to prop it open. They filed in like school children, in hushed decorum, and took their seats in a row. Williams closed the door behind him, and all eyes turned in unison toward the glass. They stared at it intently, waiting, with no words to break the silence.

Soon Williams entered the interrogation room with McGuire, offering him the seat facing the mirror. He set a tape recorder on the table, pushed the controls, and began. "We are at the Franklin, North Carolina sheriff's substation at 11:08 on July 10, 1997. Present are Adam McGuire and Detective Steve Williams of Asheville." Williams read the suspect his rights in a perfunctory manner, then spoke loudly for John's benefit. "Are you comfortable, sir? Please state your name and address."

"What do ya think, John?" the deputy whispered.

John stared at the suspect through the glass. "I'm not sure. His hair is right. He's bald like Johnson, with that island in the front of his head. But something's different." John began to talk faster and faster. "The scar's in the same place. His nose—that's it. It's not as big, and he's not wearing glasses." John put his palm on his forehead, plastering back his dark hair. "It's hard to tell, without the beard."

"It's okay. Just take your time," the deputy said calmly.

"But he moves his hands exactly like Johnson, holds his head the same. Sure seems like Johnson."

Detective Williams stopped his questions abruptly. "Mr. McGuire, I have a matter to attend to. I'd like you to wait here for me." McGuire flopped his hands on the table and stared blankly ahead.

Williams rushed into the observation room. "Well, John, what do you think?"

John hesitated. "I'm not really sure. Looks like him and moves like him, but some things are different. No glasses and no beard. His nose, too—I swear it's smaller. Used to take up his whole face."

"What about his voice?"

John shook his head. "I forgot about that, I was so busy looking."

"I'll go back in," Williams said. "Close your eyes and forget about his face. Just listen. Okay?"

Detective Williams returned to the interrogation room. "Sorry for the interruption, Mr. McGuire. Now let's continue."

"First, detective, let's talk about legal representation. Of course, I have a right to an attorney. You and I both know that. But I don't suppose I'll need one, since I have nothing to hide." McGuire spoke the lines as if rehearsed during the night.

John leaned back in his seat and closed his eyes, as McGuire spoke.

"I do believe that you're required to tell me why I'm here and what you're charging me with. If you *are* charging me, that is."

"We certainly owe you that much, Mr. McGuire. You've been identified as a suspect in a child abduction case." Williams blurted the words out, as if he were impatient with the progress, anxious to get on with it.

John's eyes opened wide, and he moved close to the glass, pressing his palms flat against it. McGuire appeared shaken, but quickly restored his composure, the demeanor of a fine gentleman.

"Perhaps I do need an attorney. Who is your witness, sir?"

"I can't disclose that yet, but you're free to call your attorney."

While McGuire was arranging for counsel, Detective Williams went back to the observation room. John had dropped his head, limp over the back of the chair, and stretched his lanky legs out straight, stiff with his heels resting a distance from the chair. He looked totally vulnerable, as if his defenses had been stolen, his bravado gone.

Williams' face twisted with concern, and he turned to Dr. Bozeman. "Okay to go on?"

Before she could answer, John spoke in a mechanical tone, as if programmed by a secret hand. "It's him, Detective Williams." John's voice quavered, distorted from the pressure on his larynx. "It's him."

Two hours later, McGuire and his counsel sat on the far side of the interrogation table, opposite two empty wooden chairs with thick slat prisons across their back, initials and curses carved into the heavy brown varnish. Diane stared at the two-way mirror, holding tightly to Mel's hand.

As John entered the room, he glanced in McGuire's direction, then darted his eyes toward the mirror. Detective Williams motioned for John to sit across from McGuire's attorney, a small-framed man with receding gray hair, whose forehead stretched into a scalp glistening with sweat.

"This here's Mr. Clark, a local attorney," Williams said, directing his attention exclusively to John.

McGuire fidgeted his broad frame in his chair, which squeaked in protest, and his attorney cleared his throat. John sat stiffly, looking down. When the room was still and the silence, unsettling, Williams set the tape recorder and began.

"This is the second interview of this day, July 10, 1997, with suspect Adam McGuire, now accompanied by his attorney, Mr. Clark. It's 13:10, and I'm Steve Williams of Asheville Missing Persons." He placed his arm protectively on John's back. "Sir, have you ever seen the young man sitting beside me?"

Mr. Clark cupped his bony hand over his mouth and whispered into his client's bulbous ear. Then, he moved his cupped palm to his own ear and motioned to McGuire, who whispered back. The attorney nodded his head in short, confident jerks, and McGuire answered, "I have not."

"Are you aware that what you say can be held against you in a court of law?" Williams thundered, startling John, whose body jumped involuntarily. "This is no longer a simple interview, and you'd best resist any stretch of the truth. Counsel, advise your client. The *truth*! Is that clear?"

"It is, sir," McGuire answered in a self-assured manner, as if he held the upper hand. He puffed his massive chest and fingered the tabs on his dungarees with the aplomb of a Wall Street executive smoothing the silk of his pocket-handkerchief. McGuire dwarfed his attorney, who nevertheless leaned toward him protectively and glared at Williams with blazing eyes.

"Let me give you another chance," Williams said, drilling away. "Are you certain that you have never seen this boy?"

The attorney raised a well-manicured finger at Williams. "I believe my client has answered that question."

"I'll answer again," McGuire said, raising his voice for the first time, forcing his words on John. "Do you know me, son? Tell them. You don't know me, now, do you?" His tone was impassioned, threatening, and his demeanor, that of a parent who, in public, controlled his child's behavior with a familiar glare that promised retribution.

John slumped his shoulders and looked helplessly at Detective Williams. He pushed his hair from his forehead with a heavy hand. "I don't guess so, mister."

Detective Williams searched John's flushed face. "Son, this man can't hurt you. All you have to do is tell the truth."

Diane felt a cold chill as McGuire's eyes locked tighter into John's. His presence was overpowering, mesmerizing, demanding obedience.

"It's not him," John stated emphatically.

McGuire, vindicated, bloated his chest in triumph.

"Well, then," his attorney said, rising, "we'll be on our way. Come along, Adam."

As they left, John spread his upper body on the table, cushioning his head in folded arms. He began to sob. "I'm sorry. I'm sorry."

Diane bolted out of the observation room, and Dr. Bozeman clicked along behind, her short legs flying. Diane watched helplessly as Dr. Bozeman patted John on the back. "It's okay, son. It's okay."

John raised his head, tears streaming down his long, drawn face. "I want to go back to the hospital," he said quietly. He rose as if by rote, in slow motion, his arms limp at his sides. He stood slumped like a scarecrow.

Diane hugged him gently. "We'll see you soon, John. Take care of yourself."

Dr. Bozeman put her arm around John's back, reaching up to his shoulders, struggling to support his weight as she guided him toward the door. John shuffled his feet, off balance, walking blindly, as if empty inside, his spirit gone.

# Part Two

# The Family Business

## Chapter 11

Buck Stanley uncapped his first beer that morning at nine-thirty, chasing his coffee. A shipment was arriving from South America tonight, and he needed someone he trusted to count inventory. He scratched the back of his head, untangling blond thick curls, matted from a restless night of tossing.

Buck usually worked at home, ensconcing himself in its masculine den with custom oak-paneled walls. The room, with its under-the-counter refrigerator and wet bar, was a perfect refuge. Stanley could drink at will, without the disapproving stares he received at business and social gatherings.

Buck phoned his secretary, an attentive Southern belle he'd met at a bar. "Lureen, can you locate Mr. DuRoy for me? I need to talk to him—yesterday."

"Yes, Mr. Stanley, I'll get on it. Are you home?" Her voice clicked efficiently.

"Yeah, honey, I'm home." Buck cradled the phone against his shoulder, craning his neck as he reached for a cigarette. "And, Lureen, you know I'm a patient man." Buck's lips drooled a trace of beer. "But tell my dawdling half-brother he'd best step lively."

"Yes, sir," Lureen's voice saluted. "I'll make it clear to Mr. DuRoy." Buck slammed down the phone and lit his cigarette.

Buck Stanley had a self-effacing country bumpkin charm, boyish face, and a deadly sarcasm, which he used for surprise attacks to demonstrate that he wasn't so dumb after all. Seemingly jocular, his lips frequently cut into a pat smile that did not fade, as most smiles do to relish the aftertaste, but turned off like a light, automatic. His words were slurred, a mixture of Southern drawl and liquor override.

In fifteen minutes Buck's half-brother, sounding winded, reported for duty by phone. "Needed to talk with you anyway," DuRoy began cryptically. "There's a new development."

"Well, Laffey," Buck cut in quickly, "why don't you just mosey on over so you can take care of business—no later than one o'clock this afternoon. You got that?" His voice was cold, and the words, biting. "You can update me then on whatever new nonsense you've come up with." Buck's best sarcasm was devoted to the humiliation of his half-brother, although he usually savored his venom, reserving his strike for an audience.

Buck had acquired his position in life through no effort of his own. The family aircraft parts business, which was lucrative and well organized, offered him a title, but no job. As the family means were immense and Buck, easily bored, he pursued recreation with a passion. He was a magnet to women, who were drawn to his frisky flirtations and expensive gifts. He used his charismatic charm to wine and dine any woman he chose, daring his wife to protest.

"I'll give you a divorce, sugar; just say the word. But you'll never get a penny of the Stanley money, or ever see your children again. I'll dig up dirt you can't imagine—manufacture it, if necessary."

Buck retained a chauffeur, not just for prestige, but for transportation when he was soused, which was much of the time. Essentially, Buck's life ran without him.

At noon Buck heard a car and walked to the window, pulling back the heavy drape to watch Laffey DuRoy's shiny black Corvette pull into the grounds of the sprawling red brick estate. The sports car image fit Laffey as poorly as his chinos, which rode his ankles too high. His face and limbs were puffy, with skin sickly white, as if powdered.

Lawrence Lafayette DuRoy's manner matched his name in pretentiousness. Short of stature with a compensatory arrogance, he annoyed Buck. Too big for his britches, Buck mumbled, as he watched his half-brother skip up the front steps. He heard the front door open, the maid's greeting—"Why, Mr. DuRoy"—then Laffey's footsteps as he raced up the stairs.

"You need me?" Laffey asked solicitously as he reached Buck's doorway, his feet buckling to attention, which lurched his body forward. He caught himself just as Buck looked over from the window.

"Yeah," Buck said, dispensing with even a cursory greeting. "There's a shipment coming into Jacksonville tonight at eight. If you get cracking, you've got plenty of time."

DuRoy hesitated at the doorway, testing the water for entry. "I need to talk to you first. It won't take long." He puffed out his chest and approached with an arrogant air, stretching his short legs into deliberate strides, hands clasped behind his back. "My carefully laid network of contacts has paid off," he announced proudly.

Buck yawned, bored with the oratory, but Laffey gushed on.

"I got a call from one of our suppliers, that body-builder punk, Donny. He's onto an obstetrics nurse in Bradford Hospital—gal named Sheila, who favors fancy digs but is lacking in the cash flow department. She's been watching the ward for us, for unwed mothers who want to sign over their babies. Donny appealed to her sense of right-eousness. Told her that we're trying to expedite the adoption process, for those poor couples who can't do the job for themselves. After all, that's what we're about, right, Buck?"

DuRoy was prone to justify his evil work. When Buck just shook his head in astonishment, Laffey muttered, "Sheila knows what a fouled-up mess it is. And she's found us an obstetrician—an Hispanic doctor, from Colombia, no less—who wants in on the act."

"And I suppose this spic doctor just happened to walk up to her at the nurses' station," Buck jeered. "Told her he needed extra cash and asked if she knew where he could sell some babies."

"No, Buck," Laffey broke in defensively. "You know I'm more careful than that. It's all been checked out. Dr. Martinez has been at the hospital for ten years, and he's highly respected."

"How does he propose to deliver?" Buck chuckled. "No pun intended."

"He can earmark the babies born in the hospital who'll be offered for adoption. Even better, he can speak to the Spanish mothers. More and more young Hispanic girls are showing up pregnant, Donny says. Some of them would carry to term, just to make a few bucks, and Martinez could get word out on the streets. This could be an ongoing process, a real gold mine."

Buck poured himself a shot of scotch, for it was afternoon and he was on to the hard stuff. He downed it with one gulp and stared at Laffey with the empty shot glass still in his hand. "And why would any doctor risk himself like that? Last I heard, doctors do a little better than just making ends meet."

"Sheila suspects that he has a habit and taking any more drugs from the ward supply could be risky for him. The hospital has cracked down."

Buck tapped his chest with his forefinger. "So why are you telling me all this?"

"Just following protocol, Buck. I need your okay to hire this doctor." Laffey raised a stubby finger to his thinning hairline and messaged his temple.

Laffey's finger gave Buck the creeps. Looked like a stick of chalk with joints. "Not a bad plan," he said. "I like it—no planes, no customs. But watch yourself, brother," he cautioned. "In South America we pay the officials to ignore us. Here you rot in jail."

"Thanks. I'll meet with Donny, and, don't worry, I'll be discreet."

"Nope," Buck said, strumming his bottom lip with his forefinger, as if he were playing a guitar. "I think I'd better step in this time—too much risk. Set up a meeting for me, with Donny and this nurse, Sheila. In fact, I think I'll join you for the delivery today. Things are kinda slow around here." Buck swept a pack of cigarettes from his desk.

"Okay, boss," Laffey said, turning with a confident step toward the door. Buck followed him as he bounded down the winding stairs. Laffey skipped across the grand entry hall, panting with the effort, opened the carved mahogany entry doors, and led Buck to his car, parked down the circular drive.

Laffey dutifully drove, and Buck stared out the window, sulking. When Laffey made a few futile attempts at conversation, he barked for silence. "Shut up, Laffey. Don't push this brother stuff."

They arrived in Jacksonville in time to visit a local haunt for a few brews. Buck even managed to set up a tryst with one of the female entertainers, who flaunted her bosom in his direction.

"Don't know how you do it, boss," Laffey said, complimenting his brother's prowess.

Buck grinned. "Just talented, I guess."

The jet landed on schedule, and the captain joined Buck and Laffey at the landing ramp, confirming the projected inventory of seventeen. "That's good, isn't it?" Laffey said to Buck.

The roster wasn't always exact, as departure corrections were frequently required. Hispanic ties were deep-rooted. The price for a baby could equal a harvest's pay for an impoverished South American family, but to let a child go— to sever an infant from his family—was often too drastic a step, even when it meant survival for those remaining. Many a tormented mother, heavy with guilt, appealed to an authority at the last moment, begging at his feet for mercy, for the release of her child. Sometimes the official would consider such a plea, but often he would not.

The count could go up or down. A doctor examined the adoptees before departure, and sick or infectious candidates were detained. A mother might deliver early and add to the head count, or a baby might die before the plane arrived. But tonight's count was on target, a shipment of fifteen strong, healthy babies and two toddlers—a profitable load.

They stood in the shadow of the plane, the sun almost down. Buck smiled as he watched the efficiency of the crew—pilots, drivers, nursemaids, and bodyguards—as they delivered their cargo. Nurses dressed in street clothes transferred the babies in padded satchels, resembling luggage from a distance. A woman, her hunched back silhouetted against an outbuilding like a hovering crone, herded two toddlers into the side-door of a van, which inside was equipped like a nursery.

DuRoy whistled in awe. "It's a beehive of activity, isn't it, captain?"

"You should have heard the commotion during the flight, crying and whining, and the nurses scurrying around, mixing bottles and changing diapers." The pilot looked down at his dusty shoes, shaking his head. "I even had to help load, because the locals were short-staffed."

"Well," Buck said, "thanks for getting here safely. Our inventory is priceless."

Laffey added, "It's important work. We're dealing with human life here."

"Yep," the captain smirked, "a real specialized business."

⁓

The Stanley family had a tradition of hard work. Buck's grandfather, Poke Stanley, dirt poor as a young man, had slaved for a peach farmer in central Georgia, hoeing the orchards, watering the trees, protecting them with sheets when cold threatened. During the summer harvest time, Poke had the worst job at the packing shed, culling the rotten peaches as they tumbled onto the assembly line, protecting his neck with a blue-checkered bandanna from the itchy peach fuzz, fresh from picking. Poke wasn't afraid of work, but he fixed his eyes higher, aiming to set other men to work, to meet his ambition, to combine a keen mind with a powerful follow-through.

When his bossman hired a crop duster to come in to spray his orchards, fighting phony peach vector and other enemies of his crop, Buck's grandfather started snooping around the trailer where the pilot slept. He was intrigued by the small Cessna crop-dusting plane and looked to the sky for a way out of the god-forsaken mess of a life he lived.

Poke quit working for the farmer and moved to town where he got a job at the local filling station sweeping floors, filling the drink machines with bottles of cola and grape soda, doing the dirty work in the bays—anything to hang around engines and learn how they worked. Once a week he drove to a vocational school thirty miles away, to study to become a mechanic. Poke met an entrepreneur who owned a fleet of automobile service centers across the South and had come to set up classes for his employees. Seeing an opportunity, Poke mentioned to him how the local stations, isolated and all, were stymied at moving the cars through the bays, how the cars sat there idle, wasting the bays, because the mechanics needed parts. Parts were the name of the game. Poke suggested that the real money was in distributing. He knew how to make it happen, but he needed a backer.

Never successful in his schooling, Poke's genius was reading people, not books. He had picked the right man to fill the till of his ambition. The entrepreneur's eyes grew big, glistening with greed, and he answered Poke with a hand-shake. "Well, Mr. Stanley—partner—guess we've got business to do."

Stanley Distribution grew rapidly, soon covering a territory of six Southern states, and Buck's father picked up the banner when his grandfather reluctantly retired in poor health, at the age of only sixty-one, from cancer of the throat. The doctors said that years of smoking had done it, but the local folks suspected that he'd breathed a mite too much of those peach-dusting chemicals.

The company expanded into parts for airplanes as well as automobiles, and Buck's father wielded monopolies with American manufacturing companies in South American countries. Stanley Distribution acquired five DC-8s, retired from the airlines, that flew international deliveries into Atlanta, and fifteen feeder planes that serviced the main headquarters in Athens, where Buck lived.

The family tradition faltered when handed down to Buck who, spoiled and lazy, didn't see the wisdom or pleasure in slaving away, when the rewards were already won. Buck fancied himself smarter than his predecessors and left the well-oiled operation alone. He would hang his thumbs under his armpits and chuckle, as he recited, "If it ain't broke, don't fix it."

Bored with the *modus operandi*, Buck added a new twist to the family business. On a rare trip to Colombia, quite innocently, he had met a rough unshaven young man from home, sitting at the bar of the America Club, a hangout for English-speaking expatriates who gathered to bet on American sports events and drink American beer. His tongue loosened by alcohol, the fellow bragged about how much money he was pulling in, preying on poor South American families—not poor by American standards, but really poor, starving, in fact. All he had to do, he said with a shrug, was talk them into giving up their kids. Or some-times, when the parents were working and the older chil-dren looked after the younger children, he'd just snatch the babies right out of their cribs or baskets or whatever pitiful thing they were sleeping in. He boasted about the big fees baby-smugglers paid for a healthy baby, even a bonus for a pretty little girl. Oh, he made it sound easy—easy to escape clean from the helpless families, and easy to elude the authorities, who became disinterested when their palms were greased. The devious child-snatcher caught Buck's attention. He talked with him, long into the night, learning the rogue's tricks of the trade.

"It's so simple," Buck exclaimed to Laffey after his return. "We have the tools for the operation, planes with legitimate business in South America. And live inventory is worth far more than parts. A baby can bring as much as fifty thousand dollars."

Buck hit his cupped palm with his fist. "Think of it, Laffey. Twenty kids times fifty thousand, a million-dollar load a few times a month—not a bad sideline. And money the government can't tax. Even better, money that Dad won't know about."

Buck smirked at the thought. "My own stamp on the business."

# The Colombian Connection

## Chapter 12

Donny snapped his fingers at a passing waiter, pointing without words to the icy wine cooler on a stand beside his chair. "More wine, Buck? How about you, Sheila?" He smiled at the plain-featured woman across the table, drab as the dull gray suit she wore.

Sheila pushed her wineglass toward him, tripping it up on a wrinkle of the tablecloth. She grasped awkwardly for the base, and the glass teetered in her hand. "Never could hold my liquor," she said, looking at Buck, giggling.

Nurse Sheila McMann had become a crucial element in Donny's scheme, and Buck could see that he cared not a whit that she was homely.

"That Prissy's baby was a beaut, wasn't she?" Donny said, reaching for Sheila's hand. "What a job you did handling that one. You're getting to be a pro."

"I'm happy that you're pleased." Sheila blushed at his compliment and played with her glass, dipping her forefinger into the wine and circling the rim. "Frankly, the money comes in handy. Seven-hundred dollars isn't bad for ten minutes work—delivering a baby to the nursery and giving a few extra pills to the mother, to make her sleep."

Donny looked shocked and pretended to protest. "What? You're doing it for the money? I thought it was because you're crazy about me."

"That too," Sheila said, laughing giddily, flushed from the wine.

"What about this Spanish doctor you've found?" Buck asked, getting impatient with the show Donny was putting on.

"You mean that good Samaritan to the adoption cause?" Donny asked. He cupped Sheila's lean hand, his thick fingers overpowering hers in an affectionate squeeze.

My God, Buck thought, next he'll pull a bouquet of roses from up his sleeve. He looked at Sheila's gawky limbs, which enhanced her homeliness, and her long, slender fingers. Although her nails were scrubbed and even polished, the ends were broken and ragged.

"Dr. Martinez is a good doctor really," she said, "but he never seems to have enough money, always complaining about it. I had a talk with him, about the poor state of affairs in the world—babies crying for homes and parents begging to adopt, but government agencies just standing in the way. Red tape and investigative services, and all that."

Sheila took a deep breath and pulled her hand loose from Donny's grip. She held it tightly to her neck, as if choking, and quickly covered her mouth as a cough erupted. "Water," she said in a gravelly voice. Her cough broke loose again, and she cleared her throat for air, wheezing. Finally, she started again, her voice hoarse. "Must have swallowed wrong. Anyway, guess I chose the right doctor, from what he said."

Donny feigned concern for her cough. "Are you okay, Sheila?"

Donny deserves a bonus, for all this romantic rot, Buck thought. "What did the doctor say, Sheila?"

"He said that he had ways of getting babies, and he'd like to help the rotten system. Did I say he's from Colombia? Anyway, I guess there are jillions of illegitimate babies there, and the people are so poor." She reached for her water glass to avert another coughing spell, rumbling in her throat.

"Sounds like a real do-gooder."

"I don't really think so, Buck; it's not that." Sheila paused as the waiter stopped at their table to remove their dinner plates.

"Finished, ma'am?" he asked, glancing down at Sheila's barely touched plate. The breast of duck, topped with cherries swimming in burgundy sauce, was still plump, and a mound of wild rice with mushrooms looked perfectly turned from a bowl. A thin orange slice, twisted like the blade of a pinwheel, garnished the plate, undisturbed.

"Go ahead and take it," Donny said, waving off the waiter. "You take a lady to the fanciest restaurant in town," he said to Buck, mockingly, "and she doesn't even appreciate it."

"No, it was delicious," Sheila protested. "I just wasn't hungry." She sat back and pulled the gray suit jacket smooth across her meager bosom. "But back to Dr. Martinez." She leaned across the table and whispered, "I think he has a drug problem. The word's out that he's on something. He probably wouldn't mind selling babies for the money."

"Sheila, Sheila," Donny teased, "and I thought you were naive. Sounds like you know all about the cruel world."

"Just work in a hospital. You see everything," Sheila said, pulling at her ear lobe and massaging around a tiny pearl stud. "But, Donny, what happens to these babies? I don't get any paperwork, and you never say where they're going."

"They all end up in good homes; don't worry about that. They're better off with their adoptive parents."

"Besides," Buck added, swirling the wine in his glass, "the less you know, the better."

"That's just what I thought. I could get in big-time trouble for this, couldn't I?"

"Get in trouble for what?" Donny asked. "You're just rescuing innocent babies. Consider yourself a Girl Scout, doing a good deed." Donny leered at her small breasts. "Course, you don't look like a Girl Scout."

"Yeah, I'm just over the age limit."

Buck returned to the subject, wanting to get on with it. "Tell me more about this doctor."

"Well, I've told Donny most of it. The guy's an obstetrician; he might even be able to tailor deliveries for you. He's in a position to know the circumstances of the mothers, to identify the ones who might sign over their babies for adoption."

"Good work, girl!" Donny lifted his glass in her direction.

He's actually enjoying himself, Buck thought. Must be the wine.

Sheila hugged her knees, taking a moment to luxuriate in Donny's approval, then set to finishing her wine. After a few moments, she asked playfully, boldly, "Donny, do you take me out only because I help you?" She crossed her legs, and Buck imagined her stocking foot reaching for Donny's calf, her toes rubbing up and down. "Or is it because you like me?"

"You know the answer to that," Donny said, evading the question. "It's going to take a while to get this operation going, Sheila. So you just be patient."

Donny's chest heaved as he leaned back, placing his elbows on the arms of his chair. "Now, honey, how about some coffee?"

# The Taste of Fresh Mango

## Chapter 13

Laffey DuRoy wore black reflective sunglasses and a Panama hat, perched dramatically forward on his broad head, almost concealing his puffy cheeks and bulbous lips. Buck groaned at Laffey's ridiculous attempt at undercover disguise. Embarrassed, he glanced around the dingy bar populated by scruffy patrons in torn jeans, many with greasy hair pulled into ponytails. At least they'd found a table in a corner, out of the way.

Just then, Donny sauntered in and swaggered across the room. So unmistakable, that macho bodybuilder's walk, like a Sumo wrestler's waddle, when the legs just couldn't come together for all the muscle.

"Hello, Donny," Laffey said, without offering his hand.

"This better be good," Buck mumbled under his breath.

"It's good, plenty good," Donny said as he sat down. He pulled his chair closer and planted his elbows on the Formica table, resting his chin on cradled hands. "This guy, this Martinez, is the doctor of your dreams, the missing link in your operation. You're going to love him, Laffey." Donny's words had started in a whisper, but crescendoed as he spoke, so that Laffey's name boomed out across the floor of the bar.

"Don't call my name out in public, you idiot," Laffey sneered, sideswiping his elbow into Donny's. The blow upset Donny's balance and slammed his chin toward the table. Instinctively, Donny clenched his fist and punched at

Laffey, stopping just short of his face. Laffey ducked his head backward and fenced with the palm of his hand.

"You shouldn't have done that," Donny warned. He rubbed his knuckles with his cupped hand, his powerful biceps taut and bulging.

Laffey's hands trembled, and his face turned even pastier than normal. Humphrey Bogart, he's not, Buck thought.

Laffey spoke, first softly, with a slow cadence that built, faster and faster, as his tone rose. "Don't you ever raise a hand to me!" Safe, with the danger past, he barked like a dog after wolves, once their pack had moved out of his territory. No longer cowering, back in charge, Laffey pointed a stiff, threatening finger in Donny's face, oblivious to stares from the bar.

Donny withdrew, silent for a moment. "Hey, man, back off. I know when I'm beat." Donny held his palms in the air, feigning surrender to this arrogant weakling half his size. "You're the boss. Sorry, man."

"Just don't let that happen, ever again," Laffey said, wiping sweat from his forehead. "Is that clear?" Laffey spoke as if scolding a child.

"Enough, enough," Buck said. He lit a cigarette and reached for the ashtray, crowded with butts, stubbed white columns set askew in a layer of gray dust. "I never knew we had such an intense operation. Take it easy, Laffey."

Buck turned his attention to Donny. "Why are we here? What's happened with this doctor of yours?"

"He's everything we hoped for. He's got a habit and needs to support it. A junkie obstetrician, for God's sake."

"Okay, okay," Buck snarled, hitting two fists on the table sharply. "We've heard all this before. Did you make the connection?"

"This nurse, Sheila McMann, got to be real friendly with the doc. Like with me, remember?" Donny gave Buck a lascivious wink.

"Yeah, I remember. Sat through a whole goddamn disgusting dinner," Buck said, frowning.

"Anyway, Sheila set us up, me and Martinez, to meet

for cocktails at some fancy club downtown, just so I could feel out the situation." Donny gave a convincing grin and shrugged his broad shoulders. "There was nothin' to it."

"Is there a point here?" Buck asked.

"Yeah, we hit it off real good. Dr. Martinez is ready for his first delivery. He's promised us about fifteen babies, and that's just a start. This guy's got the goods, there for the taking."

"So when is this coming down?" Laffey asked.

Buck chuckled at the lingo. Laffey must watch some cop show on TV.

Donny sat forward in his seat, and his voice rose in enthusiasm. "I just wanted to get your final okay, before I set up a time and place. I've got the go-ahead, right?"

"You're sure this guy's no plant?" Buck asked.

"Out of the question. Sheila has known this doctor for years."

"Okay, Donny, let's do it," Buck said, his face hard as stone. "You've done some good work, but don't forget, there're a lot of volunteers for your job. Keep your mouth zipped. We don't need stupid people."

"Right," Laffey scoffed, rubbing his powdery hands together, with the stubby digits held straight. "Don't mess with us."

"Shut up, Laffey," Buck said in disgust. He stared into his beer mug, mesmerized, as if, at least for the moment, the connection had little interest for him. He began to hum, distractedly, as if he were alone.

But Buck was a chameleon. He suddenly exploded into fury, turning in a flash toward Donny. He reached for his collar, clutching it in his fist at the throat. "But, Donny, if you get the slightest suspicion that things aren't right, the faintest whiff of a rat, back off. I wouldn't make a mistake on this one." He released the shirt, pushing Donny's chest back against the chair. "No," he warned, "if you screw up this one, you're dead meat."

Donny frowned and his face turned red, but he nodded obediently, straightening his collar.

Unruffled, as if nothing had happened, Buck rose and strolled leisurely toward the door. Laffey sneered disdainfully at Donny's brawny frame, then sauntered after Buck, snickering.

⁓

Gabriel Martinez's Colombian background had dealt him inside knowledge of the politically favored cartels that smuggled babies out of the country. His own cousin, who lived in a remote area, had suffered at their hands. Upon the horror of discovering his child missing, his cousin had related the shocking details to the authorities, who received the news with apathetic detachment. They gave him little encouragement, and he never heard from them again. Victims of the cartel were quickly forgotten.

Gabriel himself had felt a traitor when he immigrated to the United States. He knew that his native land was desperate for doctors, but he wanted more for his family than his country could offer, the freedom to follow their dreams. Sometimes Gabriel ached for Colombia—for the taste of fresh mango, for a midday meal of fried bananas and rice under the avocado tree in his dusty courtyard, to gather with his friends and family in the early evening, young men straddling the front brick wall to watch pretty girls strutting by to buy a Coke at the corner grocery store, with starched white blouses and raven hair sleeked back, carefully preened to earn admiring glances.

Dr. Martinez shared his Latin background with Detective Williams in the basement of the doctor's Atlanta apartment building, where they met as arranged by the FBI. They sat at the manager's metal desk, the lone object in an expanse of empty space, like a Navajo hogan in the desert. A small desk lamp sent out dusty rays.

Williams set his coffee down on the desk. "Trying to keep awake," he said, glancing at his watch. "What is it, almost midnight?"

Gabriel Martinez's Spanish accent was barely perceptible. Born to a prominent Colombian family who promoted language skills, he'd spoken English as a child. "Americans don't understand the joy of Latin camaraderie," he said, wistfully. "I left my country and my friends behind, but I'd do anything to protect them." The doctor's raven-black eyes glistened with passion.

This guy is a nobleman, a silent hero, Williams thought. "You're proving that by helping the FBI to set up a sting operation, which is not without personal risk. Maybe you know, maybe you don't, we put a police plant on the ward, posing as one of the cleaning staff. He's the one who left word for this meeting, on a note buried between pages 132 and 133 of your medical book."

"Yeah, the FBI mailbox, I call it. I'm reviewing *Female Anatomy & Physiology* a lot lately."

"It was only after careful surveillance, they tell me, that you were tapped as a colleague who would be sympathetic to the cause, precisely because of your empathy and your courage." Williams reached for Martinez's hand and sandwiched it between his own, shaking it vigorously. "It's not often I'm this proud of anyone."

Dr. Martinez looked down, embarrassed. "It's hard to believe, isn't it, detective, that—even here in America—babies are not safe, that babies in my own hospital are vulnerable to being snatched, virtually out of the arms of their mothers."

"But it's true, doctor." Williams glanced up at the tangle of pipes on the ceiling of the deserted basement, the bowels of a huge building, gurgling and steaming. "What's most frightening is that these kidnappings are part of a much bigger problem. The pattern and frequency shows organization. Child abduction, like any thievery, requires an ultimate buyer, or fence, for what is stolen. Bogus adoption services, like this Sunrise Adoption Agency, are probably widespread, far-reaching."

Martinez shook his head in disbelief, as Williams paused for a sip of coffee, then continued.

"As you know, the legitimate adoption process is slow and often disappointing. Many couples unable to conceive are wealthy, or desperate, willing to pay for a child—easy prey for these criminals. I've read the FBI reports, which indicate that we're only beginning to scratch the surface."

Williams looked squarely at Dr. Martinez, his eyes steady with resolve. "Unfortunately, I see the victims of this crime every day—mothers who have lost their children, not knowing if they are dead, neglected, or tortured. These mothers are distraught, and their lives are empty, broken. I'm hoping that we'll dig up some trails that will help solve some of my cases. What can you tell me about the nurse, Sheila McMann?"

Martinez put his elbow on the desk and rested his chin on his hand, his eyes cast downward. "She's a darn good nurse, too good to get hooked up with a scam like this. I guess she must have fallen head over heels for this young punk, Donny, from the agency." Martinez sighed, glancing back at Williams. "He must have talked a good game. Sheila seems to worship him. She lost sight of what she was doing."

"How'd you connect with her?"

"An FBI agent told me what to do, how to act around the obstetrics ward—to appear desperate for money, for drugs, like I was a real junkie. He said that I'd be bait, and the fish would come to me. Sure enough, wasn't long before Sheila started hanging around when I was at the nurses' station. I confided in her about my drug problem, and we began to talk together more and more. She was real sympathetic, told me she'd had money problems, too.

"One day, out of the blue, she brought up the baby issue, like it was a social cause, an opportunity to help the world. She said she needed a doctor who could determine which mothers would be motivated to give up their babies, a doctor who would help to provide healthy babies to fine adoptive parents. She told me that these babies wouldn't have a fair chance with their real mothers, who were too immature or too poor, sometimes drug addicts."

Williams pulled out a small pad and ballpoint pen, jotted some quick notes, then stored the pen in his shirt pocket. Williams caught Martinez, who was a dapper dresser, staring at his shirt, which was blotted with ink stains.

"Habit of mine, ruining shirts," Williams said, chuckling. "Just can't seem to remember to put the top back on my ballpoint. More than a few times it almost led to divorce. Now my wife just lets me wear spotted shirts."

Williams' smile faded into a scowl. He rubbed his

chin, back and forth, scratching the late night stubble of his heavy beard. "Seriously, though, I'd like to meet with Sheila McMann. She may hold some pieces to my puzzle."

"No problem," Martinez said quickly, nodding, as if he anticipated the request. "I'll set it up in the morning."

# Deeper Than the Surface

## Chapter 14

"What made you do it, Miss McMann?"

Detective Williams sat behind an office desk at a suburban Atlanta police station, glancing at the chaos on the other side of a glass partition—uniformed officers, dashing here and there, handcuffed suspects, undercover cops and witnesses, secretaries, all milling about. The rather homely woman in front of him, Sheila McMann, seemed a decent enough sort. He scratched his head in wonder as he continued the questioning.

"You took an oath, a solemn oath as a nurse, to heal sick people, didn't you? How could you steal a baby from its mother?" Williams spoke softly, his tone not judging but searching, as if he, the master crime solver, could not fathom this culprit's motivation, could not solve the mystery.

The sallow cast of Sheila McMann's ill-favored face began to redden. She drooped her shoulders, hanging her head, as she defended herself meekly. "But I didn't know. Donny told me we were doing a good thing for the babies, and the adoptive parents. He said we were saving lives, that otherwise the babies might be abused or unloved, left with a druggie for a mom, or a young girl, a child herself. I thought I was doing the right thing."

Sheila's tears broke loose and slow streams fell down her cheeks, separated by a jutting nose with an unfortunate mole dotting one nostril. She lifted her hands to her eyes. Two index fingers with jagged nails masked her lower lids and wiped the tears, leaving the flesh of her cheekbones with a wet shine.

Through reddened eyes, she peered at Detective Williams. "I know it was stupid," she confessed, "but I thought Donny had fallen for me. I believed that he really cared." Sheila's face scrunched painfully, and Detective Williams offered her a tissue to intercept the tears.

He looked down at his hand, dotted with liver spots. With a forefinger he manipulated the skin on top in a circle, producing wrinkles that saddened him. The hand of a stranger—the skin thinner now, with the same dark splotches that he often noted in his criminal profiles, indicating advanced age.

Martinez was right; she didn't deserve this. Let's give the girl some hope. "Maybe it's not too late to make amends," he said softly. "Maybe, just maybe, you can do some good."

Sheila sniffled loudly, her chest heaving erratically as she tried to control her breathing. "I know I'm in real trouble, the kind that puts you in jail. But I deserve it. If only I could make up for being so stupid. If I could just do something right."

Williams crossed his arms over his large chest, trying to look stern, and Sheila hung her head again. Man, he thought, poor girl has it tough. He moved around the desk and sat on the corner, his leg swinging freely in front of Sheila, but she didn't look up. A tear landed with a soft tap on his boot.

"Well, Sheila, you do have quite a bit of information about Donny, and about his operation. We could use that information." She lifted her head, and Williams set the bait. "We could try to make a deal for you, maybe get you probation or less time in jail."

"My life's over anyway, detective. But what can I do to help those mothers?" Tears flooded Sheila's face. "It's those mothers that haunt me. If only I could bring one baby back."

"That might be possible."

"How?" Sheila pled. "Tell me how, and I'll do it. I'll do anything." She composed herself, dabbing her cheeks, and folded her hands under her chin, as if in prayer.

"You must have seen some of the adoptive parents. If so, you must remember something about them—their names, where they're from, how they got in touch with

Donny."

"I wasn't allowed to ask their names, or to know anything about them, whether they had other children, or if they couldn't have children on their own. Donny would've killed me if I'd asked anything."

She searched a far corner of the ceiling for an answer, then suddenly locked her eyes into his. "Now that I think about it, Donny never told me anything about himself, either. I had no telephone number, no address. He never mentioned his family, never divulged anything personal. Honestly, I don't know how I could have been so dumb."

Williams spoke gently. "Sheila, you should look in the mirror deeper than the surface. I see a strong face, with lovely soft eyes, and a mouth that is much prettier in a smile, with lips curled up, not down like now. Someday you'll meet a man, unlike Donny, who'll admire your sweet nature, not take advantage of it." He gave her hand a fatherly pat. "Now let's get down to business."

"I told you, I don't know anything. I wish I did."

"Try. Tell me again about that last baby, Prissy's baby girl. What happened when you snatched her away, right after delivery? Where did you take her?"

"I took her to Donny, for a quick look. He was waiting in the hall near the nurses' station. The nurses have gotten used to him hanging around—you know, as an agent for the adoption service. Donny wanted to be sure that the baby was perfect, no problems for the adoption. After he checked her out, I carried her into the nursery."

"But how did the baby get to the adoptive parents? How were the papers signed without the mother knowing?"

Sheila was silent, and Williams listened to the ticking of the clock.

"I drugged Prissy," she finally said in a whisper. Williams leaned closer. "She had no choice but to sleep. And she was underage, so her mother had custody." Sheila bit the nails on her right hand, democratically chewing the fingers from left to right, drawing blood from one cuticle. "While Prissy was out cold, I delivered her baby to the adoptive parents in the nursing supervisor's office. Donny was there, too."

"What did they look like?"

"They looked nice, maybe my age, in their early thirties. The mother had flowing hair, red like Prissy's. Donny
always tried to match the adoptive parents physically with
the child, just like a legitimate adoption agency. The father
was handsome, thin, with curly dark hair and, I think, dark
eyes. They were so excited to be parents, cooing over the
baby. She was a beautiful baby, too—no freckles, of course,
but she did have silky red hair, just a trace."

Sheila paused to study a fingerprinting chart on the
wall. She stared intently, her eyes boring into the chart, until
a thought burst through and she pointed a finger into the
air. "They looked rich, that's what. Dressed in fine clothes,
the mother, and jewelry that would blind you, diamond
rings on both hands. She was gentle with the child, so as not
to hurt her. She cradled her in her arms like the baby Jesus
himself. I knew in my heart that she'd be a good mother."

"Did they say anything about themselves?" Williams
asked. He walked over to a sidetable, where a glass coffeepot
gurgled on the heat ring of an electric coffeemaker, and
poured Sheila a fresh cup. No more for me, he thought. The
inside of my stomach must be black lacquer by now.

"Thanks." She glanced back at the paneled wall, as she
blew into the cup, then sipped. "Let's see, now. The man
held the baby, too, while Donny was going over things with
the woman. I remember him talking to the baby in a
singsong voice, rhyming words, telling her she'd be safe.
Maybe it was a lullaby I'd never heard. Something like,
'You'll be safe, little one, we'll take care of you. You'll be
happy, little girl, we'll watch over you.' He said it over and
over, so softly, and lulled that baby right to sleep, happy in
her new father's arms."

She frowned, trying to remember more. "But then he
said something kind of funny, like 'You'll go rafting when
you're older. I'll show you the water,' or was it 'whitewater'?

"Then he mentioned the Olympics. I remember that
particularly, because it was so odd. 'You'll miss the
Olympics, but someday . . .'" Sheila's voice trailed away.
"Not exactly that, of course, but something like that. Strange
that he would mention the Olympics, don't you think?"

Williams pursed his lips and manipulated his cheek with the flat of his fingers, turning his face lopsided, contorted as if he'd lost his muscles to a stroke. "That's strange talk, all right, to a baby. The man must be really caught up in whitewater rafting, or canoeing, or kayaking. Could he be an athlete in the Olympics?"

She shook her head. "Not likely. Not that he was paunchy or anything. He seemed in really good shape, but maybe too old. Aren't most Olympic athletes in their twenties?"

"Yeah, you're right. Probably too old. But you never know where this information may lead me. That's enough for today."

"I guess I should get back to my shift."

"I'll be in touch," Williams said, patting her shoulder softly as he pointed her toward the door. He watched her progress through the maze of desks and called out a warning, "Don't forget to use the rear door of the building."

Williams leaned over the desk to scribble some notes on a yellow legal pad. He chewed the eraser on the tip of his pencil, then spit a particle into the air, cocking his head. Whitewater racing. Man against the rapids. The Olympic committee is building a whole new course, up at Ocoee, for the canoe/kayak slalom competition. Hey, he thought, grinning. That's one event that I just might attend.

# Does the Day Die?

## Chapter 15

Florida's endless sky welcomed Diane home. Stunned and heartbroken over John's cold, abrupt parting, she took the dune crossover to the beach at sunset, seeking solace from her sadness.

The early evening was misty, and the sun was perfectly centered between the crossover railings as Diane stepped down onto the sand. The huge red ball radiated a dramatic palette, orange and scarlet, with a background of baby blue and soft touches of murky white. The dusk dawned as the sun fell—a beginning and an end. In the failing light, she wondered. Does the day die in that brilliant burial fire? Do joy and fear and pain and hope simply vanish in the blazing inferno? Or is the day ceremoniously bedded down for the night, tucked in tight, surrounded in darkness, only to rise in a fresh-lit sky with its baggage in tow? Was her sorrow new every day and yet to be faced, or was that the familiar sorrow of yesterday, awakening refreshed?

Mel ran barefoot down the dune crossover, calling to her. In better, happier days they had often walked at sunset with Matt and Chris—a family, complete, at peace beside the lapping waves. The beach had been their playground during the day, and, at sunset, their refuge.

They walked south to the beach preserve where sunset groupies gathered in the evening. An old man and woman, with pale and wrinkled skin, sat shielded by an umbrella, sectioned like a beachball into citrus wedges of lemon, orange, and lime. They watched their grandchildren belly-flop in the surf.

Two boys, hard at play, built an ambitious fort in the sand. Using paper cups as tools, they fashioned parapets and capped them with scallops, fortifying the buttresses with pin shells. Struck with a masterful brainchild, one yelled, "A moat, we need a moat!" and they bent over to dig by hand, feet straddling the trench, as sand flew between their legs.

Mel and Diane reached a line of Australian pines, where Mel threw his lure into the sand shallows. A snook took the bait, flailing against the hook, and contorted wildly as it leapt high above the water. Mel whispered under his breath, easing his prey into shore, "Come here . . . come on." When the fish was safely beached, he yelled to her, proud as a child.

Diane remembered how Chris had called to her to photograph his first catch, skinny legs standing tall as he held forth his prize, his rod and reel tossed to the ground. His smile was broad, spaced with teeth, as he jutted his chin forward in triumph. His curly hair, streaked with blond, was tousled by the sea breeze, and his freckled cheeks and nose had turned pink from too much sun. Her memory snapped with the shutter, a moment frozen in time.

She remembered cleaning the fish—a sheepshead weighing in at two pounds—and frying it for dinner. "You can thank me for tonight's dinner," Chris bragged. Mel praised the fisherman, complimenting him on the flavor of the fish, and Matt complained that there wasn't enough.

"Let's walk back with the fish," Diane said, smiling through her memory. "I'll clean it for dinner."

They took the path over the sand dune, separating the budding sea oats gently with outstretched arms. Mel rinsed his feet off with a hose, and Diane stomped her feet on the back terrace, to shake the sand from her sneakers. She heard the phone ring and hurried inside, leaving the snook to flap madly against the paver brick terrace.

It was Detective Williams.

"Diane, I got a call from Dr. Bozeman. You're aware, I know, that John has been severely depressed the last couple of weeks, didn't even speak for days on end. Well, he's coming out of it now."

"Thank, God," she said softly. "I've been so worried."

"The doctor feels that there are some things I should

hear. She mentioned that she'd like you to be there, too, but didn't want to put any pressure on you."

"I know. She's called several times about John's setback, trying to make me feel better. I think she places all the blame on herself." Diane walked to a chair and, carrying the long twisted telephone cord with her, jerked it like a whip to hurdle the telephone table. She sat down and brushed a remnant of sand off the sole of her shoe onto the tile floor. "When are you going?"

"You know me; no time like the present. Thought I'd go first thing in the morning. Can Mel spare you?"

"We do have a closing scheduled, but he can manage it without me. I'll see if I can arrange a flight. If I can get the early one, I should be at the hospital by ten o'clock."

Diane hung up the phone and sat still, staring at a wall of electronic equipment—the wide-screened TV, a VCR and CD player, the woofer and speakers. She felt as tangled as the mass of wires, winding their way from the floor to the back of the shelf to the guts of the boxes. This day is going to die, she thought. Tomorrow I'll have a chance to see John, to straighten out some of the mess. But first, I have to call the airline, and pack, and go over the closing papers with Mel. If only I had the energy. She rose, her body heavy, and turned to the stairs, feet dragging, to climb to her bed, to rest. She would find peace in the new day.

The next morning, on schedule, Detective Williams and Diane met with Dr. Bozeman in her office, where they sipped coffee as they considered the next step. The office was spacious, with feminine touches, live plants and photographs, at the window a wicker chaise in the shape of a fish with a thick flowered cushion. Diane could imagine John lying there, his head propped up as he searched the Atlanta skyline—free to speak his feelings in this safe shelter, his privacy guaranteed by a trusted confidante.

Dr. Bozeman opened the meeting with a solemn confession. "I now believe my first instinct was correct. John was not ready for a confrontation with his abductor." She lowered her eyes to her lap and fingered the crease of her slacks. "He had to lie about Johnson's identity; it was the only way to protect himself. The mind is astonishingly self-protective." Her eyes rose to meet Diane's. "But John is an honest young man. He suffered so much guilt that he became mute, to prevent his tongue from uttering any more lies—in essence, to cleanse his soul."

"Then McGuire *is* Johnson?" Detective Williams asked abruptly, unable to contain himself any longer.

"Yes, detective, I believe so."

"What is John's condition now?" Diane asked, her voice heavy with concern. "Is he less depressed? Talking more freely?"

"Well, it's a slow process, but he's coming along. Perhaps seeing you will do him some good."

"I hate to seem callous," Williams said, "but can John help us in the case? Will he be able to finger this character?"

"The staff has met on this matter." Dr. Bozeman thumbed through John's file on her desk. "More than once. Our conclusion is that the sooner he can identify Johnson, the better. We believe that he must pass this milestone—resolve the issue by dealing with his guilt and his anger toward Johnson—before he can move forward with his therapy." She raised a finger to the air. "But only John can tell us when he's strong enough to face it."

John was studying in a corner of the bright solarium, the sun shining through the blinds, slatting his face with thick, dark lines. He smiled when he saw her and rose quickly to give her a bear hug. So different, Diane thought, from the last time he had left her, with his spirit gone and his actions, low-key and perfunctory. Now he clutched her hard, his eyes shining. "Miss Diane," he announced to the empty room and sat her on a chair beside him.

Although she wanted to keep the talk small, without pressure, John began to confess. "I lied, but I'm not sure why." His words flowed uncontrollably, as he rocked back and forth, faster and faster.

"At first I was upset that I couldn't stand up to Johnson. I really wanted to, but the words wouldn't come. Why did he pretend not to know me? He didn't even seem to care that I was in the room." John lowered his head and rocked in silence. He flattened his long fingers on his legs, and Diane saw that he had chewed his nails to nubs. He clenched his fists. The knuckles bulged and the veins popped, mapping the top of his hands in blue, and he looked up with angry eyes. "I hate Johnson. I hate him for locking me up, and I hate him for leaving me."

The anger out, John rested his elbows on his knees and cradled his chin in his fists, spent. "I feel bad that I lied to Detective Williams. I'll try to make things better, tell him the truth. But I'm also going to tell him that Johnson's not a bad man, not really."

Diane saw the struggle on John's face. "Perhaps you need some rest. We can explore all of this later, don't you think?"

John began to rock again and chewed on his lower lip. "No, I want to set things straight with Detective Williams as soon as I can."

Diane touched his shoulder gently, to slow his rocking. "John, Detective Williams met me here today. He's in the hospital, talking with Dr. Bozeman. Would you like to see him?"

"Will you stay?"

"Of course," Diane said as she rose, nudging John's hand. He stood beside her, his lanky body already over six feet, so that she had to reach up to plant her hands on his shoulders. "We don't want you to feel pressured to say anything. The truth has a timing of its own. It's for you to decide when you want to talk."

John nodded and locked her hand into his, tugging her down the hall to Dr. Bozeman's office. He dropped her hand at the door and hurried into the room, greeting Detective Williams with a firm handshake. "I'd like to dig right in," he said, glancing at Dr. Bozeman for approval, "if that's all right."

Dr. Bozeman nodded, and Williams motioned to the chair beside him. John raked his fingers through his hair and, without urging, began.

"I lived in one room, a bedroom with the window boarded over and the door always locked. But it wasn't so bad, really. I slept on a twin bed with a real thin spread, checkered in brown and blue. The floor was wood with no rug, or anything. There was no heat, and my feet got cold, so I'd mostly wear socks. No need for shoes when you're not going nowhere.

"Sometimes Johnson would stay gone for lots of days, and I'd have the radio for company. But I'd just get so lonesome . . ."

Dr. Bozeman supervised, occasionally breaking John's train of thought when he became agitated. John related everything he could remember—a stream of random events, one memory prompting another, like rocks toppling as they gathered momentum, rolling down a cliff.

Detective Williams interrupted from time to time, fleshing in some of the details he had uncovered. "The creep's real name is Adam McGuire. He made up the name *Johnson*."

Dr. Bozeman checked Williams with a stern glare, then directed her words to John. "This man gave himself a special name—just for you, John. And he gave you a new name—just for him. The combination of *John* and *son* suggests that he viewed you as his child. We know that the two of you had a strong bond, similar to a family." She looked back at Williams and scowled.

"Sorry," Williams said, glancing meekly at Diane and then back to John. "I guess McGuire was like a father to you. We dug up some of his earlier photographs and, just like you said, his nose did appear larger. We haven't found the medical records yet, but we're pretty sure that he had a nose job—you know, plastic surgery. We know that he's wearing contact lenses now; we've located the optometrist to verify that. One thing we can't figure out—what led him to kidnap you. Doesn't seem to fit with the rest of his life. He never mentioned anything to you, did he?"

John squinted his eyes, trying to remember. His pupils darted as he touched his lips. Diane could see the memories flashing by and wanted to wrap her arms around him, to protect him from the hurt. Finally he spoke. "Johnson did say that, before me, he was real lonely. That might be the reason."

"But why you?" Williams asked. "Why a boy of your age—ten at the time, as I recall? This is hard to ask, son, but Dr. Bozeman understands that I must. Did he ever try to touch you where he shouldn't, take pictures of you undressed, or anything like that?"

John turned red and rubbed the side of his neck under his collar. "I already told the doctor. He hugged me, no different than my uncle. That's all, except . . . sometimes he hit me. One time, I remember, he'd made a big steak, special for the weekend, and I wouldn't eat. Just wasn't hungry."

"He spanked your bottom?" Williams asked.

"There and just about everywhere else. He was really mad. Whacked me hard in the face. Slapped me sideways. My eye was swollen shut for a few days, but I guess I should've eaten."

"Did he hit you with just his hand? Ever with anything else?"

"Yeah—his belt, a lot of times. Once with a big old board, slammed me hard across the back of my legs. I couldn't move for the pain. Thought he'd broken them." John began to chew his nails. "I couldn't walk for a long time."

"The son-of-a-bitch," Williams muttered under his breath. Diane nudged his elbow, not wanting to lose the progress they were making.

John's eyes brimmed over with tears, and he wiped them with his fists. "Most of the time he was real nice, though, especially when I couldn't talk."

"Couldn't talk?" Diane and Williams asked in unison.

"Yeah, he was real worried. Somehow I just couldn't talk. Johnson said it was 'cause of what he had done to me, locking me away. Myself, I don't know why. But those days, when I couldn't talk, just ran together, and I'm not sure how long it was. I remember feeling real bad, and all I could do was sleep."

"We've talked about being depressed," Dr. Bozeman reminded him. "Remember how bad you've been feeling the last couple of weeks? Was it like that?"

"I guess so. But, with Johnson, I didn't see no other folks. So my mind had nowhere to go, just inside."

Dr. Bozeman complimented him. "I'm awfully proud of how you're getting to know yourself." John smiled weakly and nodded his head.

"John," Williams said, "would it be all right for me to ask just a couple more questions? I know you're getting tired, but it won't take long."

Diane wanted to scream, "Don't make him suffer anymore." But John answered, " It's okay."

"Did Johnson ever mention other children? Do you think you were the only child he ever kept?"

"I know I was the only one; he told me," John said defensively. "He did mention that sometimes he took care of lots of kids, even babies, but only for a day or two. Those children weren't so important; they went to other homes. But I stayed. I stayed home with Johnson."

Dr. Bozeman spoke in a firm and steady voice. "We know. You were like a son to him." She pushed John's file aside and turned to Detective Williams. "Now, can we call it a day?"

Williams flipped his notepad closed, and the loud slap called the session to an end, like the bang of a courtroom gavel. All rose quickly, as if anxious to stretch, and the heavy tension in the room seemed to lift.

Dr. Bozeman motioned to John. "Let's go see what's for lunch. Maybe our guests would like to join us."

# Déjà Vu

## Chapter 16

"We know how you did it now, McGuire. All the pieces fit together."

Detective Williams glanced around the interrogation room at the Franklin substation—the same thick-railed chairs marked with graffiti, the familiar rectangular mirror on the wall, through which John and Dr. Bozeman and Diane observed. *Déjà vu.* The same suspect with the same attorney, Mr. Clark, but this time would be different. McGuire looked worried, his cocky attitude gone. And his attorney was silent.

Williams started the tape recorder, pointing a thumb toward it for the attorney's benefit, like a tennis player warning that new fast balls were coming. He stated the day and hour of the meeting, identified the participants, and then began to bark at McGuire, who looked stunned. "You kept your residence in North Carolina, but actually lived in Georgia most of the time. Didn't you, McGuire?" Williams voice could boom when he really let it loose. "Only a hundred miles outside Atlanta, isn't that right? No need in denying it; we have the proof."

McGuire started to speak, but his attorney stopped him, extending a flat palm like a football rusher, holding off a tackler. "What proof, detective?"

"We have a lease signed by you, McGuire, about four years ago." Williams searched through a thick stack of papers on the desk and slammed a document down in front of McGuire's attorney. "That's what our handwriting experts say, after examining the paperwork you filled out way back then. We traced it all back to a man who represented the landlord, an old codger in Peaceton, Georgia. Seemed to have a penchant for holding on to old papers and stuff—a real packrat. Even though the name was fictitious, he recognized you from one of your earlier snapshots. We have lots of your photographs," Williams sneered.

"You rented a house, beside a river there—a house where a kidnapped boy was stashed. Counsel, we have documented evidence that your client attempted to change his appearance. And the boy has agreed to identify him. It's strong, sir, real strong stuff."

Mr. Clark looked incredulous. He pinched the bridge of his pointed nose, hard between his thumb and forefinger, as if he were trying to squeeze out a defense strategy. His client must have left him in the lurch, Williams thought.

"Let me talk to my client. Will you excuse us?" He bent forward and began whispering to McGuire. His voice grew louder, agitated, and he stopped to glare at Williams, who shuffled his chair back and left the room.

Williams walked to the observation room where John sat stiffly, Diane's hand on his shoulder. "Could I see you, just for a moment?" he asked Dr. Bozeman, who stepped outside to the corridor.

"Doctor, I hope to get a confession. We've got a stack of evidence, and I'm trying to spare John another confrontation with McGuire."

"Good. I don't want to chance anything," she said firmly, "unless absolutely necessary. John says that he's anxious to talk to Johnson, but then he vacillates. One minute he's ready and the next, he's nervous, hesitant."

"I just need to confirm McGuire's identification—that's all. A quick *yes* or *no* will suffice. I don't think John should hear what's coming next, anyway. He might get upset when we talk about McGuire's punishment, that he's going to face jail time. Plus, I may have to use some rough language to get a confession."

"Thanks for your discretion, detective. Let's go see John."

The observation room was narrow, with chairs lined up, facing the two-way mirror only a few feet away. John sat there, his rangy legs contorted, knees almost bumping the wall. He turned his head in the direction of the door, as it opened, and nodded emphatically, his long hair bouncing in agreement. "That's him. I'm sure of it now."

"Would you be willing to say that in court, in front of a judge, if we needed you to?"

"I think so. Couldn't I just hold my breath and point?" John smiled at his own feeble joke, but his young eyes looked frightened.

"You sure could, son," Williams said, patting John's shoulder, just as he heard his name paged over the loudspeaker. "Well, I guess I'll say good-bye now, for a while. You all probably want to get started back. John has done his work here, and a mighty fine job it was."

Diane stood to shake his strong, callused hand. "Steve, you'll never know how much this day has meant to me."

Williams winked. "Oh, I think I have an idea. You take care, and say hello to the fisherman for me." He stepped vigorously out the door, back to the interrogation room.

Words stirred between attorney and client, but hushed when he entered. Before Williams could even take a seat, Clark spoke, anxious to share the fruit of his dialogue with McGuire. "My client has some information that may prove valuable to you."

Williams responded with disinterest. "Every two-bit criminal wants to trade his confession for a deal." Nonchalantly, he wandered over to the mirror and stared at his face, examining the pockmarks dotted with whiskers. He flashed a twisted smile into the void.

"My client could have knowledge of other child abductions," Clark pressed on, pleading to the detective's back. "Perhaps he performed only a small role in other abductions, merely as an employee of the key players. Just doing his job. Would such information buy him a deal?"

"Only one way to find out. Shoot."

"I'm afraid I need more encouragement than that, detective." Clark studied a pen in his bony hands, rubbing it back and forth in his palms. "We need at least a guarantee that Mr. McGuire won't be incriminated for the additional abductions, with a plea bargain in this case. My client has never before been in trouble with the law."

"Oh yeah," Williams said, turning to glare at McGuire.

"You're really a nice guy who was just misguided." He walked toward the table and leaned close, face to face with McGuire. His eyes knifed the suspect. "By some terrible mix-up, you locked a kid away for three years—held him prisoner and smacked him around. Otherwise, I'm sure you're a bloody boon to society." Williams paused, eyes still locked on McGuire. "But I'll see what I can do. The kid wants us to go easy—God knows why—and his recommendation pulls weight with me, a lot more than yours, Mr. Clark."

"Okay, Adam," the attorney said, motioning to his client. "You can start."

The fluorescent light above illuminated the top of McGuire's bald head. He dipped his chin down to the table, nearly touching it, his elbows spread like wings and his face lost in shadow.

"Okay, I wasn't making much money. I'd been working at a furniture company, but they laid me off when the economy got lousy. So I was doing odd jobs, not very challenging and certainly not rewarding, monetarily. For a while I was a gofer for a local builder, who won a big contract in Georgia. He told me that I had to transplant, if I wanted to keep my job. I did, because I could see I was becoming more and more valuable to the company. I counted material, and I noticed when lumber was missing, or a plumbing fixture was damaged when it was shipped. I probably saved the contractor more money than he paid me, and he was thinking of making me permanent." He looked up at Williams, but only for a moment. His eyes, cowards against the detective's piercing stare, retreated quickly to the table.

"One night in a bar I met up with a real weasel, guy named Donny. Stocky young punk, weightlifter—short, but with bulging muscles. Turned out, being a small town, we kept running into each other. We became acquaintances and got drunk together one night." McGuire looked at his attorney, crossed his fingers over his overblown midsection, and said apologetically, "I don't normally drink that much."

First bit of remorse, Williams thought. Strange set of values—drinking's bad, but it's okay to kidnap kids.

McGuire sucked up his chest and started again, this time with more confidence, his carriage haughty. Well, at least he's a dignified son-of-a-bitch, Williams thought.

"Donny said he wasn't from that town, but lived close by. Said he liked being anonymous, better for picking up women. He fancied himself a woman's man, and he did have, I suppose, a brassy charm about him." McGuire paused, this time searching his attorney's eyes. Clark squeezed his client's forearm reassuringly and nodded for him to continue.

"I told Donny about my financial dilemma and the work I did. He put me down, sneering, and said he could do a lot better for me. Was I interested? Said it wouldn't require much time, just a few days here and there. He wanted me to help look after a bunch of kids, in different places—sometimes Georgia, sometimes Florida or North Carolina."

McGuire held his hands up in surrender, re-living his reaction to Donny. "I wasn't a likely candidate, I told him. I'd never had any kids of my own and didn't have any qualifications to be a babysitter even if the idea appealed to me, which it didn't. Donny assured me that was fine; there were nursemaids for that. He needed me to drive and to watch after things."

"So you took him up on it?"

McGuire nodded.

"Tell me what your work was like."

McGuire clapped his hands together, just under his chin, as if happy to perform. "We'd go to an airport to meet a jet, a private one, without the usual support staff on the ground. The flight attendants weren't in uniform, just wearing jeans or regular street clothes, and the pilots were dressed in fatigues. The biggest surprise was the cargo—it was live. The airplanes brought in children, mostly infants. Many of them were Hispanic."

McGuire rotated in his chair, pointing his portly body directly at Williams, to plead his case. "Don't get me wrong, detective. Donny told me that everything was on the up and up, that these were arranged adoptions and that we were doing good work in the world. I had no reason to doubt him."

Williams scoffed. "So then, why the hell are you telling me all this?"

"Because I began to get suspicious." McGuire cupped his hands in front of him, bouncing the tips of his fat fingers off each other. "Is it getting hot in here, or is it just me?"

Now he thinks he's the guest speaker at a convention. It's going to get a hell of a lot hotter, Williams thought, but said nothing.

"A couple of tough guys always met the planes. After a while they got comfortable with me and let a few things slip. For one thing, I learned that they packed guns; I saw holsters under their coats. Guess they eventually got to trust me, because they didn't attempt to hide them anymore. They'd unbuckle their holsters and take the guns right off, to lessen their load. Said the buggers were heavy."

"Did you ever see them use the guns?"

"Nope."

Williams reached for his legal pad and pulled a pencil from his ear. "Let's get some specifics here. How much did they pay you? Did they pay in cash?"

"Yeah, only in cash. Every job took a day or two, by the time we secured the delivery, and I made seven hundred bucks, sometimes more."

"Not bad pay for a crud."

McGuire raised his shoulders. "I beg your pardon."

"Calm down," his attorney said, "and stay put." He motioned to Williams, and they stepped to the corner of the room to confer.

In a few minutes Williams returned to the table, reeling off demands. "I want physical descriptions of everyone—plus names, accents, addresses, vehicles, all that—and information on the planes—where they came from, where they landed, and when. I need to know precisely what happened, from the time you arrived at the plane until the disposition of the children. If you want a deal, you'll have to work for it. The better witness you can be, the better break we can give you."

McGuire glanced toward his attorney for guidance. Clark gave none, still hunched in the corner, hands lost in his pockets.

Williams continued. "One more thing. Did you ever pick up any kid near here, maybe up by Lake Glenville?"

"Don't reckon I did, sir."

Williams leaned close, taking in the words like a breathless man in need of air. "You may want to search your memory real good. Could be important to your future."

"I'll think real hard," McGuire said as he cracked a smile, loosening up. "Hey, boss, I'm not doing too badly, am I?"

Williams leaned over the table and thrust his fist in McGuire's face, holding it there, within inches, as if he were going to use him for punching practice. McGuire's smirk faded as Williams stared deep into his eyes. "You're a son-of-a-bitch, and don't you forget it."

McGuire backed away, instinctively cringing, sweat dripping from his brow. He twisted his lips into a bow, between his thumb and forefinger, slowly shaking his head.

That's better, Williams thought. I like that look of anguish. He turned and walked away, with a click of triumph in his step. On his way out, he turned off the overhead light and slammed the door loudly, as if to seal the fate of the wide-eyed suspect, sitting stunned in the shadows of the dark interrogation room.

# Whitewater

## Chapter 17

The mountain sliced vertically, a wall of rock jutting up just inches from the narrow road, succumbing to an outcrop of trees at the top—tall pines with soft pincushion branches, red maple, their leaves draping like ivy, and river birch with white trunks that peeled like sunburned skin. Traffic slowed almost to a halt in a profusion of sport utility vehicles, pickup trucks with trailers hauling kayaks and canoes, and buses, filled to capacity, with puffy orange rafts strapped on top.

On the opposite side of the curving road, far below, lay the Ocoee River, cutting into a steep cliff of huge boulders, some gray in the sun and others polished by the water, slick and green. The water moved swiftly, fighting the rocks, churning in whirlpools, grappling the rafts and canoes, white fountains bursting in the air.

Detective Williams pulled off the road onto an overlook and, spotting some picnickers on a flat rock below, began the treacherous descent, hopping from rock to rock. He stopped within speaking distance of the group, who were laughing and joking in a distinctive Tennessee twang.

"Hi, there," he called out casually. "You know when the tryouts start?"

"You mean the 'lympic trial runs?" a tall man in jeans answered, standing with one leg propped up against a rock ledge.

"Yeah."

"Not for a while, I guess. They're trying to finish the racecourse. Got a whole section of the river closed off."

"Are those people practicing for the trial runs?" Williams pointed down at the river where two kayaks were slicing through the water, creating geysers as they slid and turned rapidly. The kayakers wore helmets with decals and silky tank tops in red and blue. Their biceps bulged with their effort.

"Really don't know. Trying to figure all that out ourselves. They look official, don't they? You might want to check at the outfitters—Shoal Outfitters, 'bout a quarter-mile back."

"I'll find it. What about the check-in area? Do you think they'd know anything?" Detective Williams' voice took on the easy cadence and soft patterns of the man's accent. "I'm looking for some people I met, down in 'lanta. They just adopted a baby girl from the hospital there. That's how I came to meet 'em. They're from this area, I think, and the man's crazy for whitewater. A nice-looking couple— wife's got long, flaming red hair; husband's thin and dark. Ever see 'em?"

A teenage girl sitting on the rock piped up, to no one in particular. "Sounds like Rita and Furman, don't it?"

The man ignored her input. "She don't know what she's talking 'bout, half the time." He stared at Williams for a second, then said, "Guess I better go join that rowdy group and grab me some fried chicken, while there's still some left." His last words trailed as he turned his shoulder. "Nice talkin' with you, mister."

Detective Williams started back up the precipitous slope, keeping his balance by holding onto protruding boulders, resembling a toddler conquering a flight of stairs. He climbed without a break and reached the shoulder of the road, his breath only slightly labored. Not bad for an old man, he thought. He got into his car and waited for an opening in the traffic, then pulled onto the narrow road, retracing his route.

The bearded proprietor of Shoal Outfitters was hunched over a tall wooden counter, shuffling a stack of invoices and feeding numbers into an adding machine. Red-faced and flustered, he sneered at Detective Williams' interruption.

"Sorry to bother you, sir. I'm looking for some friends of mine, a couple with a baby—Furman and Rita."

"Nope, don't know nobody named Furman or Rita. Anyway, I figure that, if folks around these parts want company, they'll find it for themselves."

The outfitters store was a cavernous log cabin, wrapped by a wide porch lined with tall rockers and a sign on the wall, inviting rafters to "Laze a Spell" after their strenuous whitewater tour. Although the establishment was practically deserted—two couples poked around the aisles, cheerfully needling one another about their misadventures on the river—the proprietor proclaimed that he had to attend to business. As proof, he called out to the couples, "Y'all need anything over there? Just give me a holler." Then, with a show of immediacy, he attacked the pile of bills on the counter and sent the tape of the adding machine flying.

"Thanks anyway, man."

Williams dismissed himself and drove to the official Ocoee check-in station. The building had the bland architecture peculiar to the national park service—concrete block without stucco, the whitewashed green over gray not visually rewarding but preservative, and free-standing walls that identified the restrooms with stick figures of a man and a woman, the latter draped with a skirt triangle.

Williams walked toward the building down a concrete ramp and onto the front terrace, an intricate puzzle of flat rocks from the local streams. Some kayakers congregated there, dripping onto the rock, turning its pattern dark. One slicked his wet hair back, using his fingers as a comb.

Now Williams saw the sign, "Information & Check-In." The entry door had a small rectangular window, with thick glass that encased what looked like chicken wire. The window, which appeared to be placed at random, was too high for a glimpse of the interior. Williams opened the heavy door and stepped inside.

Behind the information counter stood a uniformed ranger, with pony-tailed chestnut hair and a pretty face, unadorned with makeup. "Welcome," she called, stating her purpose with a smile and a pert toss of her head.

"Good morning, miss. You sure have a beautiful spot here."

"God blessed Tennessee, didn't he? Can I help you?"

"I wanted to get some information on the Olympics—the trial schedule and the summer events. Do you have anything?"

"On the far counter," she said, motioning to a stack of pamphlets. "See, there."

"Oh yeah. Thanks." He opened a tri-folded leaflet, thumbing down the categories, feigning interest. "I'm looking for some friends of mine who are here observing the athletes. Man's dark and thin; woman has long red hair. They have a newborn, an adorable little girl with red hair, too. Haven't seen them, have you?"

"Not for about ten minutes, I'd say." The ranger smiled and covered her mouth, tickled with her surprise answer.

Williams shrugged, chuckling. "You aren't serious?"

"Yes I am, sir. Your friends were here just a few minutes ago. Better look around outside."

"Gee, thanks, miss. I think they drove their van, didn't they?"

"Don't know. The park service isn't big on windows, as you can see."

He glanced at the solid concrete-block walls, then up at a tall skylight with large sliding glass frames, through which emanated the room's only natural light. "Yeah," he said, moving quickly to the door.

Some small groups were milling about in the parking lot. Williams approached the kayakers he'd passed on his way in. "Did you see a couple with a baby just now?"

"Woman with red hair?"

"Yeah, long red hair."

"Couldn't really miss her," one said appreciatively, his face reddening.

Beside him a young woman, bent over from the waist, was towel-drying her hair, which fell toward the ground. She peeked out from under the towel and rolled her eyes. "They just left."

"What were they driving? Did you see?"

"A beige Mercedes. Nice car. Don't see many in these parts."

"Which way'd they go?"

"Up river, that way," she pointed. "Just left a minute

ago."

"Thanks," Williams called, as he rushed for his car. He broke into a line of traffic, the cars and buses inching along, timid drivers, wary of curves and gawking at the river. "That's great," he mumbled to himself, frustrated with the pace and unable to pass.

He watched the scenic overlooks, and, after a mile, hit pay dirt—a parked beige Mercedes, with a man leaning through the door into the back seat. Williams pulled off the road and parked two spaces down. He strolled over to the observation deck and sat on the guard wall, hiking up one leg leisurely. The lean man lifted out a baby and passed the infant along to a woman with flowing red hair. Williams walked casually in their direction, stopping to admire the child.

"What a beautiful baby," he said. "Girl?"

"Why, yes. She's our little angel," the woman replied sweetly, holding back the brim of the baby's sunhat so that her face could be admired.

"How old is she?"

"Just six weeks now," the man chipped in, bursting with pride, "and healthy as a horse."

"I've got three grandchildren myself," Williams bantered. "She looks good size, bigger than my friend's baby. Yeah, my friend adopted a child down in Atlanta, born at Bradford Hospital, just a few months ago. She'd been waiting years, as a single parent, you know." Williams moved to step away.

"That's just too big a coincidence," the woman said, startled. "Our baby was born there, too. Did you happen to meet Donny?" she asked gregariously, as she shifted the baby to her other hip. "He was our adoption counselor."

"Guy obviously lifted weights," the man offered, sounding peeved.

"Maybe it's the same agency," Williams said, feigning surprise. "What was the name of it?"

The man hedged. "Well, we're supposed to maintain confidentiality. Part of the process."

"What do you mean?" Williams pushed for more information, but gently. "Why would the name of an adoption agency be confidential?"

"I'm not sure," the man said, deflecting his eyes toward the river.

"Now that you mention it," the woman mused, "Donny didn't tell us much about his company. But he sure produced a beautiful baby." She gently bounced the infant, sleeping soundly in the cradle of her arms.

"Ma'am—Rita, I believe—"

"How do you know my name?"

"I don't want to alarm you, but I'm Detective Williams, a special investigator on the trail of an illegal child-smuggling operation." He lifted his identification badge from a shirt pocket and held it steady in front of the man.

The woman peered over her husband's shoulder, her face peaked. "God, Furman, do something."

Detective Williams reassured her. "Don't worry, ma'am. Nothing's going to happen to your baby. No one wants to take your baby from you." He paused and then spoke slowly, softly. "I just need information, that's all. These child-smugglers are the cruelest criminals of all. They kidnap babies at birth from their mothers, grab kids playing in their own yards. We have to stop them."

"But what can we do?" Rita was incredulous. "We can't jeopardize our baby."

"All I need is for you to agree to an interview. I'll conduct it right here, if you want, right now. Then at some point I'll probably need you to testify. But the important thing is that I've spoken with the mother of your child; I can assure you that she doesn't want to interfere. She never got to see her baby, though, and would just like to see her, maybe talk to you. It's only fair, for the baby and the mother, don't you think?"

"No, I don't," she answered, raising her voice. "I'm Lucy's mother—no one else. She can't have two mothers." Tears began to graze her cheeks, and her shoulders sank.

Furman reached over protectively, engulfing his wife and child in his arms. "Are you sure, detective, absolutely sure that they won't take our Lucy away?"

"I can guarantee it," Williams answered with authority.

"Honey, we can't hide Lucy from the world. If we've learned who her birth mother is, we have to think about what's best for the baby—how she'll feel, years from now. Maybe we'll be able to learn about her background, her medical history. We're Lucy's real parents; we know that, and so will Lucy." He grasped his wife tighter and looked Williams in the eye. "I have your word?"

"You do."

His wife sobbed softly, as he reached for the detective's hand. "We'll help if we can."

# A Bundle of Softness

## Chapter 18

Detective Williams paced the main entry hall of Bradford Hospital, watching the revolving door. He spotted a pencil-thin girl with hair the color of copper, silky strands falling loose from a barrette at the nape of her neck. A tall, gangly young man walked closely behind. He headed toward them. "Prissy?"

"That's me. Are you the detective?" she whispered, as if she didn't want to be overheard.

"Yes, I'm Detective Williams," he said, offering his hand, "and I'm awfully glad to meet you." She shook his hand limply. He could feel it trembling, like a frightened bird.

"This here's Bud," she said. "He's the father."

Williams extended his greeting to Bud. Just a boy himself, he saw. Bud locked the detective's hand in a tight grip and shook it profusely.

"Nice to meet you, sir."

Prissy wore a denim dress with pearl buttons clasping the gathered bodice, its fullness falling in folds from her small breasts. She hugged her midsection. "My stomach is turning over—feels like I'm on a roller coaster. Hope I don't faint."

"Let's take a seat," Williams suggested, gesturing toward benches lining the entry hall. They obliged, assuming stiff postures against the wall, and he sat down beside them.

"Prissy, your baby is upstairs in Obstetrics, in the nursing supervisor's office. Your baby's new mom and dad brought her, as they promised they would. If you think you're nervous, you should see them."

She smiled wryly, looking relieved.

"When you're ready," he said, "we'll go up. But first, do you still feel the same about everything? Do you think you'll be satisfied just to see Lucy, and nothing more?"

"Lucy. That's a pretty name, ain't it, Bud?" She ignored his question.

Williams continued. "I kinda assured the parents that you just wanted to see your baby, with no strings attached." He hung his head, embarrassed at the boldness of his words.

"Detective, I'm not stupid. I know I can't handle no baby—not yet. I'm too young. I think you understand, though, how much I want to see her. Just see her, that's all." Prissy's green eyes clouded. "Maybe, if they like me, they'll let me see her some more, someday. But I won't ask to, and I won't bother them. I'll sign something, if they want me to. Bud will, too."

Williams looked at Bud. "Will you, son?"

"Yes, sir," he said with conviction.

"Well, then, if you're ready." Detective Williams rose and held out his hand to offer Prissy a lift. "You're a brave girl." Prissy's freckles hid in her blush.

They entered the office where Rita sat, holding a bundle of softness, rosy skin amidst layers of pink cotton, trimmed in lace white as chalk. Furman hovered down over his family, poised to shield them from the unknown. His head turned abruptly toward the door.

Prissy took only one step into the room, as if an invisible barrier retarded her progress. Detective Williams offered a gentle nudge, and she moved a few more steps, hesitantly, before the barrier blocked her path again.

Perhaps Rita discerned that her competition was no more than a scared child. She beckoned Prissy over with a wave of her hand. "Come here." She held the bundle upright, cushioning the infant's head with one hand. "This is Lucy."

Prissy stared, her face pale, wooden. Her eyes slowly filled with wonder. Seconds passed before she whispered, "She's tiny, so tiny."

Rita reassured her. "The doctor says she's real healthy,

a good size for her age."

Prissy held a crooked finger to her baby, cooing softly. "Little Lucy, sweet little Lucy." She reached behind her to grab for Bud. "Look, Bud, she's smiling. She's smiling at me."

In a helpless gesture Rita offered her bundle up to Prissy. "Want to hold her?"

Prissy gathered the baby into her arms and began to sob, tears glistening like pearls in the softness of her face. Detective Williams saw that the tears came from joy, and perhaps relief.

Furman stared at Prissy and clasped his hands together under his chin, as if praying for closure. Rita cast her eyes into her lap, her shoulders slumped and fragile, lost in the disappointment of long fruitless years. Williams felt their fear, and the room stilled in silence.

Finally, Prissy spoke longingly through her tears. "Someday I'll have another baby. Won't I, Bud? Just as beautiful . . ." Prissy's voice cracked, her words forgotten somewhere in her throat. Gently she handed the baby back to Rita, with a needless warning, "You take care of my baby, okay? You be good to her."

Rita's tears, at last liberated, puddled at the swell of her cheek as she smiled, her shoulders rising rhythmically in unison with her pronounced sniffles. "I'll love her with all my heart. I'll always protect her." She looked up into Prissy's innocent eyes. "And, when she's old enough, I'll tell her what a wonderful mother she has. She'll understand."

Prissy turned away, covering her mouth with a fist, and forced her steps toward the door. She hesitated at the sound of Lucy, who began to cry softly, but she never looked back.

# Red and White Balloons

Chapter 19

Diane's timid voice groped for the right words. "Dr. Bozeman, we've all missed John and," she cleared her throat with a nervous cough, "we'd like him to come to Florida to visit us at Thanksgiving." She paused, then hurried to confirm, "If you think he's strong enough, of course."

"That's a wonderful idea. For how long a visit?"

Diane, not sure herself, wound the curls of the telephone cord around her index finger. She had not anticipated that Dr. Bozeman would accept the invitation so readily and, somehow, had not thought that far ahead. "Well, it's too long a trip for just a weekend," she rationalized. "How about a week?"

"That sounds perfect. John will be ecstatic; I know without asking."

"I can arrange for a flight from here," Diane said.

"Great. We can get him from the hospital to the airport, and the airline staff will assist him in flight, if you can meet him at the Ft. Myers airport. Then we'll keep in touch and, if he's doing fine, we'll stretch the visit to a week." Diane smiled in victory, clenching a fist triumphantly in the air.

Diane had been forced to face the reality that she might never see Chris again, although his image beset her mind. Her days were filled with jumbled snapshots, her nights with dreams of endless, irrepressible images of Chris, as if her memory thumbed through an old photo album, rifling the pages. His face was young, ripe with wonder, unfinished, and she tried to carry him forward in time, to see his face as it matured, but she could not. She was haunted by the face of a five-year-old—a cherub with freckles, frozen in time.

The emergence of John in her life had sprouted new growth in Diane, feeding fresh thoughts, nurturing hope. The void of her lost son could not be filled, but somehow John bridged the emptiness.

⁓

Mel and Diane's fine beachfront home amazed John, who'd seen nothing to compare in his sheltered environment. The cottage, as understated as its designation, sat on the edge of the Gulf of Mexico, its buffed walls mirroring the soft sand. The grounds were left natural, with verdant sea grapes, waving sea oats, sporadic bunches of sea ox daisies, and dainty bouquets of wild periwinkles, pink and white dots on the dune. The home had open decks that captured the steady roll of the waves, the rhythm of a gentle sea.

Diane led John up the stairs to a two-story great room with floor-to-ceiling Palladian windows that framed the Gulf through a foreground of palm fronds. The fireplace surround was coral-stone, sliced smooth, etched in its natural state with marine fossils, lending eerie decoration. A kaleidoscope of furnishings emulated the beach—whitewashed bamboo upholstered in taupe and white duckcloth, sprinkled with seashell prints, and a giant nautilus coffeetable topped with glass. A sweeping streamer of silk, splashed with green fronds, draped over stone sconces from the ceiling to the floor where it puddled, wrapping the room like an gigantic gift.

Matt spirited John away to his suite on the ground level—bachelor quarters, he called them—a bedroom and sitting room with white-framed French doors that led to a long screened lanai, opening the interior to a splurge of seaside greenery.

Diane followed, smiling. It felt good to have two boys at home again.

"This is our floor. Look out here." Matt grabbed John's arm eagerly, pointing to a path of crushed white shells, some perfectly formed fossils. "We can go out to the beach whenever we want to. It's really cool."

John remained agog for a couple of days, then settled into a tropical lifestyle. In the backyard one afternoon, Diane was watering her potted plants, dried by the intense Florida sun. "Just can't water these flowers enough," she said to the boys.

John was relaxing on a chaise lounge, tanning his face. In a lazy slouch best effected by a teenage boy, Matt lolled beside him, arms folded back to cushion his head and one overgrown foot slung to the ground.

"You're lucky to have so long off from classes," Matt said wistfully. "We only get a four-day weekend for Thanksgiving." He reached for a small shell and threw it on John's chest. "I guess that's the advantage of getting kidnapped."

John kidded back in the same easy manner. "Yeah, maybe you should try it."

Diane pretended not to hear. Somehow, John had caught on to Matt's unbounded banter, and she was surprised, but pleased, at his spontaneous reactions. He seemed to relax around Matt, to let down his guard.

"Hey, I bet you got all wimpy at the hospital," Matt teased. "I'll beat you to the beach."

"Right, shrimp," John said, as he jumped up and ran down the shell path, his long legs sprinting. Suddenly, feeling the sharp shells in the path, he started hopping on his tiptoes. "Ouch."

Matt's soles were tough from going barefoot, year round, and he passed John easily, laughing. Diane called after them, "Watch out for stingrays. If you go in the water, shuffle your feet." She was struck by Matt's apparent acceptance of John, with no jealousy, at least on the surface. Perhaps he was ready for a new juncture.

Late that afternoon, Diane discovered herself in rare quiet, alone in the house. She guessed that Mel and the boys were at the dock fishing, probably trying to catch the fat black drum that shadowed the pilings at sunset. She headed for a solitary walk on the beach.

The tide was extremely low, but Diane had scant hope for shells, as the earlier beach-goers had likely absconded with the better specimens. Her most rewarding shelling was at full moon, low tide, at daybreak before the beach was combed. Sometimes she waded the sand flats to observe the burrowing mollusks, bands of Fighting Conchs with uncanny feet that stretched blindly from their cocoons to the sand, advancing with clumsy slaps.

Tonight she took long strides at a fast clip, wanting to reach the pass before the last good light. Beyond the preserve, a mile from home, the beach was deserted.

Before rounding the curve of the pass, she spotted two balloons—one red, one white—bouncing along with the break of the waves. The evening breeze tossed them onshore, joined a few inches down by their strings. As if holding hands, they pranced across the sand dunes, playfully touching, mimicking one another, dancing, softly skipping.

Lost in thought in the darkening mist, Diane was startled by two blurred figures, just around the bend. Perhaps thirty-five feet away, they didn't appear to be moving. She should turn back; Mel didn't like her to walk the beach alone at night. Anyone from a boat could be lurking there or hidden in the mangroves beyond.

The figures grew larger, and now it was too late to turn. She thought she heard her name, muffled in the wind. Matt and John appeared, out of the gloaming, greeting her with shy smiles and laughing eyes, as if they recognized her dilemma.

"Mom, John thought it was you."

"Did you hear me calling?" John asked softly. "Nice sunset, huh? I guess you've seen millions of them."

"But each one is different, John. It's impossible to say which one the most beautiful." She turned now and started to walk back, inching slowly, reluctantly, with a small first step. "Did you see the balloons?"

"Balloons?"

"A red one and a white one, dancing across the beach." She pointed back toward the dune, but the balloons were lost from sight, probably burst by the prickly Australian pine cones.

"Yeah, Mom, you're okay," Matt said, playfully circling his ear with his forefinger.

They started walking back toward the cottage, and the boys took off in a race. Diane stared into the misty gray, the silvery, sweet evening that had burst balloons and spawned brothers in spirit. The last light of the sun illuminated their lithe bodies, as they pranced across the dunes, playfully touching, pushing each other away, then coming together, laughing—two boys, running free.

⁓

John was enchanted by the sea. He had always lived inland and, during his tenure with Johnson, inside four stark walls in solitary confinement. Diane felt that, like her, he loved the freedom of the sea, the boundless space and the endless sand that edged the world. Every day he brought word of a new discovery.

Today he ran into the kitchen, begging, "Please come down to the beach. I want to show you something." John grabbed Diane by the hand, practically dragging her down the path to the beach. "This way," he said, pointing to a spot where he'd been fishing in the surf. His rod and reel was propped against a folding beach chair, beside a yellow and white bait bucket.

He pushed back the door flap of the bait bucket, shook it upside down, and out tumbled a crab, taking a defensive stance as he hit the ground, like a paratrooper landing in enemy territory. The crab's papaya-seed eyes bulged high, as he danced on long, mechanical legs. His claws were mismatched, one twice the size of the other, both held ready like traps baited to spring. He moved stealthily to the side, then backed up so suddenly, when Diane approached, that he tumbled backwards onto the sand.

"What are you going to do with him? Keep him for bait?"

"No, ma'am." John picked up the bait bucket and started back toward the house, the tie rope dangling in the sand. "I just wanted to show you. I wouldn't keep him from his family."

As they walked, Diane spoke to him about his departure the next day, for a week had passed. "We're going to miss you, John. We've really enjoyed having you."

"You know, Miss Diane, I've already stayed at the hospital longer than I'm supposed to. Dr. Bozeman said they made a special exception, but I don't think I can be there much longer. I don't think I need to be, do you?"

"I don't really know." A nerve popped in Diane's forehead, as if to warn her that she was entering unexplored emotional territory. "Have you spoken to Dr. Bozeman about how you feel?"

"She says I'll know when I'm ready." John grimaced as he stepped onto a sharp shell. The path was pretty, but treacherous. "I think that I *am* ready. I just don't know where I'm going." He hopped up and down on one leg and rubbed the sole of his foot.

After dinner on this, the last, night of his visit, Diane sensed that John shared her despondency. She felt an urgent need to speak to Dr. Bozeman, and, while Matt and John were watching a movie downstairs, she and Mel, each at a phone extension, shared their thoughts with the doctor.

"You'd be amazed," Diane began, "how naturally John fits into our lives. We've all come to care for him, haven't we, Mel?"

"He's like a son to me."

"I'm pleased that you concur," Dr. Bozeman said. "But what about that missing piece of the puzzle? How does Matt feel?"

"Surprisingly, Matt doesn't seem to be jealous. He says that he would like to have a brother again." Diane added softly, "He misses Chris, too, you know."

"Yes, I'm sure that he does."

Diane forged on, with determination. "This afternoon we had a family powwow—Mel and Matt and I. We talked everything over, and I think we're all in shock over the outcome. We agreed unanimously, and without pressure—I held back for once, Dr. Bozeman, and let the guys decide for themselves." Diane's voice filled with excitement. "We want to ask John to come to live with us, to be our foster child. Of course, we know that we'll all have to adjust, especially Matt—"

"What do you think, doctor?" Mel asked.

Diane continued anxiously. "Do you think it's a healthy situation? Do you think it's a possibility?"

Dr. Bozeman paused—interminably, it seemed to Diane—then spoke in a voice touched with tenderness. "You and Mel are naive when it comes to your own strong-points. We at the hospital couldn't order a more suitable parenting team or a more therapeutic living environment. Having John become your foster child is a natural extension of the strong bond you've established with him. And, as you know, we had hoped for a sibling. I'm thrilled, absolutely thrilled, at your suggestion. Have you mentioned it to John?"

Mel broke in, "Good heavens, no. He's had enough disappointments. We weren't sure how you'd react, whether he was ready."

"More importantly, let's see how John reacts to the idea. Do you think you could call him to the phone and let me speak privately with him? Perhaps I can spare him the heartbreak of tomorrow's separation."

Diane called John to the phone and walked into the kitchen where she sat, nervous and unsteady, on a barstool beside Mel at the counter. In only a few minutes, John ambled in, his arms hung limply at his side. He looks stunned, Diane thought. His eyes were hollow, and he looked tired—like a weary traveler, home at last from a long journey. He gazed into Diane's eyes, and a smile began to break on his lips, then broaden until his face was awash with joy, his eyes glistening. He said simply, "You want me?"

Diane stood and walked around the counter, her arms held up to her tall young son. She touched the smooth skin of his young, innocent face. She would share this precious time, accompany him on his trip from child to man. She smiled at his blistered nose, as her finger traced his cheekbone, brushing aside a tear.

"And you want us?" she answered softly, her own eyes collecting tears.

Mel stretched his arms lovingly around the girth of their embrace, just as Matt loped into the room. "Hey, what's going on? Did I miss something?"

Diane turned. "Meet your new brother. John has

agreed to be our foster son."

Matt grinned broadly and approached John with his hand in the air. "That's cool."

John grabbed Matt's hand and pulled him over to join the communal hug, their first as a family. As their arms intertwined, Diane, for a fleeting moment, felt a happiness that she'd forgotten. If only Chris could be here, she thought. He would be giggling deliriously. And with that image, her happiness faded into a foggy memory of long ago.

⟶

Diane spread the bed, smoothing wrinkles with the plank of her arm, then karate-chopped the pillows and tossed them against the headboard into some semblance of order. No act was perfunctory today. She did her chores deliberately, orchestrating them relative to the main event of the day—the last time I'll make the bed before John comes home, the last breakfast I'll cook until John is part of the family, the last heart-to-heart talk with Matt until he becomes a sibling again.

Diane worried about Matt, who would once again, from this day forward, share his space, his parents, and his life. He would have gains, of course—a friend, a peer within the family—but she feared that jealousy would loom, as it had toward his lost brother.

"Matt, honey, how're you doing?" she asked at breakfast. "Are you excited about John? I'd understand if you were anxious, maybe had some mixed feelings." Diane threw the ball in Matt's court. She wanted him to explore his thoughts before his emotions took over.

Matt lowered his head over his cereal. "I suppose it's a little late to have second thoughts." He swallowed a huge helping, then raised his spoon in the air for emphasis. "Guess I'm feeling good about everything. Let's put it this way—I won't have trouble finding a partner for beach volleyball."

Matt tended to couch most situations in athletic terms. Mel had once told her that sports parallel all of life's struggles, and perhaps he wasn't too far off. Matt used the same theory, without the analysis.

Diane walked over to the breakfast table and stood behind Matt, bending to give him a hug. "You know you're my number-one son. I love you."

Matt chose that moment to depart, rising to dribble an imaginary basketball across the kitchen floor, then turned to shoot in the direction of the refrigerator. "I know, Mom. I know." When he reached the door, he tossed parting words over his shoulder. "See ya later."

⁓

They entered the airport terminal a half-hour early and checked the arrival schedules. John's flight was running a few minutes late, so Matt took off to buy a pretzel to appease his growling stomach. At the arrival gate Mel and Diane sat on a bench beside a floor-to-ceiling picture window, to watch for the Delta flight from Atlanta.

Diane had a thousand thoughts. Not often did destiny deal a singular act that would change your life forever. Had she been a good mother, even an adequate one? Could she handle another child? She picked at a cuticle, tearing skin loose from her nail.

Mel reached over, pulling her hands apart, and pecked her cheek. "Love ya, hon."

Let it go, she told herself—the guilt and self-doubt. Remember what the North Carolina group said—about her being a good mother, to Matt, as she had been to Chris. She'd played no part in his disappearance. She had protected him in every way she knew how. She had been tormented, bereft, for the past three years. Was she going to beat herself up forever?

Diane often gave herself silent pep talks, which usually fell flat. But today was different. She was here, as in childbirth, to welcome a new child. She must embrace this moment and never look back, never question. A warm smile crossed her face, clearing her thoughts. She could handle this. She felt strong and whole—fulfilled, a sensation she recognized from long ago, an emotion stolen from her by

Chris' abductor, now rushing blissfully back, renewed.

A plane rolled to the gate, just as Diane spotted Matt's loping stride. "Is this John's flight?" he called from a distance, oblivious to the waiting crowd.

Diane grinned at his artlessness as he yelled, chewing, then popped half a pretzel into his mouth, clamping it between his teeth. Airport waiting gates are always stilted, she thought. She watched a hovering Oriental family stack luggage to build an imaginary wall around their space. A businessman protected his reading material, clasping his arms around it, as if he feared a literary mugger might be lurking about. Two women took turns at each other's ear, as they whispered a secret conversation. Parents sequestered their children. The atmosphere was hushed.

But now the arriving passengers emerged, and all bonds broke loose. The waiting parties cast aside their self-consciousness, as they matched up with passengers, greeting them loudly with effusive hugs, conversing in capsules, yelled in unison—

"How was the flight?"

"Bumpy."

"How's Grandma feeling?"

"Not well."

"You must be exhausted."

"Here, let me get that bag."

The confabulation rose to a roar.

Matt spotted him first, his head towering over the passengers around him, long strands of hair swinging from side to side as he walked. "John!" Matt called, running forward. "Hey, man." He gave John an embarrassed hug, as they touched chests and bounced back.

Mel and Diane caught up. John bent down to engulf Diane in a bear hug, reaching around her to shake Mel's hand. "Gosh, it's good to be here," he said, scanning his new family with pride.

"Well, son," Mel said, his eyes moist, "we're awfully glad to have you here."

Diane stubbornly held back tears, rubbing the outside corners of her eyes with clenched fists. "You can't imagine how we feel, John—how happy we are."

His dark eyes pierced hers. "Maybe I can."

Diane grabbed him again, without words, to hold him to her.

"Enough of this mush, guys," Matt said, lightening the moment. "Let's go eat."

They walked arm and arm through the terminal, a family of four. Diane held onto John, who talked ceaselessly about the flight and the view from the sky. She smiled, remembering how quiet he had been the first time she met him. He had come out of his shell and, as he broadened his horizons, so would she. She squeezed her arm tighter around him. Life would be fresh, for both of them.

# Part Three

# A Weak Link

## Chapter 20

Buck Stanley tilted back in an overstuffed leather chair, his legs sprawled atop a large desk, crumbling stacks of paper. He looked up at his half-brother, Lawrence DuRoy, standing at attention on the other side of the desk.

"Laffey, I like the prospect of in-state deliveries, less expensive and less risky. What's happening with your new crony?"

"Donny? He's setting things up with the Colombian doctor, like you said."

"Something about that punk worries me." Buck stared at the beer can in his hand—ubiquitous at any hour of the day—and took a swig. "Are you sure we can trust him, not only his judgment but his mouth?" Buck's eyes flashed in the dim light of the desk lamp.

"Don't worry. I gave him another warning about how we deal with rats. He's too scared to talk, and in too deep." Laffey looked down, nervously fingering his nails, then slid his palms roughly down his thighs, wiping clean the sweat. "We may have a problem though."

"Lord God, what are you whining about this time?" Buck gazed toward the ceiling, and in a dramatic gesture, craned his head back and turned his palms up, splashing beer on his shirt.

"I received some inside information, from one of my deputy stoolies. The police arrested a suspected child abductor in North Carolina a while ago, after his description went out on the wire."

"So?" Buck countered impatiently, motioning his forearm in an inward swirl, gesturing for his brother to get on with it.

"His name was Adam McGuire. Does that ring a bell?" Laffey shuffled his feet. "They got hold of a thirteen-year-old boy who'd been abducted. Called himself John."

Buck sipped his beer. "Did the boy identify McGuire?"

"Just the opposite. Said he wasn't his kidnapper."

"Then what's the problem?" Buck shrugged offhandedly.

"The kid changed his mind later. Must have seen through the cosmetic work. He fingered McGuire, and some detective named Williams arrested him." Laffey glanced at the chair facing the desk, but Buck's face offered no invitation to sit down.

"It gets worse," Laffey confided cautiously. "McGuire chickened out—probably made a deal, because his attorney kept him out of jail—and he could snitch on Donny."

"Not very good timing, is it?" Buck's voice was heavy with sarcasm. "Just when Donny is about to expand our territory."

Laffey nodded. "What worries me"—he hesitated, as if couching a heavy blow—"Donny's not so clever, but he thinks he is. That's dangerous. If they get him in custody, he could squeal like a rat." Laffey stated the issue nonchalantly, offhandedly, as if he were detached from any consequences.

Buck, his eyes aflame, shot Laffey a wicked glare. "Dear brother, you haven't handled this one very well. Sounds like you've got a weak link that might break up our plan, bust everything apart." Buck slugged his beer and smashed the can inward with his palms, then folded it slowly, deliberately. "We better pull Donny back, end this operation before it begins. We have to sever all connections."

"No, no," Laffey stammered. "I've worked too hard to put it all together. I told you I'm keeping Donny quiet. I can take care of him." Laffey's lips twitched. "No problem."

"Yeah, you handle Donny. I'll get someone to ditch McGuire. If he's not around to testify, we're clean."

"But what if he's already testified?"

"Then we'll have to ditch Donny, too. That's one way to keep him quiet." Buck shifted his legs off the desk and sat upright, glowering at Laffey, unconvinced by his tough talk.

Buck was getting bored with the dilemma. His attention span was short and his need for a drink, powerful. He rose and sauntered to the refrigerator, reached for another beer, and returned, sneering again at his brother, as if he hadn't yet expressed enough disfavor.

Blood flushed Laffey's wan face, like burnt sienna running amuck, stark against a fresh white canvas. "One more thing about that kid, the one McGuire kidnapped. Apparently, he's still talking to the detective, and we don't know how much more he'll blab."

"Doesn't sound too promising. Laffey, I'm disappointed in you." Buck's mouth was set in a frown.

"What could I do? It was totally out of my control." Laffey's chalky plump hands rose in surrender. "What do you want me to do?"

"I want you to take care of him."

"Take care of a kid, a thirteen-year-old? Come on, you don't mean that." Laffey's eyes widened, and he shook his head from side to side. "Can't do it."

Buck looked at his brother in amazement. "And why not, if I might be so inquisitive?"

"Got another little problem."

"More bad news? How could you botch up any worse?" Buck curled his hands, elbows on the desk, and played fisticuffs with his puckered cheeks.

Laffey twisted his face awry. "Not really a problem, just an inconvenience. The kid is living with a family in Florida, some building contractor on the West Coast. He's just become their foster child, and they're probably hovering over him, like a mother hen her chick. Makes it more complicated."

"Tell you what," Buck said in disgust, standing. He walked around the desk and looked his brother in the eye. "Get some good inside stuff on that contractor. I'll figure out a way to keep the brat's mouth shut. If we have to threaten him, or his new family—hurt somebody, whatever—so be it."

He patted his brother's slumped shoulder, soft taps that grew into heavy hits. Buck's frown lifted, and a smile bloomed on his boyish face. "I could use a Florida vacation, maybe a little excitement. Don't worry your pretty head about it. I'll take care of this one."

# A Quiet Black Descending

## Chapter 21

Diane and Mel sipped wine on the second floor of Lou's Beach House, watching the setting sun nod to a stormy night, churning the sky. Wisps of clouds rolled against the glistening gray horizon, a shiny negative, white on gray. Sitting on their favorite barstools beside a wide picture window to the Gulf, they had front-row seats to watch the sun's performance, a quiet black descending as the curtain fell.

At the next table sat a middle-aged man with a boyish face, intent on a frosty pitcher of draft beer, which he was downing without the benefit of drinking mates. He mumbled something under his breath, as if he were talking to himself, dribbling his words. Then he repeated his muttering, louder still.

"Pardon?" Mel replied, his voice hesitant. "Were you speaking to us?"

"S'pose so," the man answered offhandedly, his words slurred. "Don't see anybody else to talk to." The man stared into his beer mug, drooping his upper body over it, as if succumbing to its power, hypnotized. He neither moved nor spoke. Diane looked out the window at pink neon reflections on the dark Gulf water, relieved that the sad, lonely man's attention had decided to stay home.

A waitress passed by, her heels clicking on the wooden floor strewn with peanut shells. The man perked up, like an actor responding to a cue. "Hey, young lady, how about another pitcher?" He called over to them again, loudly this time, unmistakable. "Why don't you join me? A pitcher looks lonely sitting on a table for one."

"Oh, thanks, but that's okay," Mel answered. "We've got to get going."

"We're walking," Diane added, as she glanced around the barn-like room, planning an exit through the tall tables, some square, some round for larger parties of patrons, with empty barstools propped against them. "The storm's really coming up now."

"Walking?" The man's eyes focused hazily on Diane, his head rocking on its base. His words dragged, out of sync, groggy from too much booze. "Where to?"

"We live down the beach," Mel said. "Walk up about twice a week."

Diane broke in, suddenly uneasy. "I'm sure he doesn't want to hear our life story."

"Sure I do. Come on over and sit down." He jerked his arm, elbow bent, toward his table, a crude stroke against the smoky air.

"No thanks, really," Diane said, as Mel extended his leg to search his shorts pocket for money to pay the check. She slid her stool back, preparing to leave.

"I'm looking for a place on the beach myself."

"What kind of place? Condo?" Mel asked. Diane gave him a disapproving nudge with her elbow.

"Not a condo. My wife looked at half a dozen of 'em." He paused to light a cigarette, its tip disappearing into an exuberant burst of flame from his gold flip-top lighter, which he shut off with a practiced twist of his wrist. "Nope, I'm looking for more privacy—a house, or maybe a villa."

"I build houses on the beach," Mel said. "Three-story homes, just to the south of here."

"You mean in Sandpiper Sound?" The man's words were suddenly sharp, the notes hitting soundly after a shaky warm-up on the keys.

"Right," Mel said, and Diane patiently sat back down.

"Looked at one home in there, but it didn't have any view. I'd like to feast my eyes on the water every night." He gestured toward the black sky. "Just like from here." Without invitation, he lifted his beer mug and moved to join them, standing beside their table. "Maybe I could come see your place. Got anything for sale?"

"Well, we have a beachfront model we could show you."

"Good. I'd like to avoid that yappy real estate girl tomorrow. Just see your place, if that's okay." He riffled the back of his hair with his hand, his eyes twinkling, then extended his hand eagerly. "Hi, I'm Buck. Buck Stanley."

"Glad to meet you," Mel answered, as he shook Buck's hand. "This is my wife, Diane."

"Pleasure, ma'am." Buck acknowledged her with a wobbly bow.

"You sound Southern," Diane said.

"Yep, from Georgia—Athens." He drained his mug, then glanced desperately over at his abandoned pitcher. "You don't mind if I join you?"

Diane nodded reluctantly. "I guess not, but I have a sinking feeling that we're going to be walking home in the rain."

Buck grabbed greedily for his pitcher of beer on the next table and tilted his mug for a refill. "I'll give you a ride home if you need it," he said, pulling up a barstool.

Trapped by the stranger, Diane made an attempt at polite conversation. "Do you visit our area often?"

"Just discovered it, attending a convention here. I fell in love with your beach and was thinking about buying a winter place." He took a healthy gulp of beer and smacked his lips loudly.

"I know what you mean. My husband and I still feel like we're on vacation, every day."

Buck offered Mel a drink, solicitously poising the pitcher above a mug. Mel nodded his acceptance. "Hard not to be in a good mood," he said, "with this much sun."

"How long y'all been down here?"

"Forever," Mel joked.

"Eighteen years actually," Diane said, "except for a year in North Carolina." She looked down, without further elaboration.

"Why North Carolina?" Buck pressed. He lit another cigarette and leaned his stool back against the wall, balancing his knee against the table edge in an easy slouch.

"It's kind of a long story," she whispered.

"I've got all night," Buck smiled, as if eager to be entertained.

As rain pelted the tall windows of Lou's Beach House, Diane shared her life with a stranger, telling him secrets she'd hidden from old friends. Her words fell like an endless summer drizzle. She spoke into the night about Chris and his abduction, about her vulnerability after losing her child.

"How could anyone snatch a child from his family?" Buck bellowed in a burst of outrage. But his fury was quickly spent, and his face became lethargic, with muscles too lazy to register further emotion. He stared at Diane with curiosity, as a bystander might observe the aftermath of an accident—apathetic, detached, not willing to help the victim, yet unable to look away.

Diane appeared defenseless, crushed by defeat like a soldier in battle. "I don't know why I'm telling you all this." She rested her arms on the table, fingers dangling, and hung her head from her shoulders like a heavy burden. Mel patted her arm and looked out into the dark night.

Buck gleamed devilishly. "My friends say I could strip a 'possum bare of its soul."

The next morning Buck's reddened eyes squinted in the Florida sun as he laboriously climbed the front entry steps, skimming the rough stone balustrade with the palm of his hand. Diane greeted him at the double doors, graced with two herons etched in glass bowing to each other, their skinny legs bent in servitude. Buck complimented her on the landscaping, glancing back at the front garden, then rattled the early-morning cough of a heavy smoker. He rested at the landing, wheezing as his shoulders rose and his chest ballooned with deep, catching breaths.

"We try to retain the indigenous plants and the natural beauty of the land," Mel explained, talking over Diane's shoulder. "That's what you're buying—the beach."

"Couldn't agree more. And I like the architecture; looks grand, European."

"Well, come see the rest," Diane said, leading the way.

Buck effused over the view, the sunlit rooms, and the

tall Palladian windows, finding nothing to fault in a cursory walk through the home. "I like it. You wouldn't believe the junk I've seen." He reached for his wallet in the back pocket of his shorts, handing Mel a business card scrolled in gold print. "Just write it up and fax it to my office. I know when something feels right."

"Does your wife need to see it?" Diane asked, accustomed to feminine input on the final decision to buy a home.

"Oh, no. She'll love it." Buck grinned, making his way back to the entry, circling his head around the rooms he passed. "What's not to love?" He was out the front door in no time.

Mel stood behind Diane at the top of the steps, his hands on her waist, as they watched Buck Stanley gun the motor of his XJ6 Jaguar sedan, its polished British-racing-green body sparkling in the intense Florida sun. He sped off down the shell driveway, sending sand and tiny crushed shells flying.

Diane waved a limp good-bye. "It seems too easy," she said, feeling numb. "Buck Stanley asked no questions, had nothing negative to say. He didn't quibble about the price. Most buyers are at least a little cagey. Never saw a buyer like that, so ingenuous."

"Maybe he just fell in love with the house and didn't want to beat around the bush. Probably knows what he wants and makes up his mind quickly."

"Hmm," she muttered. "Maybe."

"Seems like a heck of a nice guy," Mel said.

Diane stared at the tire tracks, long grainy streaks, darkening the pretty white shells like rain in a sandbox. She shook her head slowly in dismay. "Drinks too much."

⌒

Coming to contract wasn't quite so easy. Buck Stanley's accountant dickered and squabbled and squawked and whined, finally agreeing to pay the price for his client's dream house on the Gulf of Mexico. Next Buck hired a local real estate attorney, Hank Jackson—a methodical, disagreeable deal breaker—who spent weeks tailoring the transaction, miring it in procedure with no purpose except to embellish his fee, then insisted, due to the lengthy delay, that his client move in before closing—to try out the house before parting with his money, "paying a handsome rent, of course." Although early occupancy was unusual, and ill advised in their experience, Mel and Diane, beaten down by the bickering, reluctantly agreed.

Buck Stanley moved into his grand new home on the Gulf with a flourish. Lady decorators in short skirts bounced up and down the steps with swatches of fabrics, and interior designer vans with fancy logos frequented the front drive, belching streams of uniformed delivery men, *objets d'art* cradled in their arms—bronze statues and marble planters and Italian wall frescoes and imported tapestries and fine oil paintings in gilded frames.

And then, Buck changed colors like a chameleon. Though cordial on the surface, he became elusive when asked to honor any part of the contract. He failed to pay his additional deposit and hedged about when, or if, he intended to close on the house. He acted paranoid, suspicious, and sometimes refused to speak directly to Mel or Diane at all, deferring instead to his attorney, Hank Jackson, who wrote letters with vague references to unsubstantiated "structural problems" and "misrepresentation."

Mel and Diane consulted with their attorney, Scott England, who was known around town to be tenacious and, when challenged, ferocious as a bulldog. England suggested that they meet with Buck, in an informal attempt to get to the bottom of it.

Buck agreed to the meeting, on his terms and in his own good time. Setting up the date and place proved to be a minor power struggle, with Buck throwing up obstacles— "Just don't know when I can fit in a meeting. I'm a busy man."—like a third-world country negotiating the shape of the table at an international diplomacy meeting, vying for even a semblance of supremacy. Finally, Buck acquiesced, and the meeting was set to take place at Mel's construction company.

Buck arrived, twelve minutes late, in a flurry, loose

legal papers riffling in his hand. He barged past the receptionist, and, without invitation or apology, hustled to the conference room.

Scott England sat at the conference table, briefing Mel and Diane, but he barely batted a lash at Buck's interruption. He quickly rose, his tall frame towering, to greet the intruder. "It's a pleasure to meet you, Mr. Stanley." Diane sensed that he was prepared to be deferential, to smooth any ruffled feathers, to get this closing accomplished for his longstanding clients, regardless of his disapproval of Buck Stanley's dealing.

England's slender stature and courtly manners distinguished him, despite his ruffled clothes, which bordered on unkempt, in the way that Abraham Lincoln obtained dignity with articulate words that overshadowed his backwoods appearance. Diane smiled at the incongruity, well aware that any nod to weakness was calculated, any apparent lack of shrewdness, strategic. He was clever, her country lawyer.

"Well, Mr. Stanley," he began, "do we have any obstacles to overcome before we can complete this transaction and get you settled in your new home?"

"I'm already settled. Didn't you hear?" Buck answered, smirking.

"Oh, right, you have occupied early," England said, stroking his chin. His lanky body dwarfed the armless chair he sat in, and he shuffled to one side, his legs askew. "But we've received letters from your attorney, Mr. Jackson, suggesting problems with the house and even with our client's disclosure. There have been no concrete complaints, just innuendo. What is it that you're trying to say? Do we have an issue here?"

"I can't speak for my attorney, now, can I? If we have issues, I'm sure they'll come up." Buck's grin turned ugly, in a flash, and he glowered at England. "Sooner or later."

He's threatening us, Diane thought. She shivered at the coldness in the room.

"I'm wondering why you came today," England said, bouncing a pointed finger on his chin. "You seem to have nothing to offer this discussion."

"Shucks," Buck said, wiping the scowl from his face, "I

was just tryin' to cooperate."

"Well, next time you better bring your lawyer. You might need to defend yourself." England spoke in a steady voice, without a ripple.

"As you wish," Buck answered with a smirk, as he picked up his papers and tapped them on the table to straighten the edges. He rose abruptly and hurried out the door, without a word or even a glance as he departed.

Floored, they sat silent for a moment. Even Scott England, the consummate rhetorician, whose fertile words were always ripe for picking, seemed at a loss. Diane searched his face for guidance, and finally he spoke.

"We can expect to hear from Buck's attorney next. Ol' Hank Jackson's known as a sort of plodder with a characteristic, rather dastardly, attack. He bombards his opponents with demands for documents, stacks and stacks of documents. In your case, he has rich territory to mine—county permits, invoices, houseplans, estimates, proposals, contracts, warranties, faxes, letters—"

"But why?" Diane interrupted.

"It's a legal ploy," England said, "designed to drain and frustrate the opponent."

Diane visualized hours standing by the copier, reproducing volumes of paper. Suddenly tired, she stretched her arms stiffly. "Well," she said wearily, "it's working already."

England cautioned, "Don't let it. Jackson prolongs every issue with a profusion of paper. His tactic is to wear down his opponent and delay, delay, delay. But it never really helps his case in the long run."

"Maybe he should spend his time practicing law, instead," Diane answered, her words leaded with bitterness.

"Maybe," England said, chuckling. "Keep in touch."

A few days later Buck Stanley stormed, unannounced, into the reception area of Mel and Diane's office, in no mood to wait his turn. Diane stood there, talking with customers, but he brushed past her and threw an arrogant glance at another group of clients seated in the waiting room. He scowled at a young boy who tugged on his mother's arm, pointing at the Lions Club display, which offered mints for a twenty-five-cent contribution. "Come on, Mommy, buy candy. Please, Mommy."

"I need to see Mel," Buck demanded of the receptionist, as if no introduction or explanation were required.

"And may I tell him who you are and the nature of your business?" the receptionist replied politely, biting her lower lip.

"Tell him Buck." He scratched his neck with a rough paw and swayed his shoulder forward over the counter, planting his elbow and peering down at the receptionist with disdain. "He'll know who I am."

The receptionist was, in fact, well acquainted, by reputation, with Buck Stanley and his imperious attitude. As she rose reluctantly to summon her boss, Diane interceded. "I'll take care of it, Beth," she said, apologizing to her clients as she left the room.

She slipped into Mel's private office and whispered, pointing back through the open door. "Buck's out front. Wants to see you, and he's not in a very good mood."

"What could he want now?" Mel moved from his drawing board to his desk, shrugging his shoulders complacently. "Bring him back, I guess, and it's probably best if you stay. But can you slip this note to Beth? I'll tell her to buzz me in a few minutes, to remind us of a meeting or something." He jotted a quick message, tearing off the top sheet of a note pad.

Diane returned with Buck, who took a commanding stance, opposing Mel at the front of his desk. Buck's arms were triangles on his hips as he shook his head from side to side in disgust. "You're in trouble, man." Without invitation, he drew back a chair and plopped down, crossing a leg and leaning forward to drape his arm across his knee. "My attorney says we've got a strong case against you," he threatened, chewing his gum vigorously.

"Well, Buck, so far neither you nor your attorney has had any specific complaint." Mel started calmly, but Diane saw his jaw ripple as he clenched his teeth. "I hear innuendoes and sarcasm, but nothing concrete. If you've got a problem with the house, give it to me in writing, and I'll deal with it.

"If you've decided that you don't want to buy the house, that's okay, too. Frankly, I'm sick of dealing with you and your attorney. We can sell the house twice before the weekend." He looked to Diane for confirmation, and she nodded, her head bobbing emphatically. His voice rose in a crescendo. "If you don't want the house, just say so."

Mel sat upright in his revolving chair, his feet grounded forward. "I've responded to ridiculous requests for paperwork from your attorney. I've followed our contract to the letter." Now his voice was thundering. "Why don't you just speak your mind?"

Buck's head fell to the side, as he chuckled quietly. "You just don't get it, do you, Mel? At least not yet. But you will. Stick around—you'll *get* it." Buck rose, cutting his words sharply, and marched out, his eyes focused on the door as if blindered.

Dumbfounded, Mel stared after Buck, then looked at Diane with wide eyes. "Maybe we've got a mental case here."

"He scares me," she said, picking up the phone to dial Scott England's office. His secretary answered and, without asking any questions, put Diane through to her boss.

"Buck Stanley just paid us a visit," Diane began hesitantly, searching for words to describe the scene she had just witnessed. "For no apparent reason. He didn't speak in specifics, but his words and his attitude had an undertone, like we were dirt under his feet. He asked for nothing, yet clearly threatened Mel. Said, in a really menacing voice, 'Stick around—you'll *get* it.' It makes me uneasy. I'm afraid for Mel."

"Maybe Buck's more than a disgruntled client," England said. "He seems to have a dangerous edge, an explosive side. Whatever else, Buck Stanley is an enigma."

Diane glanced out the window at the parking lot and motioned to Mel. Walking to his car, Buck broke into a run when he spotted a few kids admiring his Jaguar. "Get away from there, brats!" he yelled, then jumped in. His tires screeched and dust flew, as he raced away.

# The Little General

## Chapter 22

It was a typical morning—the smell of coffee wafting through the office, a few chat sessions going on in small groups, workers kicking into gear, following their ritual morning steps as the workday took shape. Isolated in his office, Mel leaned against the drawing board, concentrating on a floor plan illuminated by the blazing spotlight of a study lamp.

Diane heard the company's entry door crash open, and she got up from her desk to investigate. As she entered the reception area, she was stunned to see a deputy sheriff, standing with authority, legs planted wide, accompanied by four men in street dress. The deputy called out loudly, "Mel Rath. Is Mel Rath here?"

Mel stepped out of his office into the hall and grinned at the sight. Diane smiled, too. One of those charity arrest gimmicks, when they take a citizen to a fake jail cell, usually a banquet room contributed by a restaurant, where he must call his friends and associates for donations, to pay for his release an hour later. She wondered who was behind the charity gag. Who had given Mel's name?

"Okay, officer," Mel said, "what's the deal?"

"I have a search warrant that I need to read to you. These are my men, undercover officers." The young deputy pumped up his short stature, as if demanding his due respect. As he read, his voice quavered.

"Would you like a glass of water?" Diane offered.

"Sure, ma'am."

Diane's hand trembled as she lifted the water jug from the refrigerator, despite her belief that this could only be a ruse. When she handed the deputy a glass of water, he paused to look at it, as if disarmed, then set it on top of a filing cabinet, without touching it to his lips. The glass apparently didn't have a solid setting, and he grabbed for it, fumbling with hands that appeared to be suddenly struck with palsy. He continued, leaning stiffly against the wall. The other officers rocked on their heels and stared at the floor, looking sheepish.

As the deputy rattled on, each word *staccato*, Diane caught a swatch here and there until finally his voice droned into a sea of legalese. "Judge Wright signed order . . . to search premises . . . to seize records . . . Stanley files . . . computer data . . . failure to reveal hidden defects . . . failure to disclose . . . attempt to defraud." Diane watched her employees as they stood around dumbfounded, powerless. The company's front doors were locked to the public, and a nightmare unfolded inside.

Once she discerned that the surrealistic scene wasn't a joke, that these men were actually serious, Diane looked helplessly at Mel. "Call our attorney," he said. Calmly, she walked to her office and softly shut the door.

"Don't shut that door!" the deputy yelled. "No doors are to be closed in this office. Do you understand?" Now he was barking like a platoon sergeant.

She opened the door, the telephone already to her ear, and threw a glare in his direction. The other men remained in the background, passively regarding the bravado of their leader, who was strutting about the room like a rooster, his feathers ruffled by an insouciant audience.

Scott England was shocked. "How the judge could possibly justify an 'attempt to defraud' is beyond me. Buck must have fabricated some funny stuff, or he has some friends in high places. But it sounds like they have a valid warrant. Say nothing at all; let them go about their work. Call me when they've left."

With a wide flourish the deputy removed his jacket and fingered his holster, eyeing the secretaries, who registered disinterest. He directed a heavy-set companion—a "computer expert," he bragged—to search the computer disks and ordered the other officers to scour individual offices, while he swished around, overseeing.

With prudent foresight Mel and Diane had well documented the Stanley transaction, retaining conversation notes, faxes, contract changes, and correspondence. Diane told the officers that the files were no mystery. "You won't find a scrap of paper that we haven't already shared with Stanley's attorney. You wouldn't believe the paperwork we've sent him."

Genuinely dismayed, she motioned Mel over to a corner. "What could they possibly be looking for?"

He lifted his shoulders, elbows bent and palms up. "Who knows?"

Ignoring England's advice, Diane led the officers to the thick files and explained that it would be futile to search the computer, which had been discontinued the year before, while the company developed new software. The deputy spoke his distrust with a suspicious glare.

Diane grinned and whispered to Mel, "He thinks we have dark secrets hidden deep in the guts of the computer."

"Let them waste their time," he said.

After an hour of frustration, the computer ace had to admit failure. "There's nothing here," he mumbled in timid disappointment.

As the morning passed, and the deputy tried to seize papers from the Stanley file, Mel's anger grew, until he finally lost his patience. He stood over the deputy and demanded, "Any documents taken from this office must be copied immediately and returned. We'll need the original paperwork to sue Stanley for this action. We'll sue the pants off him." Mel's eyes flared, as his voice rose. "I don't want anything lost. I won't tolerate it."

The deputy cowered under Mel's glare, and authority passed like a relay baton into Mel's hands. Crumbling in defeat, the deputy ended a four-hour search for secret files that, he was certain, had been cached. Eventually the officers left with Mel's secretary and two boxes of original documents to be reproduced at the station and brought back intact by closing time. The secretary told Diane, upon her return, that she had felt captive in the back seat of the deputy's car, with no inside door handles and the rooster in the front seat crowing to his companion, as if she weren't present, about his recent spectacular pursuits in the cause of justice.

Later a friend from the police department gave Diane the true story on the caliber of the little general and the reputation he had earned. "Seems his wife left him, with ample grounds for divorce. She took up with a fine fellow in a decent relationship. One day this fool deputy stormed into his ex-wife's home, grabbed her lover by the throat, and shoved a loaded revolver in his mouth." The act had been reported and reprimanded, yet the deputy was still performing in the line of duty, suspected to be on the take. The other officers thought the little punk was a joke, a dangerous joke.

# The Bulldog

## Chapter 23

Scott England, a reedy six foot six, had lean discombobulated limbs that sprawled haphazardly, as if out of his control. Wire half-glasses sat on the tip of his conspicuous nose, and his beady eyes were ever X-raying the situation at hand. His family had pioneered the town, and his office exhibited the proof—early photographs, in sepia tones, of the small village it had been before the roads were paved, with his ancestors prominent in the foreground. Antique scales, tools, and maps punctuated stacks of law books and incongruous modern equipment, England having recently dived into the sea of advancing electronics. He had a doting secretary who kept him on cue, but did no typing. England keyed his own computer pad, cranking out inspired letters and documents.

He ushered Mel and Diane into his office, a disarray of files, tall stacks of dusty books, and aimless winding cords. "Watch your step, there. Please have a seat," he said, as he grabbed an accordion file stuffed to the gills, spilling its guts as he looked for a clear space to set it down. He started to pick up the mess of papers, then swatted his hand in the air. "Forget it. My gal will put it all together later."

Diane sat forward in her chair as England spoke. "Buck Stanley's complaint to the police was total fabrication; the charge of fraud is outrageous. He definitely deserves to be sued, and sue we will.

"I have information from the police on how these trumped-up charges came about. Seems that Buck's relative, his half-brother, put together a portfolio, with letters from you and the contract and ledger sheets contrived by his accountant. The half-brother's name is Lawrence Lafayette DuRoy—that's quite a Southern concoction for a name, isn't it? Anyway, he and Buck's attorney, Jackson, delivered this portfolio of sorts to the police station and accused you of fraud."

Diane shook her head in disbelief. "But what could he put together that would incriminate us? You know we haven't done anything, except sell him a house."

"That's just it, Diane. The portfolio was clever. It twisted words and falsified figures enough to fool a stupid investigator into thinking that there was some meat to their accusation."

"But what does Buck want?" Mel asked. "Is he trying to get the house for less money?"

"That's the apparent motive, but it just doesn't smell right."

"I agree," Diane said. "He acts vindictive, enraged— out of control."

Mel nodded. "I don't know what I did to make him so angry, but his actions appear to be directed at me personally."

"We may not be able to discern Buck's motive, but his attorney's tactics are clear," England said. "Jackson is using subterfuge, distracting us with mountains of meaningless paperwork, because he has no case. A modern-day Shylock, obviously milking his client. His reputation precedes him around town. The creep has even pulled this search warrant routine before. He'll break the law himself, just to make his opponent humble." England sorted files on his desk as he spoke and slammed one down in disgust. "When lawyers— who should be the stalwart champions of justice—let their ethics go, everything is lost. Justice must be served," he avowed, pounding a fist on his huge chaotic desk, sending papers flying.

Requiring impeccable attention to detail, England directed Diane to prepare a chronological file documenting the case. He attacked his own homework with vigor and mapped out a strategy. Cutting right to the quick, he issued his first summons to depose, serving papers on Lawrence Lafayette DuRoy.

Across a massive, polished mahogany conference table in an Atlanta legal office, Diane watched Lawrence Lafayette DuRoy squirm as he was grilled by Scott England. He's probably accustomed to genteel Southern handling with, at least, politeness on the surface, she thought. England's rough questioning must strike him as crude.

"Isn't it true that you instigated a portfolio accusing my client, Mel Rath, of fraud? Don't look at your lawyer, Mr. DuRoy; it's too late for that. Speak up, sir."

England's towering frame commanded the conference table. His rangy arms sprawled over an impressive array of files, and his bold voice confirmed that he was in charge.

DuRoy, with his stunted body hunched low in his seat, looked defenseless. His answers were stammering and imprecise. "But . . . uh . . . I don't really think I want to answer that question. I . . . uh . . . protest . . . that it's improper."

"Thanks for the legal guidance," England barbed. "I'll take it under advisement." Then, lifting his shoulders, he raised his voice, stern and threatening, "Now, answer the question."

DuRoy turned with a sweaty desperation to his attorney, who reflected a helpless shrug and echoed humbly, "Answer the question."

Diane surveyed the faces around the table. England was rock solid, demanding, his chin jutted forward in determination. DuRoy was flustered, picking at his fingernails in his lap, and his attorney appeared resigned, his shoulders slouched in surrender. A court reporter sat expressionless beside a machine on a stand, her fingers flying soundlessly.

Mel was smiling. His eyes twinkled, crinkling at the corners, and his lips curled in a satisfied grin. She reached for his hand under the table and gave it a squeeze.

"Yes," DuRoy continued timidly. "I made up a portfolio . . . if you will . . . accusing Mel Rath of an attempt to defraud my half-brother, Buck Stanley."

"Defraud your half-brother of how much money?" England's voice thundered, as if struck by lightning. "Speak up, sir."

"Well . . . I'm not sure. Thousands of dollars, I guess."

England stood and began to pace back and forth beside the table, like a lion stalking his prey. He bent his lanky torso slightly at the waist, with his hands folded behind him. "And how did you determine this accusation?"

"How? Mel Rath misrepresented the home's value, by not disclosing . . . you know . . . hidden defects and such." He spoke mechanically, as if carefully coached. The deposition room was quiet for a moment, and DuRoy wriggled in the stilted silence. Diane admired England's use of the dramatic pause.

"Let's be specific, Mr. DuRoy. What did my client misrepresent? How did he fail to disclose? What defects did he hide?"

"Well, it's all in writing. Buck's attorney referred to these things in some letters."

"And this is proof?" England laughed, flopping an upturned palm into the air. "Letters from an opposing attorney, unsubstantiated letters? An attorney can write anything in a letter." He leaned over Diane's shoulder and muttered, "At least, that's my experience with Buck's attorney." He shook his head and raised a forefinger at the court reporter. "No, let's keep that off the record."

England turned back to his prey. "Mr. DuRoy, isn't it true that your portfolio, in fact, presented *no* evidence to support these accusations? And isn't it also true that you were selective in your quotes of letters and documents—that you omitted important context, so that the substance of the written material might be misconstrued?"

DuRoy's mouth moved, but no sound came out. England cupped his hand to his ear and stretched his head in a comical attempt to hear DuRoy's unspoken words. Mel and Diane chuckled quietly, and DuRoy's attorney tapped the table with his hand, to restore decorum, as a judge would rap his gavel to silence the court. But a grin broke through even his stern demeanor.

Sweat dotted DuRoy's pasty face, as he tried again to speak. "What were you asking? Oh yes, I included excerpts from faxes and letters, back and forth. Well . . . yes . . . perhaps I failed to include everything germane. I . . . may have left certain parts out. Misleading? Not really. Well, I suppose

. . . it might have been misconstrued. But I think this line of questioning . . . should be . . . uh . . . struck—"

England, chortling now himself, chimed in, "Mr. DuRoy, you've been watching too much TV." He dropped his smile with a flick of his head and sneered at DuRoy as if he were muck in the swamp. "Now, this portfolio." England turned his attention to Diane. "It's pretty professional, so I hear—hard covered and spiral bound, even has an index."

DuRoy puffed up with the compliment. "I was editor, you know, of my college yearbook."

England's eyes burned into DuRoy's. "Back to the business at hand." The disgust in his voice implied that the deed was as dastardly as ever committed by man. "What did you do with the portfolio? What, sir? Tell me—*what?*"

DuRoy cringed at the rat-tat-tat of England's grill. "Oh yes . . . the business at hand."

"Did you deliver the portfolio to the police?"

"Well, now, maybe I did." DuRoy swayed his head prissily.

"Maybe? Are you saying that you don't remember?"

"Okay, okay . . . I did."

"Did you not, in fact, instigate the whole series of events that led to the search warrant?" England bellowed, as he rounded the table to approach DuRoy. Diane realized that he was done toying with the creep.

DuRoy was pale, and he clutched the table tightly. "Who's on trial here?"

"Next, it may be you," England thundered. "Do you realize that, if you lie, you can be jailed for perjury? You should be aware of that fact and carefully consider your responses."

DuRoy's pudgy frame crumpled further down in his seat, so that his chest disappeared below the table line. His eyes glistened and beads of sweat dotted his round face. He threw his head back and massaged the nape of his neck with pale, stubby fingers. "I'm aware. Let's just say that I . . . put together . . . the portfolio."

"Where is that portfolio now? May I see it?"

DuRoy answered with a smirk. "I'm afraid that's impossible. It's been lost, or mislaid."

England lost patience. "You have a short memory. You *must* turn over the portfolio and any other pertinent documents. If you do not, you will be held accountable. You will face trouble that you can't imagine. But you haven't turned over anything yet, have you?"

"I just don't think it's proper—" DuRoy's words trailed to a whisper, and his shoulders sank in defeat.

"Shut up," his attorney said in disgust. "You'll get your documents, Mr. England."

# The Impostors

## Chapter 24

Raccoon eyes peered out from black shadows behind the Roman tub, and Diane could hear small, restless squeals. "Must be a mother, with babies."

"I can't do this," Mel said, lowering the handgun he'd borrowed in desperation, after all other attempts had failed.

The raccoon had plagued the construction of Mel and Diane's new model home from the beginning, even embedding its paw prints in the freshly poured concrete of the entry landing, marking its territory. Later the cured concrete would be coated with a troweled design, so the raccoon's spoor would not become a permanent fixture, but its physical presence was turning out to be. At first, the workers thought the raccoon was a male, because it was large and aggressive. They had to defend their lunches, and the raccoon had bared its teeth and stood ground against their taunts and attempts to push it back with a board. In the evenings, the raccoon had relieved itself in various choice spots around the home—the master sitting room, the study, a guestroom, the master bath. Now its motivation was clear—a mother protecting her little ones, nested in the dark shadows behind the Roman tub, protected by the tile surround and beyond the reach of human hands.

Mel and Diane had tried to reclaim their territory, as the house was nearing completion. They had played loud music and poured ammonia into the nest to uproot the animal, but to no avail. The pursuit was getting less comical; the raccoon had chewed through the guest bath wall.

Finally, they turned to an animal trapper, unique to his profession, who never killed his prey. His panel truck had an official-looking logo, a badge encircling his motto, *Arrest a Pest*. When he drove up, Mel joked, "The animals in the woods must be shaking in their boots."

The animal arrester gravely observed the nest, the mother raccoon's approaches and escapes, and cupped his hand on his chin in thought. "No problem. I'll set a big trap and then go in after the little ones. Got to get the mother first, or she'll tear the house apart looking for her babies."

"How many babies do you think?"

"Probably two, maybe three. You'll have to cut into the wall for me to lift them out. I'll have it done by morning. You can have your house back tomorrow."

When Mel and Diane arrived at the office, the secretaries were astir with news. Scott England had called.

"Buck's motion to dismiss has been denied," Beth said, excitement in her voice, "and the trial has been pushed forward. You have forms to fill out and fax back to Scott immediately. And he wants you to return his call."

The early laborious months of the lawsuit had passed slowly, seemingly without progress, as Buck's attorney tried to worm out of the action with lengthy countersuits, all unsuccessful. But things had started popping when they began to prepare for trial. On England's orders, they worked late hours—copying files, printing graphic charts on the computer, enlarging photographs of the house, and securing expert witnesses.

At last, Diane thought, we'll see the fruit of our labor.

England set up a viewing of the model home, which Stanley already occupied, to give their experts an opportunity to authenticate the quality of construction. The house was teeming with men and women in suits and uniforms—industry subcontractors, a young female attorney representing Jackson's law firm, a structural engineer, the construction supervisor from Mel's company, Scott England, Mel, and Diane. All were talking at once, some milling about in small groups, comparing samples, taking photographs, opening and shutting cabinet doors, running faucets. Diane giggled to herself. Buck, who was not present, was probably off getting drunk somewhere, she thought. He would be livid at the intrusion, the impostors violating his home.

The owner of Moonlight Tile was scraping at the floor grout, to counter Buck's claim that it had discolored. With twenty-five years in the tile industry under his belt, fighting to earn respect in a white man's industry, Virgil had earned his competent air. "No doubt 'bout it. Some'un's scraped this grout out 'n tried to replace it." He stooped over for a closer examination and rubbed his thick black fingers, chalked with grout, over the ruts.

"What'cha think, Virgil?" England asked.

Raising a head of curly gray hair, Virgil gave his solemn opinion, "Well, suh, I think some'un did jurst 'nuff to make a mess."

England's eyes danced in delight. "You're going to make one hell of a witness."

England joined Diane on the sofa. He flopped his arms loosely at his sides and crossed his legs, in a most relaxed fashion. He leaned closer to Diane, shielding his mouth to consult his client in confidence, for a moment ignoring the beehive.

A phone rang, and the young female attorney from Jackson's law firm, in a show of control, ran for it. "It's for you, Mr. England. Our senior partner," she announced, sounding awestruck.

England walked calmly to the cordless phone and strolled off to the far reaches of the dining room. "Yes?" he answered loudly, then held the phone for a few minutes without comment. "Well, I don't know. It seems you've gotten yourself in quite a jam—your client, too. Court's set for next week, you know. And we're ready to go," he stated truthfully.

He moved among the bodies of subcontractors, stepping over a plumber crouched under the kitchen sink, his ample buttocks peeking above a white yoke of jockey shorts, fighting for emancipation. "It's a little late to talk," England said. He might have had on blinders, for all the attention he appeared to give his audience, many of whom were grinning. But Diane knew better. He was playing the crowd and enjoying every minute of it.

"Okay, I guess I can talk to my clients. Call me back in fifteen minutes." England's voice feigned sympathy for the opposition. "It'll be tough convincing them," he said, winking at Diane, "but I'll give it my best shot."

Without consulting Mel and Diane, England took the next call upstairs behind closed doors. Walking by, Diane overheard, "You know, I've got a theory about this. That half-brother, DuRoy, might have a jealous disposition, might be envious of Buck's fancy new beachfront home. Yeah, that dimwit could have an agenda of his own." Diane smiled, having previously speculated with England on the motivation of Lawrence Lafayette DuRoy.

"Doesn't matter, though, who drummed up the case," England continued. "It's Buck Stanley who will have to pay—and pay big. My clients are reasonable folks, but they've been hurt badly. They won't walk away lightly."

About a half-hour later, another call came in for England, who exchanged a sly grin with Diane before taking the phone. He repeated his earlier promenade through the living area on the main floor, not saying much other than an occasional "I see." Once, he declared "absolutely not," shaking his head like a seasoned baseball pitcher rejecting his catcher's signal. He ended the conversation curtly. "I'll see what I can do. Give me ten minutes."

England motioned Mel and Diane to the sofa. "An interesting development. It seems that Buck has left the country and won't be available to testify."

"Probably off on a binge," Diane suggested.

"Could be. They've made us an offer. Let me say, first, that we're ready for court, and we'll win; they have nothing but slime. But there are expenses to consider. The court costs and attorney trial fees could be another $20,000, and we're already in the $70,000 range. There would be wear and tear on the two of you—not that you haven't suffered already— but I know you're up to it."

"What's the offer?" Mel asked.

"They've made two proposals. First, they offered $160,000, above and beyond the contract price, with each party paying its own attorney fees."

"That's not bad," Mel said.

England continued nonchalantly. "I turned that down flat. Knew you wouldn't take it." Diane smiled at Mel, acknowledging that they were in good hands.

"You might at least consider the second proposal," England said, winking mischievously at Diane. "Each party pays its own attorney fees, no further litigation, and $200,000 for your trouble. We might get more in court. The son-of-a-bitch deserves to pay."

"Not bad at all," Mel mused.

Diane's face was blank, impossible to read, as her eyes searched the high ceiling. Her lips gradually twisted into a smile. "It's a victory, but a bittersweet one. I'm sorry we'll miss our day in court—to expose Buck, to show his ugly underbelly to the world."

"Yeah," England added. "I really wanted to hang the bastard."

Buck Stanley returned from Paris, where he had drowned out with booze any thought of the lawsuit. By day, he had sampled the white wine and, by night, the red. Buck's face was still boyishly handsome, even though his hair had thinned in a circle on the crown of his head, and his halting French was no obstacle to romance, perhaps an advantage. He had hooked onto a pretty Mademoiselle, taken with his reckless charm, and buried his head in her bosom, safe from the world.

Finally back home, Buck lounged in a wicker chaise on his veranda, a cordless phone to his ear. "That incompetent asshole," he muttered.

Hank Jackson rationalized on the other end of the line. "Yeah, that blundering idiot crippled us. His deposition was a joke. We *had* to offer them a deal—$200,000, to keep you from getting sued and your butt out of jail."

"How'd you pay the money?"

"Well, we couldn't get hold of you," Jackson hedged.

"Spit it out. Who authorized the funds?"

"Guess."

"Laffey, that son-of-a-bitch. He'll pay it back, one way or another." Buck's eyes were on fire. "You didn't exactly do a sterling job yourself, Hank. I really don't think you earned your fee."

"Well—" Jackson began in protest.

Without a word, Buck clicked the phone off, staring at it blindly. He couldn't wait to lay into his worthless half-brother. "Speak of the devil," he mumbled, as DuRoy's Corvette rolled into the drive. "The asshole himself."

DuRoy burst out of the sportscar and ran toward the house, his pudgy legs flying. When he spotted Buck, he braked, almost toppling forward.

Buck called him over and acted downright cordial, considering the circumstances. "You're a real screw-up."

Laffey lowered his head, appearing properly penitent.

A little verbal abuse went a long way with Buck, who seemed to be suddenly distracted from his anger. "Don't pout," he said, as if speaking to a child. "So you botched up your deposition. Probably ruined our chances, resulted in me—and maybe you—losing a hell of a lot of money." Buck arched one curly eyebrow. "But, hey, I'm used to your screwing up."

"What about the kidnapped boy?" DuRoy asked hesitantly. "Wha'cha going to do about him?"

Buck didn't like being questioned. He slung the telephone across the porch, crashing it against the exterior brick wall of the house. DuRoy instinctively ducked in defense, as telephone parts flew helter-skelter.

"Hell, I know how to take care of things," Buck said, slurping his beer hungrily. "So we fell a little short. So what? Next time Mel Rath won't see me coming."

# The Tap

## Chapter 25

Sweating, despite air conditioning and the ceiling fan whirling at top speed, Diane pulled resisting thigh-highs over her damp legs. One hose ripped in the struggle, but she was in no mood to begin again, even if she could find a match, which was as likely as a Florida cold spell in summer. She unwound a broomstick skirt, which she kept twisted in a drawer to hold its wrinkled pleats, hoping it would be long enough to cover the run. Mel was away on business, and she'd forgotten to put on the coffee—normally a part of his morning ritual. She would have no caffeine jumpstart, and, without caffeine, she was a zombie.

At the office the day's hapless theme continued, with one needless interruption after another. Diane finally surrendered to the inevitable. I will accomplish nothing of importance today, she thought, as she shuffled through the jumbled stacks of paperwork on her desk, sorting the priority files and shoveling everything else on the floor.

Just before noon, Beth rushed into the office, catching her heel on the carpet as she darted toward Diane's desk. "There's a couple here, inquiring about the beachfront homes."

"Who are they?" Diane asked, as she lowered her reading glasses to the tip of her nose and peered over.

"Mr. and Mrs. Snyder, kinda young, maybe late thirties, early forties. Nice looking. Say they need a house directly on the beach."

"Okay. Give me a couple of minutes and bring them back."

Beth tugged nervously at the lacy cuff of her blouse as she ushered the clients in, stumbled through a quick introduction, and hurried off. Diane rose to shake hands.

Mr. Snyder, small framed and skinny, had a ruddy complexion and a well-trimmed reddish beard with highlights of gray stroked on the undersides, as if he'd had wet paint on his palms and absentmindedly rested his chin there. His dark eyes were riveting, deep, steady.

His wife was a pert blonde, apparently a few years younger. Controlling the conversation flow with her words and flighty gestures, Mrs. Snyder flopped her hands erratically in the air, as she rattled on about "four bedrooms, must be right on the water . . ."

Looking distracted, Mr. Snyder handed Diane a neatly typed note in clear view of his wife, ignoring her prattle.

*Please do not react to this message.*

*We are federal agents, assisting in the case of your missing son. Detective Steve Williams has sent us to you. He needs your help, but suspects that your office may be bugged and your phones tapped. As a precaution, he has asked us to speak with you elsewhere.*

*Destroy this paper immediately.*

Diane's hands trembled as she read, but she said nothing. Her heart began to beat out of control. She felt its rhythm, pulsating like the amorphous heart she'd seen in a documentary film, raw and red, loud and steady, but hers was beating faster. She plastered her palm to her chest.

"I like an open kitchen," Mrs. Snyder continued breathlessly, pulling her hair back to twist into a tight knot. "We must have a water view from the dining room, and we need a den that's private, set apart."

Mr. Snyder asked, "Can we see the home now, Mrs. Rath? Do you understand what we need?"

Without hesitation, Diane concurred, nodding as she ripped the notepaper into tiny shreds. "Of course. Let's get going."

Diane took them to the beach, where the wind tossed their words away. "What have you learned about my son's case?" she asked, knotting her fists under crossed arms.

Mrs. Snyder's demeanor transformed from babbling house-hunter to staid professional. "Perhaps it's best that you don't know everything." She hesitated for a moment, then thought better and began to rattle details, rapid-fire. "Detective Williams has tapped an obstetrician in Atlanta to assist in the case, and he wants you to be a go-between—his connection to Bradford Hospital. He suspects a snitch in the police grapevine and is afraid that the obstetrics ward is being watched. He needs a direct link, someone he can trust. Your name came up."

"Thanks for the compliment, but I don't see—"

Mr. Snyder had no patience for her train of thought. "Dr. Bozeman gave Williams the lead. Got him in touch with FBI agents at Bradford Hospital, where both she and the obstetrician, Dr. Martinez, are on staff."

"Thus, the connection," Mrs. Snyder said, picking up the train of logic. "You're in constant touch with both Williams and Dr. Bozeman, who has agreed to be an emissary, as long as you are comfortable with the plan. She made that very clear. She insisted that there be no pressure on you or your family and that your foster son, John, be bypassed completely."

"But why all the secrecy? And why does Steve suspect that our office is bugged?" The wind blew curls into her face, and Diane made a cap of her hands, clutching her head tightly.

"You'll need some background here," Mr. Snyder said, planting his thumb on his chin and strumming his beard, as he spoke. "I believe you are aware that John's kidnapper, Adam McGuire, confessed. But what you don't know is where that confession led. Detective Williams has uncovered a baby-smuggling operation, a large cartel that reaches to South America. Criminals there prey on desperately poor families, offering to buy their babies, and then they import these helpless infants to the States, where they bring astronomical prices on the adoption black market. Babies are being stolen for adoption, too, here at home—even at the

Bradford Hospital obstetrics ward, right under the noses of the mothers who deliver."

Diane nodded her head. "Yes, I overheard Dr. Bozeman and Steve discuss an FBI investigation."

Mr. Snyder ignored the interruption. "Williams infiltrated the ward with a police plant, who posed as one of the cleaning staff. Then, after surveillance, he selected Martinez as a colleague sympathetic to the cause, and he persuaded a nurse who worked for the baby-smuggling operation to serve as a witness. Nobody sets a trap like Williams."

He paused, still stroking his beard with his fingertips. "Perhaps we should sit down, Diane. You look uneasy."

"I'm shaking," she said, holding her trembling hand out, as proof. "We can sit on the crossover steps. Come on."

Mrs. Snyder spoke, as they sat at the end of the dune crossover, three across, staring out at the choppy Gulf waters. "Williams has worked hard to put the sting in place. He won't release any reports on the operation, for fear of leaks within the network. Only a vital few know his plan. He says the element of surprise is critical."

"Now," Mr. Snyder said, "for your part. Williams needs you to be a go-between. He'll send you coded data on times and places he wants to meet with Martinez, and you'll relay the information to Dr. Bozeman. There will be no danger to you or to your family. But you'll have to be careful. Williams suspects that your home is wired, too."

"But how?"

"An easy matter. How often is no one at home?"

"Well, I guess pretty often. We're always away on weekdays."

"Piece of cake. Entering your home to set up surveillance is like clockwork for these guys."

"Why would they want to listen to us, anyway?"

"Because of your foster son, John, who identified McGuire in the first place. The cartel could be worried that he has lots of inside knowledge, from the years he spent as McGuire's captive, and, worse, that he may pass it along."

"But John doesn't know anything," Diane said defensively.

"Perhaps not, but they can't take chances. They may

have even tapped Dr. Bozeman's line. As John's psychiatrist, she could be privy to how much he knows, and how much he's told the police. The cartel may be listening. That's why Steve is using coded data."

Stunned, Diane leaned against the dune railing, steadying her body, but not her fears. "Does Steve believe that the disappearance of our son is connected in any way?"

Mrs. Snyder dropped her professional air and spoke softly, with gentle and consoling words. "Williams told us about your son. I'm sorry. We won't know for a while, but there's always hope."

Although she wanted desperately to talk to Mel, Diane didn't need to think about their proposition. If there were a chance to find Chris, or to dig up new information, she had no choice, but she felt helpless, incompetent. "Count me in. I'll do my best."

"You'll do fine," Mr. Snyder assured her. "Detective Williams has complete confidence in you, and he does his homework. Steve's not known for loose ends. You'll know exactly what to do and when to do it. We'll send you a message by express mail, disguised as a follow-up to our real estate inquiry. Just remember, the code is in this order— place, day, hour. The first number will stand for the day of the rendezvous; the second number will tell the hour to meet. Then, you deliver the same code to Dr. Bozeman."

Diane nodded. "Place, day, then hour."

They walked back down the crossover and to the shell driveway, where the palm fronds were whipping in the wind. The force blew trails of railroad vines flat to the ground. Their purple bugle blossoms swayed, as if playing a tune.

"We'll leave you now," Mrs. Snyder said, extending her hand. "Please stay calm and try not to worry. You will hear from us."

As she watched their car pull away, Diane crossed her arms and massaged her shoulders, feeling so alone. Mel wouldn't be home until late the next evening, and Matt and John had already left for a weekend soccer camp. She waved helplessly to the Snyders and carried her heavy secret with her, up the stone steps into an empty house, the wind howling as she closed the doors behind her.

⌒

The next morning a strand of Diane's hair tickled her cheek, and she awoke with a start. Her hands reached for the ceiling in a yawn. Mel always held her from the back, his arm wrapped around her breasts as they slept. She rolled over to confirm the untouched pillow beside her, the sharp realization that she was alone. With Mel away, her cocoon wrested from her, she had struggled through the night, sleeping fitfully.

Her mind faded through the mist of memory to yesterday, to the Snyders and her new mission. She hadn't been able to speak freely to Mel over the phone, and she craved his opinion. Energized by the thought that he'd be home tonight, she pounced out of bed. Her calves were stiff, as they often were from walking the beach, and she reached down, the sharp jolt of a Charley horse threatening. She sat back on the bed and worked the throbbing tendon. She remembered the same wrenching pain from pregnancy.

Her small role, outlined by the Snyders—to pass dates and places along to Dr. Bozeman—did not frighten her, but was stressful in nature. Her home was no longer a refuge. Her eyes darted to the far corners of the ceiling, searching for sniper microphones. The Snyders hadn't mentioned cameras, but who knew? She grabbed her robe from the foot of the bed and tugged it tightly over her breasts.

It was Saturday, a rare free day to spend as she pleased. Diane had nowhere to go, but found no comfort in her home. She stared into the vanity dressing mirror, brushing her teeth furiously, then pulled her front curls into a knot on top of her head, which she clasped with a barrette, leaving the back tresses to fall loose. A few bouncy ringlets rebelled to dangle on her forehead. In a quick finish, she touched her lips with lipstick and stroked her cheeks lightly with blush. She clawed through the clothes in her chest of drawers and chose a pair of gym shorts and a loose sweatshirt, which she donned in the darkness of the walk-in closet.

But why let these bastards ruin her day? Mel would be

home tonight, and, in the meantime, she would spend her free time as she damn well pleased. They could listen, or gawk, all they wanted.

Yawning, she shuffled lazily down the stairs to the kitchen. She filled the teakettle with water, put it on the stove to boil, and tore the wrapping off an Earl Grey teabag, draping its string over the rim of her favorite eggshell china cup. Tea always tasted better in a thin-lipped cup, never so fine from a thick mug. When the kettle whistled, she jumped, startled, as if reminded that there was reason for alarm. Quickly, she retrieved the kettle, stopping its shrill alert, and dunked the teabag thirty times, which was *de rigueur*. Any less would make the tea too weak; any more, too strong. Diane never thought of herself as a ritualist—a perfectionist, perhaps, as Matt accused. She opened a jar of honey, its aroma as sweet as summer clover, and stirred in a heaping tablespoon.

Diane sipped the tea, then sat down at her polished white baby grand, running her agile fingers lightly up and down the keyboard. Softly, as if the keys would break, she played "Clair de Lune," and the beautiful, haunting melody echoed through the still, empty house. She'd give them a little culture, she thought, if they were listening.

She felt privileged to share classical notes with such giants as Bach, Chopin, and Mozart, to tap into a rapturous reservoir, to play the music of genius. She found the same enchantment in art and literature, to explore the passionate weaves of a Van Gogh painting or to read the timeless words of Shakespeare. Diane ached to share these great classics with her boys, to impart the joy they gave her. She began her grand finale—"Scarf Dance," a favorite from childhood— pounding the keys dramatically, but stopped abruptly with a snap of memory—a young boy sitting at the piano beside her, mesmerized by her hands as she played. She stared down at her fingers, mute on the keyboard. Perhaps someday, she prayed, she would play for Chris again.

Diane took a second cup of tea onto the lanai and settled into a chaise lounge, watching the pelicans slide across the water as they skimmed inches from the surface. If she could imitate one act in nature, she thought, it would be that. Small groups of pelicans surveyed the water from high above, diving for fish with heavy plops into the water. At dusk they would gather in troops and fly over the cottage—to nest, she supposed—always heading north, following the leader in patterned form, flapping on cue, catching the same draft paths night after night, as predictable as the sunset. A mobile of pipes hung from the porch ceiling, and the wind played their chimes like a xylophone, almost lulling her to sleep.

The doorbell rang, joining the chimes in a duet. Diane was in a hazy fog and, at first, didn't distinguish the two and, when she did, her instinct was to ignore the bell. She didn't want to destroy the simple pleasure of her time alone, but the spell was already broken. She frowned as she rose to answer the bell.

She opened the door to beautiful green eyes—Mel's eyes, locking passionately into hers. "You're early," she whispered.

He didn't say hello, but instead, "You're beautiful," the same words he'd uttered huskily at her door on their first date, many years before.

Mel seldom left her alone anymore, and she felt the loss hardest when he returned, like a baby who doesn't realize how much he has missed his parents until they reappear. This time, in his absence, her world had shattered, and she was sick with need. She reached for him, her lifeline, and they embraced. "Darling," she whispered, "darling."

# Part Four

# Plans for Delivery

## Chapter 26

Detective Williams drummed his fingernails on the desk, anxious to hear Dr. Martinez's report. He blew the steam off his coffee, then sipped gingerly, so as not to burn his lips. "So you proposed a major haul to Donny?"

Martinez nodded, raising a thumb from his fist, as in victory. "And I think I got his attention. I predicted that I could deliver close to twenty infants."

"Do you think he took the bait?"

"I don't know. He received the news rather offhandedly—playing it cool, I guess. Said he'd have to get back to me. I got mad because he was being so nonchalant." Martinez paused, his eyes alive with the memory. "I acted furious and yelled at him, told him that I had a lot at stake and was risking everything."

The phone rang and Williams picked it up, lodging it under his chin. "Detective Williams. Oh, hi, honey." He smiled at Martinez and covered the phone with his hand, mouthing "sorry" as he rolled his eyes. "What does your mom think?" Uh-oh, he thought, one of those impossibly complicated teenage daughter catastrophes. He knew he couldn't interrupt. Finally, he said, "If your mom says okay, I'll go along with it. Oh, that's all right, honey. I'll see you tonight. No, no, I won't miss it. I'll be there. Bye."

Williams shrugged his shoulders at Martinez. "Sorry to interrupt, but some things just can't wait. Back to business. What did Donny say?"

"I think he enjoyed my dilemma. He just smirked and accused me of wanting too much money. Said that he should look for another baby dealer, one not so greedy."

"So then what happened?"

"I got right in his face and screamed, 'You set the bloody price; not me.' I was ready to punch him, even though we both knew that he could knock me sideways. When he saw my fist in the air, he ducked and made fists himself, like a boxer. Then he threw some pretend punches, making fun of me. Said 'Now, now, doctor,' real sarcastic, then promised to get back to me. He told me to sit tight for a few days."

An express letter, bearing a fictitious return address for the Snyders, arrived at Diane's office. She had put herself on watch at mail time and quickly intercepted the letter from the receptionist, who opened all correspondence not marked *Personal*.

*Thank you, Mrs. Rath, for showing us your properties. We regret that we cannot pursue a purchase at this time. We are going on vacation to Duck Pond Bed & Breakfast, outside Atlanta, on the ninth and won't be back until the twelfth. We'll be in touch.*

*Mr. and Mrs. Snyder*

Later that day, Diane reached Dr. Bozeman from a pay phone on the other side of town. "Doctor, I'd like to set up an appointment for John, on the ninth. We're planning to be in the area, staying at Duck Pond. Would twelve noon be possible?"

"Mrs. Rath, it's good to hear from you," Dr. Bozeman said, effecting a detached, professional tone. "That's only three days away; let me check. Yes, twelve o'clock on the ninth is free. I'll put it down. Can you tell me how our patient is doing?"

Diane answered nervously, "He's just fine. No setbacks."

"Excellent," the doctor affirmed. "How's your weather down there?"

"Oh, the usual, sunny and hot."

"Well, you'd better bring a jacket when you come up.

It's getting downright chilly here."

"Will do."

"See you soon, then. Good day."

Diane pushed the accordion door aside, then hesitated, lowering her head toward the ground. "Please, God, let this lead to Chris." She left the shadow of the phone booth and blinked at the bright sunlight, which blazed a golden trail on the sidewalk, as if bidding her on.

Detective Williams sat on a deserted park bench in a sleepy suburb of Atlanta. The Georgia weather was brisk. A barren oak blocked the stiff breeze blowing across the pond, but the cold permeated the detective's clothes, chilling his limbs. He'd had a small breakfast, and his stomach growled, just as he spotted Dr. Martinez approaching. Williams, by habit, checked his watch. It was precisely noon.

Martinez sat down on the far end of the bench and engrossed himself in a newspaper, spreading his arms wide. He spoke to the newspaper. "I think we've got'em."

Williams glanced over at the doctor's dark olive hands, holding the newspaper steady. He was struck, once again, by the Colombian's barely perceptible accent.

Martinez continued briskly. "They took the bait. They want to set up the delivery."

"When and where?" Williams asked, hardly moving his lips. His eyes followed a wadded candy wrapper, lifted by a capricious breeze and skipping in the dust. He stood, as if to leave, but paused to zip up his jacket, waiting for an answer.

"We'll meet at an undisclosed Atlanta warehouse. They won't tell me more than that, or even when. They said for me to concentrate on the cargo." Martinez hacked a cough, then cleared his throat. "Should be soon, though. They think I've got the babies lined up, so they won't waste time. Have that cleaning guy check *Female Anatomy & Physiology*. I'll leave you word." He paused. "By the way, detective, he'll probably get a kick out of the pictures."

Williams swallowed a smile and walked away without

responding or looking back. God, I'm hungry, he thought—hungry for lunch, and hungry to get these bastards. His step took on a bounce, and he grinned as he crunched through a pile of crisp leaves. Probably won't take long for either.

# The Right to Remain Silent

## Chapter 27

Detective Williams' brow furrowed as he glanced at his watch. "Just like that bastard Donny to be late," he muttered to his partner, who sat in the driver's seat of an unmarked van.

Williams' partner, Phil, was a tall, burly young fellow, his head topped with wild black hair. He was a follower, not a leader, and he never disagreed with his lead man. "Yeah, just like that bastard."

A swat team, dressed in black to move surreptitiously through the night, stirred restlessly in the back of the van, which was partitioned from the front seat. Williams could hear muffled laughter over the intercom, as they tossed disparaging jibes at each other, for they were a sharp-witted crew. Their training honed them to be vigilant—quick, as well as deadly—and he had seen them drop their derision, on cue, to step into action, turning vicious as a mother rattlesnake protecting her young.

Donny had instructed Martinez to meet him outside an Atlanta produce warehouse, which buzzed in the mornings with deliveries to the Farmer's Market close by, but was deserted at night. The van was parked a block and a half from the cavernous warehouse. In the dim light, Williams could make out the high, massive doors designed to swallow tall, hefty trucks spilling over with green tomatoes, bins of potatoes, or watermelons piled into a giant haystack. Dr. Martinez manned a six-wheeler parked on the curb outside.

Phil leaned against the headrest, tipping the brim of his cap forward. "Yeah, Steve, if it was a normal drop-off, like a bag of money in a trashcan, you wouldn't care. But these are supposed to be kids—babies. You can just picture them in the back of that truck, lying in boxes, or baskets or something, crying their eyes out with hardly anyone, just a nurse or two, to comfort them. Poor babies, stolen from their folks. The guy's scum."

"I'm counting on Donny to rat on the big boys," Williams said, "and if he doesn't show, we've lost. Maybe I should have just arrested his ass, whether the cartel moved or not." He was beginning to sound nervous.

"Don't worry, boss. He'll be here—and he'll turn yellowbelly. He'll squeal to protect his own ass."

A black Ford Bronco drove by slowly, hesitating as it passed the six-wheeler, but didn't stop. From a distant corner a lonely lamppost cast a lean shadow in the faded yellow light. A second Bronco crept up and pulled to a halt behind the six-wheeler, but failed to yield its occupants.

"Shit, they've got two vehicles," Williams said. "Wonder how many guys?" The Bronco's doors flew open, as if to satisfy his curiosity, and four bodies emerged. Three figures hulked over the fourth. "Looks like one short guy, probably Donny, and three goons."

Williams spoke into the intercom, "There're four of them, three huge. Even the little one's tough. Get ready; they're approaching Martinez." Phil turned the ignition and, without headlights, pulled into the dark street. The engine purred as the van prowled toward its target.

"Easy now, easy," Williams directed, still a block away. "When they move to open the back of the six-wheeler, we've got to be there. If they see it's empty, Martinez is a goner."

The short figure moved to the driver's side of the six-wheeler and motioned for Martinez to let down his window. The doctor obliged, gesturing furiously in protest to the delay. Martinez plays that Hispanic temperament to good advantage, Williams thought. Quite a performance, especially for opening night. After a minute, the short man pointed to the rear of the truck, and three looming figures started in that direction.

The van sped up and Williams called to his team, "Hit the three goons at the rear of the truck. I'll handle their fearless leader." At that, the van's side door slid back in a flash, and the swat team pounced with guns drawn. Williams grabbed Donny's arms and twisted them behind his back. He could feel the flex of hard muscles, rippling in protest as Phil snapped handcuffs around his wrists.

The contest was quick and efficient. The swat team easily cuffed the other three hoods, wrestling them to the far side of the six-wheeler, and briskly, one on one, read them their rights. A fleeting disturbance to the silence of the night.

Williams stepped to the driver's seat of the truck, to have a word with Martinez. "We're holding these creeps in the shadows for a minute. Are you all right?"

Gabriel Martinez gave Williams an anxious look. "I'm okay now." His breath escaped loudly through his nose, as he exhaled in relief. "I was getting worried when they didn't show up."

"The other Bronco will probably get suspicious and want to investigate, if we don't move out soon," Williams said. "You stand behind the truck, with the swat team and their new friends. I'll take your place and wait on the street side. With my back turned, I won't be too bad a stand-in for you."

Williams manned his post for ten minutes, with no sign of the second vehicle, then pulled a walkie-talkie from his back pocket and whispered into it. "If they get wind of the arrests, they'll throw Donny to the wolves and high tail it home." He perked up at the sight of a sport utility vehicle approaching. "Wait, looks like our Bronco's back." He kept his back turned, but glanced over his shoulder. "Yep, it's them. Get ready, boys."

Williams stepped to the front of the truck, further into the shadows, as the Bronco stopped beside the cab. "What's the hold-up?" a Southern accent asked from the driver's open window.

Williams cocked his hand like a gun and pointed to the back of the six-wheeler. "They're behind the truck," he said gruffly, muffling his voice with a cough.

The front doors of the Bronco opened in synchrony, and two men emerged, one stretching his arms lazily in the dusk. Oblivious, they chatted softly as they ambled to the back of the truck.

"Everything okay, Donny?"

The swat team replied with lightning speed, and, within seconds, a gun was pressed against the skull of each man.

"You have the right to remain silent . . ."

Williams needed information, and quick. The incompetent goons had delayed the delivery schedule by forty-two minutes. Donny, his hands cuffed behind him, sat upright in the back of the van, nervously surveying his interrogators.

Williams swigged a soft drink, as he nonchalantly served up Donny's options. "Well, it's you or them. 'Course, personally," he commiserated, "I wouldn't like your choices. You can hold your tongue and rot in jail. You can tell us what you know and basically save your butt, so your ass will spend less time in jail. Or we can just let you go and give your bosses the pleasure of taking care of you themselves." Williams curled his fingernails inward and stared intently at them, as if he were contemplating a manicure.

"I don't want t-t-to say anything, till I see my lawyer," Donny stuttered, his eyes darting back and forth, first at Williams, then down to his lap.

Williams' laughter erupted from deep in his throat, and he rared back in his chair, as if he had lots of time to relish this joke. "We've got a long night ahead of us, creep." He leaned over in his chair and, dropping his smile, grabbed Donny by the front of his collar. "By the time you see your lawyer, you won't be in any shape to talk. Better tell us where you were delivering that cargo."

Williams sneered at the word *cargo*. The bastards treated innocent babies with all the compassion they would heap on a cache of cocaine.

"Yeah, better tell us where you were heading—now—or there's no deal." He released Donny's collar with a shove and stared back at his nails. "Otherwise, you're dead meat, and your bosses are home free. Hope they paid you enough to be the fall guy." He shrugged his shoulders. "'Course, you'll never get out of jail to spend the money, anyway."

"And if I do tell you?" Donny rolled distrusting eyes to the far corner of the van's ceiling.

"Listen, asshole, you'll at least have a chance of seeing blue sky again."

Donny resembled a sweaty boxer hunched in his corner, body spent and eyes tunneled to the punch he knew was coming, the knockout that would validate his lurking defeat. He spouted the words under his breath. "There's an old run-down factory, abandoned now, southeast of here just outside Athens. It's all set up for the kids, with nurses, cribs, blankets, even a doctor."

Williams lost no time. "So they're waiting now for you and the delivery?"

"Maybe they are; maybe they're not."

Williams slapped his open hand across Donny's cheek, which burned the color of raspberry.

"Okay, lay off. They're expecting us." It was Donny's last attempt to control a losing battle.

"We'll continue this tea party on the road," Williams said, turning to the intercom. "Take off, Phil," he directed his partner, then glared at Donny, whose eyes flashed a growing respect. "Where do we go from here, punk?"

"Take a right at the gas station onto the highway."

Williams relayed the route to Phil, in bits and pieces, as Donny coughed them up. "Oh, and Phil, call in the descriptions and license plate numbers on those Broncos."

Williams looked out the back window for the six-wheeler. "Is Martinez following okay?"

"Yeah. He's not too bad a truck driver, for being a doctor, and all."

No one spoke for a while. Even the swat team seemed to be reserving energy. "Boss," Phil called over the intercom, breaking the silence, "no record on the Broncos."

Williams muttered, "Big surprise, huh?" He settled back in his seat and checked his watch. The trip should take a little over an hour, he thought and closed his eyes, hell-bent to ignore his lowlife guest, at least for a while.

When they reached the outskirts of Athens, Williams signaled his partner. "Phil, pull up here on the shoulder. I better rearrange our seating." The van screeched to a halt onto rough terrain, and the handcuffed men, off balance with no way to stop their fall, tumbled at random in the back of the van. "Jesus, Phil, you trying to rough these guys up? Maybe do my job for me?"

Phil hopped out and rushed back to fling the van door open. Williams grabbed Donny by the back of the collar and pushed him roughly toward Phil, who forced him into the driver's seat, then uncuffed him. Phil got in the back of the van, as Williams moved to the passenger seat and drew his revolver to cover Donny. "Take off," he barked. As Donny drove to the delivery point, Williams pummeled him with questions.

"Are they armed at the factory?"

"Usually a couple of bodyguards are outside. They pack guns, but who knows if they know what to do with them?"

"You've never seen them use their guns?"

"Nope."

"What about inside?"

"No arms in there."

"How many people?"

"Not many. Just nurses, like in a hospital."

"When we get there, I want you to take me to the person in charge." Williams loosened his grip on the gun. "Who is that, anyway?"

"None of my bosses are there. I guess the doctor would call the shots."

"Doctor, huh? Some healer." Then Williams spoke into the intercom. "Get that, guys? Two armed men outside."

"Got it, boss."

Donny drove on in silence. Maybe he's contemplating all those lonely years ahead, Williams thought. If it's up to me, he'll rot in jail.

The factory was a mammoth structure, yellow brick with an ochre patina, its sprawling walls punctuated by huge awning windows, too filthy to see through, most cracked or broken out with jagged edges. Two chimneys, blackened with ancient soot, rose stark against the moonlit sky.

A six-foot-high wire fence surrounded the grounds, with two tall gates denying entry. At first glance the gates looked obsolete. The wire was rusty and twisted, but reinforced with steel bars. Donny gained easy admittance. "It's me," he confirmed, raising his left shoulder out the window and circling his arm to the six-wheeler behind him. Williams pointed his revolver at Donny's pelvis.

Two sizable guys stepped up to open the gates, straining to lift the bottom rods above the overgrown turf. Probably the same two bodyguards McGuire had mentioned, Williams thought. As the van entered, he spoke loudly for the benefit of the intercom. "Guys, we're entering the compound. I've got sight of the two thugs, at the gate. They're armed, judging from the bulges under their coat jackets."

Donny stopped the van at the old factory and got out, heading for a side door. Williams pocketed his gun and followed close behind. The door opened to another world. In contrast to the dilapidated grounds, the interior was impeccably neat, with all the trappings of a clinic—small cots, tightly dressed with clean stiff linens, cribs, thermometers and blood pressure cuffs, stethoscopes, a pharmaceutical stand of jars and vials, neatly labeled, cotton balls and swabs, diapers, blankets, cans of formula and baby bottles, and a host of white-uniformed nurses scurrying around. One looked up from her work, readying the medicines, and saw Donny enter. "How many this time?" she called.

Donny hesitated, looking puzzled for a moment. "Oh, nineteen, I think." With a sharp nudge from Williams, he asked, "Is Doc Brown here? We may have a sick baby."

The doctor of the ad hoc ward, apparently within earshot, hurried in from the next room. "Here, Donny."

"Follow us, doc," Williams interrupted. "We need your medical opinion."

The doctor never got the opportunity to venture a diagnosis. The swat team intercepted him as he rounded the threshold. One covered his mouth and another bent his elbow high behind his back. They dumped the doctor into the back of the six-wheeler, where the other captives greeted their distinguished colleague with cynical frowns.

Williams ordered Phil to call for back-up, then grabbed his camera and went inside to photograph the premises. He panned around the clinic, registering the myriad medical equipment and baby paraphernalia, collecting photographic evidence to support the case. Then Williams turned his inevitable charm on the nurses, who huddled in fear.

"Hey, ladies, back against the wall. The good news—you're off duty." Williams brandished his camera with a flourish. "The bad news—it's time for your mug shots."

# The Leader of the Pack

## Chapter 28

Morning broke through a long night, and, back at the Athens police station, Williams was getting disgusted with the punk. He had expected Donny to squeal like a pig to earn a shorter sentence in the state penitentiary, but he refused to break. Donny gave only sketchy descriptions of his contacts and claimed he knew them only by nickname. He offered some phone numbers, which turned out to be no longer in service. He's not leveling with us, Williams thought, or maybe he's too low on the totem pole. Just the punk I pegged him for.

"Sorry, Donny, but what you know doesn't add up to peanuts," Williams said, prodding. "If you can't cough up the names of the cartel bosses, then you're worthless to us. No deal." Williams sneered, rubbing the scruffy mat of hair on the back of his sturdy neck. "With your pretty body, you should be popular in jail. And you can rot there, for all I care."

Williams tapped the table with his pencil, like a snare drum. "Guess your bosses have hung you out to dry." He leaned back in his chair and crossed his fingers, turning his thumbs in orbit. "There might be a chance for you yet, though. You could lead us to them."

"How could I do that?" Donny asked, slumping his stocky shoulders. "You say that my contact numbers are dead."

"But the bosses can find you, that's for sure—if we let you out as bait."

"But if they find me, they'll kill me."

Williams shrugged, indifferent to the concept, but a thin smile softened his face. "Oh, we'll protect you. We'll be watching when you meet up with them, to keep you covered." His voice turned suddenly sympathetic, as reassuring as that of a father coaxing his child to dive into the unknown water. "You'll be safe as a baby. What do you say?"

"What kind of a deal will I get?" Donny rubbed his eyes roughly, then stared solemnly at Williams. The whites of his eyes were red as blistered skin. "I better talk to my lawyer."

"You do that, kid. You do that."

⌐

Next Williams went to work on the doctor.

At his arrest, Doc Brown had remained unruffled, polite and professional, close mouthed, with the presence of mind to insist that his attorney meet them at the Athens police station.

Williams felt out of place as soon as he entered the interrogation room. At the room's lone table, Doc Brown was chatting idly with his attorney, who wore a pressed suit and silk tie. A real fashion plate, Williams thought. The attorney sat tall with a confident air, a commanding presence, as if he were presiding over the proceeding.

"Detective Williams, I'd like you to meet Mark Lawton, my nephew."

"Convenient to have an attorney in the family," Williams muttered. "Probably comes in handy, in your line of business." He sat down with a glum expression. They're a real clan, these yokels, he thought. They make me feel like a stranger at my own party.

"So, Mr. Lawton, let's hear how your client came to work for a bunch of hoods. Not his usual clientele, I wouldn't think." He waited for some smart-alecky retort from the kid, who instead sat silently, staring straight ahead, his eyes blank. Williams' thumbs began to orbit.

After an uncomfortable moment or two, Mark Lawton began. He contained information to the barest essentials. "The good doctor was hired by an adoption agency to oversee an important social need—to evaluate the health of young orphans and to treat them, if required. My uncle was unaware of any illegal proceedings."

Williams broke in, his voice oozing sarcasm, "And he found nothing strange about a broken-down factory serving as a hospital?"

With a respectful gesture in his client's direction, the attorney proclaimed solemnly, "Who was *he* to question? He was simply doing his job. The doctor has led a life of service to his profession and the community."

Ignoring the speech, Williams spoke tersely. "What adoption agency?"

Doc Brown looked to his nephew, who nodded approval, then answered. "The Sunrise Adoption Agency."

"The same Atlanta agency that Donny worked for, I presume?"

"Uh-huh," the doctor said, dipping his head into his chest.

Williams caught the body language. Is the old guy beginning to feel contrite? "And I'm sure you asked for the proper credentials, didn't you, doctor? An old hand like you?"

Doc Brown huffed his body, shoulders raised and head cocked in contempt. "I do not question my clients, sir, except as to their medical needs."

So much for remorse, Williams thought, then sneered irreverently. "If you're so innocent, you won't mind sharing information with me. You can tell me all about the Sunrise Adoption Agency—what you know about their employees and how you got paid. You may have some valuable—"

Mark Lawton broke in. "Of course, the doctor will answer your questions. He has nothing to hide." Something in this young man's smile told Williams that he was accustomed to defending his uncle, that Doc Brown's past was not all pearly white.

Williams grilled the doctor for an hour, barking at him, question after question. Doc Brown's face revealed not a trace of discomfort. If anything, he looked bored.

Finally, disgusted with the guarded answers, Williams brought the interrogation to a close. Not a trace to connect the doctor to the leaders of the cartel, Williams thought, and perhaps he really didn't have any inside information, except on the Sunrise Adoption Agency, which he'd already divulged. Probably couldn't even stick him with obstruction of justice. "Guess I'm forced to release you, doc, but I'm sure hoping to see you again." Williams laughed. "In fact, I have the feeling we'll be real chummy before all this is over."

Doc Brown started to respond, but his nephew held up a hand of caution, like a traffic cop. They marched out quickly, without a good-bye from Williams, who bent over the table scribbling notes.

The good doctor won't be lonely, Williams thought, as he jotted down names in his notepad, drafting his team. I'll send an undercover cop to keep him company.

Undaunted, Williams handpicked his undercover team and met with them the next week in his ad hoc office at the Athens police station. Sitting sidesaddle against the front of his desk, Williams briefed the officers, his brown eyes intense.

"I've arranged for Donny's release," he said, tracing his bushy gray eyebrows with a stiff finger, "and I want him tailed twenty-four hours a day. Don't let him out of your sight. Here's his address and a layout of his apartment in Atlanta. You're to eat, breathe, and sleep with the guy."

Williams grinned. "Not a pretty task, I know. But he's all we've got. And the cartel knows we have him. They'll be anxious to shut him up. If we can keep this creep alive, it just might work."

He stood, and the officers stirred in their seats, anticipating their dismissal. But instead, he walked behind the desk and began to shuffle some loose papers. The officers, as one, settled back down and watched attentively, rapt as new cadets in training, while Williams leaned over the desk to examine each page carefully. After a moment he looked up abruptly, his eyes puzzled, as if he were surprised to see the group still there before him.

"Oh, there's one other thing," he said, still bent over his desk. "I guess we should all have the whole picture." He picked up a sheet by the corner and flapped it in the air.

"You're aware that a local doctor was arrested, along with Donny and the rest of them. Well, I ordered an inquiry into Doc Brown's practice, and we interviewed his staff, patients, and social acquaintances. The early reports are quite complimentary. Apparently, his staff admires him, his patients revere him, and his friends love him. The man's just short of sainthood."

Williams floated the paper back onto the desk. "So, why would he get himself in this mess? It just doesn't figure." He scratched his head with a passion, like a dog with a burr. "So, I'm going to do some legwork myself. Just want you to keep your eyes and ears open." Williams lifted his palms and raised his eyes to the ceiling. "Just in case our saint comes crashing down."

He looked back at the group and pointed a finger, as if warning a recalcitrant child. "And keep in touch. Let me know what you have—regardless of how hot you think it is, or isn't. I've got a personal stake in this one."

Williams sat down and sunk back in his chair. "Okay, boys, I guess that's it."

The officers took their cue and, like bees to their hive, cleared the room in no time. God, Williams thought, if I could only get hold of the energy the young guys have. You can see it in the bounce of their step, the quick work of their tongue. They're so . . . so spunky, it's plain humiliating. Guess I'm getting old. This case is only beginning, and I'm just so tired.

Upper-class society in the town of Athens, Georgia, revolved around a traditional country club linked with a golf course, a few miles out of town. The two-story brick edifice had been up-dated with a crisp white portico and a deck skirting the front elevation, bordered with a low gingerbread fence. Antique rattan chairs with flowery blue-and-white chintz cushions and patio tables set with blue willow china lent the entrance an inviting comfort, without sacrifice of ostentation. Detective Williams had wangled an invitation to the club from the chief-of-police, who, as an elected official, was deemed to have an acceptable position on the social ladder, although on the lower rungs. The chief enhanced his popularity when, as a Southern gentleman, he sometimes ignored the faux pas of a fellow club member.

Unpracticed in his social graces, Williams awkwardly pawed his new silk tie, splashed with purple lightning that resembled shazam bolts on a Captain Marvel costume. He waited for the chief-of-police in the club library, which boasted a decorator's vision of a rich masculine décor, too practiced in its item-by-item detail. A mahogany game table shone with layers of polish, and a hand-carved chair rail matched bookshelves of golden oak. Jungle prints dominated the room, in the drapes and upholstery, and a prize deer trophy hung over a jigsaw puzzle of flagstones on the fireplace surround. Williams shuddered at a coffee table of thick glass, supported by elephant tusks. Hope they're cheap imitations, he thought.

The chief called his greeting out loudly, as he entered the double doorway to the library. "Good evening, Detective Williams." He offered his pudgy hand and shook vigorously. "Glad to have a fellow officer from the good state of North Carolina. Yep, we sure are."

Williams spoke quietly, smiling. "Actually, chief, I hope to keep a low profile. People tend to clam up around my kind."

"Good God," the chief said, his head nodding up and down, jowls jiggling. "Sorry. Just wasn't thinking. But don't you worry." The chief winked, although with his droopy eyelids, the effort hardly showed. "Mum's the word."

After a quick chat, Williams asked to be excused and spent the rest of the evening ingratiating himself to the regulars, maneuvering his conversation around to the doctor at every opportunity. "I don't really know many folks locally, except, of course, Doc Brown."

The responses were predictable.

"Good old Doc Brown."

"Doc saved the life of my aunt, who was on her death bed."

"The man's a saint for sure."

Around nine o'clock the doctor appeared, after late

rounds, and sat at the lounge bar. Williams positioned himself at a far table, inconspicuous in the crowded room of
spectators watching a Monday-night football game.
Drinking levels were at advanced stages by this time, and the
relaxed audience flicked careless repartee, loudly back and
forth. A fraternity of Southern men, Williams thought.
Devotees of one-up-manship. The doctor seldom spoke, but
was the frequent recipient of barbs. Williams wondered why
this upstanding gentleman was a victim of derision, the butt
of so many jokes.

One masterful voice, spiced with Southern intellect,
reigned supreme, its easy flow punctuated by nervous laughter from the group. With skill and sarcasm, the speaker
hurled shafts at his friends, then paused to relish the reaction, the brief shock of the crowd, their uneasy faces.

"Why, Buck," one brave voice said, "you're wicked."

"Yeah," another chimed in, safety in numbers. "You
sure know how to rub salt in a wound."

Buck Stanley was the leader of the pack. He targeted
one fall guy after another, aiming with precision at his most
tender frailty. Buck knew his friends.

He knew about their affairs—"Mitch's come up with a
new hobby—designer whips, I hear."

He knew about their failures—"Guess you were sick of
that job anyway, Jeep; 'sides, your family didn't really need
a swimming pool."

And he knew about their troubles—"Understand Doc
Brown's into healing the Third World."

Yep, Williams thought, this guy knows his friends, all
right. He's made a real study of them. Maybe he'd like to
share what he knows about the good doctor.

After the game, Williams took up conversation with a
drunken Buck Stanley and implied, as he had all evening,
that he was an old friend of Doc Brown's. "Personally don't
know many people here, just Doc Brown. What'd you mean
by him 'healing the Third World'?"

"Just an inside joke. Sometimes the doc spends too
much time in Las Vegas." Buck chuckled. "Has that gam-
bling fever, you know. Makes him a mite too ambitious."

The next day Williams extended his investigation to include Buck Stanley. He asked his partner, Phil, to process the necessary paperwork to get Buck's phone tapped, whether it was justified or not. "No doubt we'll discover more than we want to know about this two-bit town. Personally, I don't care much about the provincial hierarchy, or all its gossip. But, hopefully, from the dredges—after we've filtered out the garbage—we'll get something valuable on Doc Brown."

Bushy patches of Phil's wild hair bounced, as he nodded in agreement. "I'll let you know when we get the go-ahead on the tap."

"Yeah. Then get some men listening."

"I'll line them up, boss. Right away."

Williams ordered some files down from Asheville and settled into the office the chief had assigned him at the Athens police headquarters. Manning phone taps always took a toll—around-the-clock personnel, tedious surveying work, hours of fruitless waiting. His wife and kids would have to understand. Not much longer, this career of being away from home.

The next week Williams spent long hours at his desk, neat from lack of industry unlike the rest of the room, which housed his portable office and was flowing over with cartons of files. There wasn't much to do but wait—a lonely game. Guilt over his family was loading him down, and he ached for a home-cooked meal. He was relieved when his partner rushed in, breaking the boredom.

"We've got something," Phil said, as he plopped down on the only empty chair in the room, all the others occupied by boxes. "At last." He slapped his hands together, accordion style, in satisfaction.

Williams looked up with eager eyes. "What do you have?"

Phil set a tape recorder on the desk, shoving aside a pencil holder and Rolodex. "We've got Stanley talking to Doc Brown, and it's not too friendly." He started the tape turning, then fast-forwarded to the pertinent passage.

"Doc, I assumed you were on my side." Williams recognized the familiar Southern drawl.

"But Buck, you know I am. I wouldn't do anything to

jeopardize your setup. I kept quiet before, remember? At the factory?"

"Shut up, you idiot. Call me later; you know where."

"Good work," Williams said, making a circle of his thumb and forefinger in the air. "Want to take a ride with me? I've got some business at the Athens airport." Williams stood and grabbed his jacket from a hook on the wall, where it hung like a headless scarecrow.

"Do I have a choice?" Phil asked, grinning, as he followed his boss out the door.

The municipal airport was close to town, an older facility that would need transplanting when the city expanded. Williams led his partner through electronic doors, past check-in desks with long lines, heading directly for the air controller's office.

He flashed his identification, which brought immediate attention from a middle-aged woman in a dowdy dress. Williams asked for the records on private flights, "Six months worth, please ma'am."

The woman struggled on bowed legs, her back turned as her short arms stretched to reach a high shelf. Her buttocks locked to one side as she lifted down a heavy ledger. "Not on computer yet," she muttered, disgruntled, as she slammed it down on the counter and walked away.

Williams scanned the ledger for Stanley Distribution feeder flights, connections to Miami, Asheville, Jacksonville, and particularly Atlanta. "Just as I thought. The corporate feeder planes rarely fly." He scratched his head and looked over at his partner. "I know I'm a suspicious devil, but maybe Stanley Distribution has changed its thrust. Maybe automobile and aircraft parts have been passed over for more profitable inventory."

"Like babies?"

Williams nodded. "Atlanta's the flight hub for the corporation. Let's have the Atlanta team run a check on flights to South America, their destinations and frequency. You know, I'm beginning to appreciate our FBI friends. They can turn a hunch into a full-fledged investigation, in no time flat."

Williams closed the thick journal, leveraging the bulky book with the flat of his wrist and forearm. Starting for the door, he spoke over his shoulder. "And we better have Buck Stanley followed. Make a note, would you?"

# The Fishing Party

## Chapter 29

"Five minutes till dinner," Diane called to Mel upstairs and the boys downstairs, chasing up and down the steps like an athlete in training. She never lost sight of her nightly goal—to round up everyone for dinner, simultaneously—although her attempts were usually futile. She even gave fair warning, five-minute notice, but over time the warnings lost their edge, like school fire drills, and grew dull with repetition.

The family largely ignored her, although stomach-driven Matt occasionally appeared promptly. Mel, ingenious at creating last-minute delays, had a sixteen-year perfect record of never showing up for dinner on time. Tonight he had to run outside, for just a minute, to check the sprinklers. John was finishing his computer game, and Matt was talking to his girlfriend on the phone. A sit-down dinner didn't look promising.

Growing up, Diane had never been late for dinner. She and her brothers had clamored to the table, elbowing each other to grab the serving dishes of mashed potatoes, fried okra, luscious tomatoes, peeled and thinly sliced, roast beef spiced with slivers of garlic, homemade biscuits, topped off with fresh blueberry or peach cobbler.

She could picture her father smiling at his ravenous brood, staving off their hunger as he paused to read a blessing from his prayer book, its binding broken from use. He would forestall the dinner longer with "just a quick story" about how his own father had religiously done the same. Night after night of endless blessings until one night he, as a little boy, had met the end of his patience and asked, as he sat down to eat, "Father, must you pray so long tonight?"

It was the cue for his children to chime in unison, "Good question." Diane smiled at the memory. Her dad would laugh at the joke, on both him and his father, son like father, strong in faith and humble, first to laugh at himself. His eyes would twinkle as he tantalized them further. "Did I ever tell you about the boarding house I used to stay in?"

She and her brothers would groan, "Yes, Daddy, about a million times."

Her mother would laugh and say, "Hurry up, dear. These kids are starving."

"Okay," he'd finally say, like a starter lowering the flag for a race to begin, "go ahead and show me your boarding-house reaches," and hands would fly to fill plates.

I guess times have changed, Diane rationalized, knowing that Mel's childhood memories were not so idyllic. Dinner for his family had been stressful, a time for confrontation, she reminded herself again, as she had for sixteen years.

The dinner was stone cold by the time everyone appeared, Matt dragging in last. "Sorry, Mom, but that was one discussion I couldn't break up. My whole social life depended on it."

The guys fell to the task at hand, shoveling in food in silence.

"What happened to your social graces?" Diane asked, sounding haughty—even to herself—as her question fell flat, unanswered. She had prepared a special meal—succulent leg of lamb with mint sauce, each plate garnished with a mint leaf. She'd trailed a knife through the sauce, leaving green swirls dotted with grated lemon rind. "Martha Stewart would be proud of this dinner!"

Despite her goading, the closest approach to polite conversation was "Pass the potatoes, please." Finally, Diane appealed to the interests of all parties by bringing up the fishing trip they had planned for the following day.

"Should be good fishing tomorrow," she opened, drawing her preoccupied family into a semblance of communication.

Matt, with a full mouth, asked, "Where we going?"

John perked up his head with interest.

Mel answered, without elaboration, "Ten mile reef."

Heads bent over plates, silverware working overtime. Perhaps not intellectual, Diane thought, but at least an evolution of the grunts of primitive society. "That's better," she mused, as she took a dainty bite of lamb, smiling.

———

The next morning Mel jumped out of bed, walking with purpose to the deck off the master bedroom. His first order of business on a fishing day was to check the Gulf for weather conditions.

"A little choppy," he reported to Diane, foggy with sleep and turning over to pursue more. "Two- to three-foot waves, it looks like, but should be passable for the ten-mile reef." He sat down on the bed, shaking her protruding hip. "Come on, lazy, get up."

She opened a lethargic eye, dismayed by his good humor at this early hour. "Must I?" she begged, tenting her head with the sheet. Mel playfully grabbed her head in a hammerlock and rasped his knuckles across the top of her head. "Okay, okay," she said, flinging back the sheet to struggle out of bed. "I'm up; I'm up."

"Is there an echo in here?" he asked, cocking his ear as he headed for the door.

Diane tottered on tiptoes into the bathroom. She brushed her teeth with a robot's arm, her hand moving mechanically up and down, eyes still shut. She opened them reluctantly and, with two fingertips, rooted the sleep from their corners. She splashed her face with water—not exactly refreshing, the tepid Florida water with its mineral smell.

Hurry, hurry, she thought. Matt will be champing at the bit, and Mel liked to get out in the Gulf early, when the fish were feeding. She brushed her hair with a vengeance, long, curly strands falling in tufts to the tile floor. She thought of the grueling Florida sun, often with no cloud cover, and rubbed her face with sunscreen. With deft, practiced strokes she added a light mask of makeup and penciled her lips with coral liner. Finally she stumbled into denim shorts, catching one foot in the opening and bouncing on the other, like a pogo stick. She pushed her head through the neck of a snug, worn tee shirt, which she'd probably throw away at the end of the day anyway, since the grouper were always bloody.

Starting down the stairs, Diane remembered the sunscreen and ran back to put it and her fish book into a woven black bag she'd bought at the straw market in Nassau. In the kitchen she made quick work of boiled ham and baby Swiss cheese sandwiches, fast as a short-order cook, and filled the cooler with ice, dumping the ice tray from the refrigerator, blasting the sink with stray cubes. Her hands still flying, she packed the sandwiches, some nectarines, cold from the refrigerator, granola bars, and leftover banana bread. I wish I'd prepared everything last night, she thought. So much to do on a fishing day.

She was just feeling under control when Matt burst into the kitchen. "Hurry up, Mom." She heard an edge of impatience, or was it disgust, in his voice. He grabbed a cereal box and poured corn flakes in a bowl, spilling stray flakes on the counter without bothering to clean them up. "Don't worry about food," he said ironically. "Let's get going."

Matt was hyper on fishing days, and Diane was harried. "Please, Matt, calm down. All this rigmarole isn't healthy for John."

Her words were all the fuel required for a full-fledged explosion. "I'm never even considered around here anymore! It's always 'John, what's good for John?' Jeez, wasn't I here first? Don't I count at all?" She reached to console him, following him to the stair landing, but he broke from her arms and ran out of the house, down the beach, leaving the fishing party in tow.

I knew jealousy had to rear its ugly head someday, Diane thought. But that came out of nowhere.

John climbed up the stairs, his steps heavy. "It's my fault. Matt's right. You're his family, and I shouldn't always get in the way."

Saddened by his words, and Matt's, Diane sat John

down on the landing and put her arm around his shoulder. "I'm sorry you overheard Matt, but don't ever feel that you don't belong in this family. You do. Matt sometimes has his own problems, not connected to you." Words slipped out that she'd been holding back. "You're here now as our foster child, but we want to adopt you. If that's what you want." She spoke through tears, welled up from the morning's stress, falling freely. "How would you like that—to be our son?"

"I'd like that more than anything," he answered quickly. Suddenly embarrassed, his eyes fell to his knees. "I've never had a mom, not one I can remember."

The back screened door screeched open, then dragged shut, followed by the sound of Matt's footsteps bounding up the stairs. He stopped short, almost overrunning Diane and John, huddled on the landing.

"Sit down and join the crowd," Diane said, attempting to be cheerful. "Matt," she implored, "let's don't ruin the day. It's early, and we can get lots of good fishing in." She reached up and planted her hand firmly on his shoulder. "We can get past this. All right, son?"

"Just drop it, Mom." He jerked his shoulder away, irritated on the surface, but she knew that he was anxious to go fishing. "Okay, let's go," he relented.

Mel had prepared the gear and was waiting on the boat, fiddling with the bilge pump at the stern. He called to them as they approached, "About time, guys. I thought my fishing party had fizzled out." He tugged on a rope to the back piling, bringing the boat close to the dock for them to board. Matt pouted instead of following captain's orders, so Diane, the trusty first mate, untied the bow ropes and pushed off, jumping on board as Mel put the motor in reverse.

The choppy waves—bumps on the water, Chris had called them—pounded the boat as they exited the pass. Mel anchored his feet and held his knees steady against the center console. Diane held on tight as he planed for a smoother ride. Matt's mood soon turned playful and he clowned around, imitating a drunken sailor, flopping his arms in the breeze as he rocked from side to side with the boat's motion. John laughed with a spontaneity that Diane would not have believed a few weeks before.

The crisp winds and clean sky of the Gulf outshone the ugly start of the day, and Matt's angry mood was erased in the fresh face of the morning. Dolphins, as if summoned by Neptune, found the boat and mimicked its move, jumping into the waves, hugging the hull. Seagulls soared above, white flecks on a blue cloth patched with clouds. A winged fish flew in spurts alongside, keeping pace with the boat.

"Look, a flying fish!"

John must have thought they were teasing him, and he wasn't going to fall for it, until Matt pointed with a sincere plea, "No, really John, look. It's there, just over the water."

John's face lit with discovery as his eyes followed the fish, skimming the surface, jumping through the air, flying above the water. Matt smiled at John's delight, and the boys sat sidesaddle on the boat gunwale, laughing and pointing, vying for the next sighting, as the fish burst sporadically from the water to race beside the boat.

Diane was happy, although surprised, to see Matt's affability, his kinship with John so quickly restored. He will undoubtedly struggle, she thought, as he faces the daily diet of a new sibling. He had been jealous of Chris, too—aren't all brothers?—but the kidnapping and its attendant guilt prevented him from working through it. Perhaps now, the issue can be resolved. Matt seems genuinely to care for John and even, miraculously, to be happy when John's happy, to experience pleasure in his joy. Over the years, she thought, Matt has built up invisible boundaries, walls that keep him captive, stewing in bitterness and isolation. If only he can climb those walls, just to get past *himself*—to care about someone else. Diane jumped when she realized that Mel was calling her.

"Honey, what compass heading?"

As first mate, she had been designated to be the operator of the handheld GPS navigation system, a dubious assignment that no one else wanted. She entered a waypoint, which pinpointed their destination, and answered after a moment, "Go at 240 degrees."

When they reached the reef, Mel turned on the fishfinder to survey the bottom. The fish alarm failed to beep, so he maneuvered to several other spots with no results. In frustration, he decided to return to the original reading. "We marked this place. Must have had a reason."

"Aw, Dad, shouldn't we try—"

"Don't forget," Diane reminded Matt, "your dad's the captain." There was always a struggle for power on the boat, a microcosm of family dynamics. Matt's impulsiveness confronted Mel's deliberateness—petulance versus patience, son challenging father.

Mel compromised. "Okay, Matt, put a line down before I anchor. We'll see what's here."

Diane cut up a frozen baitfish, and Matt grabbed a slice to impale on his hook. Mel had rigged lines for everyone, with extra leaders for the hooks inevitably lost on the rocky surface of the reef. Diane showed John how to bait his hook and helped him immerse his line, which was weighted with a heavy sinker, feeding it slowly until it lost its tautness and began to ravel, the sign that it had reached bottom. Then, she reeled a couple of times, to hold the bait just above the rocks.

The emerald water was clear, and Diane spotted sea life floating by—first a jellyfish, an ethereal spirit in the water, then hundreds of white darts flickering under the surface, sugar trout and shiners. Their goal, prized for its delicate taste, was much lower, lurking at the very bottom, hiding in the deep holes of the reef.

Diane considered the grouper a dumb fish, fat and round, without fight, but its sheer weight forced them to work up a sweat. A bait no sooner hit bottom than a bulbous grouper, lured from its hideaway in the reef, attacked. They struggled to reel against the weight and laboriously pulled up fish after fish, all undersized. The legal length for grouper was twenty inches—a huge, heavy fish—and their catch might have been cloned, most about half that size. Disappointed, Matt complained as he threw one fish after another back into the water.

"I think I've got something," John reported hesitantly, his rod bending down, the tip almost in the water. Mel called for him to hold his rod tip up, and, as John grabbed for it, misunderstanding, the reel loosened and the line began to discombobulate, tangling itself as it unwound, out of control. Diane went over to help and felt the fish still on the line.

"Now, give constant pressure, just reel him up slowly," Mel said.

John's lean body strained, the rod handle bruising his stomach, as he reeled steadily, quietly determined, his face solemn. His lips curled in delight when the fish broke the surface, for this was a monster, a fat red amorphous glob of fine fish. "Is this one big enough to keep?" he asked innocently, as Matt groaned, acknowledging the catch of the day.

The Gulf calmed and lay a flat carpet for their return to shore. As they pulled into the dock, Mel gave captain's orders to the mates.

"Matt, hold onto the pilings; careful, watch your hand. Now, climb over to the rope."

"John, tie the rope to the bow, under the railing; that's right."

His commands were precise, gently persuasive. Matt was too tired to resist. The captain had whipped his crew into shape.

# Like the Wind

## Chapter 30

Buck Stanley scratched his brow, tilting the brim of his baseball cap. "You sure no one followed you, Donny?"

"Of course I am. The route I took would have shaken a bloodhound."

"Well," Buck said, "I felt we needed to meet again, since we invested bail money in you. Who the hell do you think contacted your attorney to offer bail?" He pointed to Donny's chest. "Zip down that jacket and unbutton your shirt."

"Sure," Donny obliged.

Buck reached toward Donny's broad chest and rummaged around roughly under his shirt. He rolled his eyes and frowned, finding the assignment most distasteful. "Just a precaution. The cops have gone crazy with wires. Can't trust anybody nowadays." He lifted the baseball cap from his head by the brim, like a player saluting the fans, and raked his fingers through his thick, tousled hair. "I've heard some disturbing news."

"What's the problem?" Donny spoke softly, so as not to be overheard. They sat outdoors at the Atlanta Underground, on the wall of a landscaped buffer where the crowd was sparse.

"The word is out, Donny, that you've ratted on us."

"I didn't say anything. I don't know anything, honest—no names, no numbers." For once, he made no effort to show how tough he was. "What's going to happen?"

"You've got two choices. We can call in one of our South American friends, and you'll be alligator bait. Or you can disappear. Personally, I like the first option, but the boys don't want their hands dirtied."

Donny bit his lip, bringing blood. "Where would I go?"

Buck looked hungrily across the square at a sidewalk cafe, where patrons were drinking tall glasses of beer. Why was he sitting here with this punk, taking a risk? If he only had someone he could trust. He would've sent Laffey, but things were getting too hot to trust that screw-up. He was going to have to take things in his own hands. Just for a while.

"I've brought you some money," Buck said, patting his jacket pocket. "Let's call it your pension. I want you to take off for Mexico, and I don't expect to see your ugly face again—ever. Do you understand? You're history, as far as I'm concerned. If you've got any good-byes to say, forget that, too. Leave now, and don't look back."

"But what will happen to me?" Donny stared at his lap.

He looks distraught—no, even worse, desperate— Buck thought. Yep, muscle-bound Donny, our steroid kid, turns out to be a shrimp. "That's up to you. You'll have to make your own way. But don't even think about opening that trap of yours."

"I wouldn't squeal on anybody."

"Not if you want to stay healthy," Buck warned. "You might be interested to hear the history of your old friend, Adam McGuire. You don't want to end up like him."

"I guess I did lose track of him."

"Well, you knew him as a decent enough guy, helping with deliveries back in Georgia." Buck thumped a pack of Marlboro cigarettes, loosening the bunch. He raised the pack to his mouth and put his pursed lips around a protruding cigarette. From his pocket he flashed a gold lighter, triggered it with his thumb to light the cigarette, and took a long drag. He held the smoke in for an inordinate time, then blew it in an exaggerated puff to the side.

"But you don't know what happened next. McGuire took on a real liability, a guilty conscience." Buck chuckled disparagingly. "Seems he wanted to be more than a delivery boy. Wanted to make more money. So he went to the mountains where everybody knows everybody. Where news gets around. He began to pick up isolated children, latchkey kids with working parents, neglected, that sort of thing."

Buck took another long drag. "McGuire set himself up as a traveling salesman, sold books and asked lots of questions. He had a big territory and was careful. Sold lots of kids. But after a while, he started feeling guilty. Lonely, too. Never had any children himself, not even a wife."

Donny listened with rapt attention. Buck leaned closer to speak in the strictest confidence, blowing a last remnant of smoke into Donny's face. "So he decided not to hand over one of the kids. Locked him up. Kept him for himself."

Donny's eyes widened. "You've got to be kidding. What'd he do with the kid?"

"No telling," Buck said, sneering. "Who cares? But then he made his worst mistake. He started fancying himself a father. He wanted to start a new life and asked us to let him out. He just wanted to go his merry way. We couldn't let him do that, could we?" Buck shot Donny a menacing glare. "So McGuire left the kid and took off, without a trace. We looked for him, but no luck. Till just now."

"How'd you find him?"

"First, he was dumb enough to get picked up by the cops. Then he got really stupid. He blabbed. He was the source that got you arrested."

Donny's eyes flamed in anger. "That son-of-a-bitch."

"We found out through our police grapevine. Easy enough, once he was caught."

Donny slouched down, drooping his shoulders. "So he's in jail."

Buck rocked his head back, laughing uncontrollably. Suddenly he stopped, and his face turned horrid in an evil contortion, his eyes riveted on Donny. "No, you punk." He spewed his words venomously. "He should be so lucky."

"What happened to him?"

Buck's face relaxed, and his words turned nonchalant. "His attorney was pretty clever. Kept McGuire out of jail by coughing up evidence for the feds." Buck scoffed and rubbed his hands together, lustily, up and down in front of his face. "So we had to take care of him."

Donny slid the sleeve of his jacket up his beefy forearm, exposing a heart-shaped tattoo, then clenched his fist tighter and tighter. The tattoo fluttered as the muscle of his forearm flexed.

"Seems he met with a mysterious accident." Buck paused to search Donny's eyes. "Fell out the window of a hotel; poor bastard broke his neck."

Donny spoke calmly, respectfully. "You won't have to worry about me. I don't know anything. You understand, don't you? I'll disappear like the wind."

Buck pulled an envelope out of his jacket pocket and handed it to Donny, who grabbed it greedily. Then Buck rose, without speaking, and walked across the plaza, past a bench where a tall young man with black unruly hair, dressed casually in faded jeans and sweatshirt, read a newspaper. The man cut his eyes at Buck's back and stood. He folded his newspaper offhandedly, tossing it into a trashcan overflowing with discarded soda cans and sandwich wrappers, then shuffled through the debris to pick up Buck's pace, following a safe distance behind.

# The Endless Wait

## Chapter 31

Buck whipped his Land Rover past a sixteen-wheeler in the driving rain, swamping his windshield with its splatter. Williams followed two cars behind, cursing the downpour, the bane of an investigator shadowing a suspect. The rain enhanced his cover, but obscured his target.

"Buck's an aggressive driver," Williams commented, without surprise, to his partner, Phil, who sat beside him, half-dozing, his bushy hair in disarray, helter-skelter against the backrest. "Granted, he's more accustomed to a luxury ride in the back seat, where he can nip a few and not worry about the road. He leaves that chore to his chauffeur. You know the guy—looks more like a bodyguard, actually. But Buck is definitely the nervous type, impatient. Keeps him moving fast."

As they neared Atlanta, the lanes on the interstate expanded and Buck zigzagged the highway like a slinky, the slightest movement in the front traffic prompting him to react with a decisive lane swing, erratic and difficult to pace. Once in the city, traffic slowed considerably, and Williams was able to stay two to three cars behind, sighting him easily. They drove out of the rain as Buck took an exit off the freeway within the downtown limits, at a slower pace now, forcing Williams to follow with no cars in-between.

A few blocks later Buck turned onto a short street of Victorian homes, historic relics that had survived Sherman's onslaught. He slowed to a halt at the curb of a stately three-story dwelling, with generous balconies and abundant gingerbread, its white trim a doily against the deep teal exterior. Buck climbed the front steps and, not stopping to ring the bell, barged in the double entry doors.

Williams parked at the curb, one block away. He sat in silence for a few minutes before speaking. "This is the part that I detest, the endless wait."

Phil looked out the window, his eyes intent on the row of decorative homes. "I get itchy, myself, sometimes. But all it gets me is chewed-up fingernails."

"When I was younger," Williams said, "somehow I was less restless. Doesn't figure, does it? I could just sit back and wait, stalk a quarry forever, carefully. I'd watch and analyze his every move." Williams rearranged his body, shifting his buttocks to a more comfortable position behind the steering wheel. "That's not me anymore, just a ghost of my past. Now I have to hold back, to keep myself from closing in too early. I get impatient."

Phil nodded. "Part of the job description, I guess."

"But, you know," Williams said, gripping the steering wheel, "this case really has me captive. I'm obsessed with finding Chris Rath and putting his kidnapper away." His voice was alive with passion. "I'd give anything to see the joy on his mother's face. She's a sweetheart, that Diane."

He bit his lower lip, gnawing it hungrily. "My career's getting old, just like me. I'd like to have this one to remember in my retirement chair, to tell my grandchildren—to feel good about myself. Yeah, it's been a long career. Guess I'm not proud of it all."

Suddenly distracted, he alerted his partner, "Wait a minute." A car pulled up in front of the Victorian house—a Lincoln Town Car, jet black with polished chrome—and four figures emerged. "Maybe we've got something."

With his baseball cap tilted, Williams viewed surreptitiously through his binoculars. "A man, maybe sixty, Hispanic," he noted. Williams had an eye trained for detail. "Short thick frame, cheeks stubbled, wearing relaxed dress pants, good cut with starched white shirt, open at the collar. He's holding onto the arm of a woman, elegant, Hispanic too, slick dark hair in a bun, a long flowing jersey dress and high heels, heavy jewelry, gold chains around her neck and wrists."

Two tall men, both muscular, costumed twins with black pants and shiny black shirts, followed close behind.

"Two goons, probably bodyguards." The group disappeared through the double doors with stained-glass insets.

Williams panned his binoculars across the front lawn and focused on the unique mailbox, a replica of the Victorian home, exact to the colors and exterior trim. Under the street numbers the name *DuRoy* was etched in decorative gothic script. "*DuRoy* mean anything to you?"

"Jesus Christ," Phil answered, bolting upright. "A guy named DuRoy was one of Donny's contacts. Our guy tailed him home. Must have been the same house."

"I'll check with downtown," Williams said, as he picked up his phone and hit speed-dial. After a short conversation with the precinct, he confirmed, "Yep, one and the same."

"I'll be damned," Phil said, whistling. "We've killed two birds with one stone." His face came alive with enthusiasm.

The guy's actually handsome, Williams thought, but you'd never notice, not with that dumb, blank mask he wears, a real poker face. Closest thing to a zombie, walking. "And I thought tailing Buck was just a shot in the dark. Funny, we may have another shadow parked on this same street, watching DuRoy." Williams eyed the curb. "Probably wondering who the hell we are. Anyway, why don't you get some shuteye," he offered. "I'll hold the fort."

Williams passed the time listening to the banter of two disc jockeys on a local station, mocking politicians, making innuendoes about the primitive state of Georgia, ridiculing rednecks—crass jokes, but funny enough to hold his interest.

More movement at the front door, first the goons, then the handsome Hispanic couple, and a short man's body, bending down, blocking part of the doorway. Williams adjusted his binoculars, but the Hispanic man was in the way. The short man held out his hand, powdery white, and a small plump arm reached up to grasp it.

"Wake up," Williams said, nudging his partner. "We've got some new players. One's a child—a Caucasian boy, I think; looks about five years old." The boy's head was down, shielding his face. Williams passed the binoculars to Phil and grabbed his camera, zooming it toward the porch. He snapped the short man, as he waved a cursory good-bye, and, as the rest of the group walked down the steps, he clicked just as the boy looked up. "Got him, dead center."

Williams photographed them all, punching the automatic feed, playing every angle. The Hispanic couple got into the back seat with the boy, and the goons got in the front, one hulking figure to each door. "Might be nothing, but I have a feeling we should follow them," he said, starting the engine just as their quarry took off. "Besides, there's another tail on this DuRoy guy. Call downtown and get somebody here pronto to cover Buck."

They followed the Lincoln at a brisk pace to the freeway, then off the airport exit to the domestic terminal, where the driver stopped to unload his entourage. One goon opened the trunk to help with the luggage, and the group rushed inside, leaving the other bodyguard to make arrangements with the skycap. A few cars behind, Williams stopped and bolted from the car, grabbing his briefcase from the back seat in an attempt to resemble a traveler. Quickly making his way to the skycap's stand, he stood at attention and appeared to be waiting, although another attendant was idle nearby.

The skycap, with a face light brown like wheatbread, rapped out the essential details. "Miami connection . . . five bags," he said, holding up five fingers. "Three passengers . . ." he added, staccato style, now touching pinkie finger to thumb, like a Boy Scout pledging, "ultimate destination . . . San José, Costa Rica." His tone was friendly. "That's s'posed to be one beautiful city, suh." The goon grunted and hurried through the rejoining double doors.

⌐

Rain pelted the windows of the cottage that morning. Diane stared with awe at the fearsome wind, rippling the wide green leaves of a banana plant as if it were tissue paper. Gusting against the native palms, relentless, it whipped the lower fronds—brown with age, some seven feet long—from their tall arched trunks, tossing them like autumn leaves from a tree. Diane heard the phone through the whistling of the wind and the banging of shutters against the stucco.

"Hi, hon. There's been a, uh, development." Mel paused, and she understood his caution. He was hedging his words, being careful. "It sounds good. Maybe what we've been waiting for."

"What?" Suddenly breathless, Diane placed her hand on her heart, feeling it quicken its beat.

"I'll come home. If the rain stops, meet me outside."

"Hurry, darling."

The rain slowed to a drizzle, and she waited under the front eave until she saw the car. She stepped into the driveway, turned up her palm to check for rain and saw that it had stopped, although the air was heavy with mist. The wind bombarded her face with long strands of reddish-brown curls. Diane cupped her forehead in her hands, protecting her eyes from the whipping. She rushed to Mel to grab his hand, leading him over the dune to the beach.

Mel didn't wait for her questions. He shared his news as they walked, pushing his words through the wind. "Detective Williams signaled me to call him, through Dr. Bozeman, so I went to the office next door. He answered right away. Said he had an unbelievable breakthrough, more incredible than he could have imagined. He started filling me in on a few background details to get to the main point. Said that the child-smuggling sting, the one you helped with, led them to other suspects—one, an aircraft parts magnate from Athens, Georgia." He stopped to face her, planting his palms on her shoulders. "Guy named Buck Stanley. Can you believe it?"

"Buck Stanley is a child smuggler?" She was incredulous. "Not that I'd put anything past him." The drizzle began again, and the wind blustered, gusting rain into their faces. Diane saluted her eyes with both hands, holding off the rain, and, by habit, stared out at the Gulf.

"Or, at least, a strong suspect," Mel said. "But even more interesting, the trail led to his half-brother, good old Lafayette DuRoy. He's already been apprehended. The whole thing's too much to take. When Williams found out that we knew these two, he started looking for a connection.

Too coincidental, he said. You know he has a nose for these things. And he's tenacious. If there *is* a connection, you can bet your boots he'll find it."

Shaken, suddenly feeling faint, Diane braced herself against Mel. Rain dribbled down the trenches of his cheeks. "There's more. Williams tailed Buck Stanley to DuRoy's place in Atlanta and saw some Hispanic visitors. They traveled yesterday with a small child to San José, Costa Rica. Williams had a hunch, and it paid off."

"But what about them? What paid off?" Diane was confused. "Does Steve think there's a connection to Chris?"

"He decided to bring DuRoy in for questioning. Sounds like he spilled his guts." Diane smiled, remembering DuRoy's weak deposition. "But the important thing is that . . ." Mel's voice cracked, "honey, we may have a lead on Chris."

Diane broke in. "Mel, please. What lead?"

"It might be good news." Mel spoke with caution. "DuRoy isn't a big player, according to Williams, but apparently he has dealt with the upper echelon of this international child-smuggling cartel. DuRoy dropped some information about an American boy, about eight years old, who's been reared in Costa Rica as a companion to the son of a cartel boss, apparently to teach his son English and the ways of America. Williams thinks it's possible that the boy is Chris. McGuire could have kidnapped him and passed him along to the cartel, for that very purpose—a requisition of sorts."

"You mean, steal a child to fill an order?"

"I know it sounds cruel."

"But why Chris?"

"McGuire preyed on kids in that part of North Carolina, especially in isolated areas. After all, he took John under similar circumstances, only a few miles away. But, honey, it may mean Chris is alive."

Diane began to tremble. "And well. Not hurt or abused. Oh God, my heart is pumping."

Mel cradled her head in his hands and, with his thumbs, wiped the rain from her brows. "Williams wants you to travel with him to Costa Rica. With the two of you, posing as a couple, he'll have greater access, a better cover with less suspicion, and he wants you there when they find the child, in case it's Chris."

"I've got to sit down." Diane fell to the ground, mindless of the rough shells on her bare legs. She stared blankly out to sea and started to cry. "Oh God, if only it could be. Please, God." Suddenly, her voice returned to full strength with renewed determination, as if she'd shaken her own shoulders to calm herself, to invoke action. "What do I need to do? Where do I meet Williams?"

"He's leaving for Miami tomorrow and will meet you at the airport at three o'clock in the afternoon. His precinct has arranged a flight for you, so you'll need to get packed tonight. Weather's pretty fair in Costa Rica year round, Williams said, but take a light jacket for the evenings."

Mel stopped his directives and tugged at her hands to help her rise. Whispering softly, "I love you," he gently pulled her toward him, and she wrapped her arms under his, around his back, his strong chest against her.

"I love you, too," she gasped, her breath caught in the embrace. "I'll go start packing." She turned to run for the house, the back of her legs speckled with shells and her heels kicking up a path of dark sand, clumped by the rain.

# The Fresh Night

## Chapter 32

Mel cast into the surf, disturbing a snowy egret poised to fish, its long ungainly beak inches from the water, a trap ready to spring. Diane stood still, observing the egret. This is the bird a graphic artist might invent—bold color accents and sleek design that appeared, in flight, to have escaped from his drawing pad, flapping away. Nature had painted the bird perfectly with snowy white feathers, stick legs of coal black with matching beak. A bright yellow patch, splotching the base of the beak, encircled the beady eyes like a mask and balanced its gaudy yellow boots. The egret scurried away on rickety legs, its head hunkered down, bobbing back and forth on a rigid neck.

The egret is awkward on land, she thought, but graceful in flight—streamlined for a single challenging environ, like so many of God's creatures. Seals waddle laboriously in slow motion across the rocks, but glide gracefully through water. Pelicans stumble along the beach on clumsy legs and flat webbed feet, but soar majestically through the air.

Diane felt like a fish out of water herself. She had bumbled into a world that she didn't know—an unfamiliar world, filled with unknowns—and she was afraid. She imagined that tomorrow's intrigue, traveling with Steve to Costa Rica, would be fraught with danger. She trusted him and knew that he would do anything to keep her safe, but she didn't trust the circumstances. The thought of Chris fueled her fears. What danger might he be in? But be calm, she told herself. Embrace the fresh hope that he is alive. She prayed that the gentle roll of the sea would ease her turmoil inside.

Diane started down the beach and began to spout poetry, as she often did—an English major's mastery of rhyme to match the moment. She wanted to be caught up in the cadence, lost in the rhythm. She marched with swinging arms, faster and faster, drowning her fears in meaningless words, the beat synchronized with that of her heart.

> *Fat black bucks in a wine-barrel room,*
> *Barrel-house kings, with feet unstable,*
> *Sagged and reeled and pounded on the table,*
> *Pounded on the table—*

Breakneck speed now, as the words, absurd rote words, drummed thoughts from her head, and the steady beat stomped away her fears.

> *Beat an empty barrel with the handle of*
> *    a broom,*
> *Hard as they were able,*
> *Boom, boom, BOOM.\**

Mel gave up on fishing and ran to catch up. "Slow down, Diane."

She halted, suddenly frozen with her arms in a catatonic swing, like a toy soldier abandoned in the sand. She turned to him, stunned. "Sorry. I was lost in my thoughts."

"More like, trying to outrun them. Can't you come up with something more mellow?"

"Okay," she said, reciting under her breath, practicing. "How about your favorite?" She sometimes recited this, walking home from Lou's Beach House in the moonlight. She began softly in a melancholy voice.

> *The wind was a torrent of darkness among*
> *    the gusty trees,*
> *The moon was a ghostly galleon tossed*
> *    upon cloudy seas,*
> *The road was a ribbon of moonlight*
> *    over the purple moor—*

---

\* *The Congo*, by Vachel Lindsay

Mel joined in the chorus. Now he's out of *his* element, Diane thought, smiling. Math major in poetry class.

> *And the highwayman came riding—*
> *Riding—riding—*
> *The highwayman came riding,*
> *Up to the old inn-door.**

They held hands, matching steps, as they sounded the words together. Approaching the deserted pass Diane heard a flurry of leaves in the seagrape bushes. Or was it in the mangroves on the bay beyond?

"Probably a raccoon," Mel said.

Diane turned but saw no movement—only an osprey, its head a shock of white, perched on a stark tree stalk. She heard a muffled blast and felt something whiz by.

Another blast. Mel instinctively threw her to the ground and fell on top of her. They crouched, using a bank of sand, built up from high tide, for cover. Her eyes searched the seagrapes, and she detected a figure, motionless in the rust of the fallen seagrape leaves.

"There, in the bushes," she pointed. They were totally exposed on the barren beach. "Let's run back toward home. Can't go south," she said, eyeing the abandoned pass, where there would be no escape except to swim the treacherous waters. "We'd get cornered."

Mel grabbed her hand and whispered, "Let's go." He darted for the seagrapes' protection, into the shadows. Another shot fired as they ran, and they ducked their heads low.

As they reached the seagrapes, she tripped on a railroad vine, landing on a prickly blanket of Australian pine cones. Mel stopped and reached down, tugging on her hands to help her rise. "Damn," she whispered as she rubbed her bleeding forearm, scraped by the fall.

And then, a familiar Southern drawl. "Not so fast. What's your rush?"

---

* *The Highwayman*, by Alfred Noyes

They turned to face Buck Stanley, clutching a handgun dangled toward the ground.

"What are you doing here?" Mel asked. Diane felt her knees buckle.

"Just looking for you, Mel. Thought you'd be alone. Sorry, Diane. I really don't have any argument with you." Buck surveyed the woods and the deserted beach. "Not a soul within screaming distance," he sneered, a smug hunter staring down his helpless prey.

"What do you want with me? I thought we'd settled our differences."

"Oh no, not all of them. There's one little matter still." Buck's voice deepened with the threat. He toyed with the gun, fingering it at his waist with both hands, pointing its barrel casually in Mel's direction.

"What little matter? I don't know what you're talking about."

"We want to help," Diane pled, her voice steady despite trembling lips. "We just don't know what you're talking about."

"Your husband's screwed me over more than once. First, he stole my money in that worthless lawsuit. And now, he's got your foster son telling lies about me. Serious lies." Buck raised the gun, pointing it directly at Mel's chest. "I can't allow that."

"I believe you've got things wrong, Buck." Mel held both palms forward, as if slowing down traffic.

Diane spoke louder, desperation in her voice. "Our foster son hasn't said anything to hurt you."

"Besides," Mel added in a clear, strong voice, "what could John say? He doesn't even know you."

"Clever, Mel, but don't pull that bullshit with me. It's over."

Diane saw Mel's face turn white, and she screamed as a gunshot pierced the night. Buck ducked his head and scurried into the seagrape thicket, running through the crusty fallen leaves.

Mel pivoted, and Diane searched his body for blood, astonished that he was unhurt. She saw a figure heading for them. "Run," she yelled, frightened beyond her wits, wanting to escape whatever underworld botchery they faced next.

"Wait, Mr. and Mrs. Rath," the man called out. "It's okay. You're safe. I'm Steve Williams' partner." The stranger rushed over, panting. "He has me following Buck Stanley. We've been tailing him for a couple of weeks."

"Good thing," Mel said, catching his breath.

"Yes," Diane agreed, collapsing on the cool sand, damp in the fresh night. She looked up at the face of the tall man, at his bushy black hair, wild in the wind. "Thanks," she said simply.

"Anytime, ma'am. Now I'll see if I can catch up with our friend." He snapped his gun in a holster and bolted up the beach, protecting his face with his hands as he entered a stand of seagrapes.

# A Country of Welcoming Smiles

## Chapter 33

Waiting at the exit gate in the Miami airport, Detective Williams waved as Diane left the baggage claim area. "Hello," he called, running to give her a hug, as any dutiful husband might. He took over the luggage cart she was wheeling and whispered when he had her close, "Your name is Diane Williams, and you're traveling as my wife. I have your passport and ticket ready. I'll handle customs. Just remember, for pete's sake, to respond when someone calls you Mrs. Williams."

Joking nervously, she replied, "Well, dear, I always had a thing for you."

He reddened as he took her arm and nudged her toward the right passage. "My pleasure. This is an old man's fantasy come true."

They hurried along, their light repartee shadowing the serious task at hand, another leg in a long and rigorous journey.

Stiff winds ruffled the national flag of Costa Rica, waving welcome to passengers arriving at the San José airport. Detective Williams hailed a taxi that drove them past the sparse outskirts of the city, then through back alleys piled with fruits and vegetables, mounds of raw yellows, glistening reds and purples, decaying browns, colors blending on a sidewalk palette. Flies buzzed, touching down on their prey, darting unsated to riper pap. Workers, patrons, and passersby milled about, kneeling, lolling, gossiping, children rolling balls of fruit, adults propping their feet on the produce, one sitting on a fresh melon to rest, holding his hands to the ground for balance.

The taxi entered the hub of downtown San José, with broad avenues and handsome shops—a modern city, brisk and clean. The sidewalks were crowded with well-dressed men and women, clicking along purposefully, eyes intent, caught in the urban rush. The taxi stopped at a hotel, enveloped by a long row of multi-storied buildings, the ground floor façades boasting elegant restaurants, salons, and banks. Across the main avenue was a city park, bursting with flowers, and the driver pointed with pride to an architectural treasure, which echoed in design the Grand Opera House in Paris. "National Theatre, *senor.*"

The hotel lobby was impeccably modern, its modest furniture arranged in neat rows as in a government waiting room. The concierge, practiced in cordiality, called out from his slick Formica counter. "You Americans must visit the casino on the top floor. It stays open all night with complimentary drinks, a pleasure for our guests."

The taxi driver had exhibited the same gracious warmth, Diane remembered. She felt at ease in this country of welcoming smiles.

Williams had briefed Diane on the plane, outlining their mission, frightening her even more. The plan bordered on danger, as she had suspected, but she would undertake any risk for word of Chris. Now there was a chance that he was alive, within reach. What if he were injured in the rescue—if, in her attempt to save him, she lost him once again? She tried not to think ahead, to concentrate on the task at hand.

For the cartel's benefit they were posing as potential adoptive parents, a plan set into place with the aid of DuRoy, as part of his plea. The FBI had arranged their accommodations through a trusted travel agent in Atlanta, but word spread fast in Costa Rica, with only one metropolitan center where much of the country's population gravitated on a business day. They couldn't be too careful, Williams said. For final details, he had set up a meeting the following day with Costa Rica's highest ranking law enforcement officer, who had guaranteed that, to avoid leaks, no politicians or government officials would be informed of the true nature of their visit.

The bellhop, half the size of Williams, insistently carried the luggage all at once, straining, and looked anxiously for approval as he leaned over to set the suitcases down, one shoulder bag toppling to the floor. As Williams handed the bellhop change from the taxi, he called across the room, "Is the suite okay, hon?" He had warned Diane of surveillance, possibly wiring, even in the hotel. "I had the travel agent book separate bedrooms, so I won't keep you up with my snoring," he said, winking.

At dinner Diane begged him for more information on DuRoy's report of an American boy growing up in Costa Rica. Williams had ordered a thick steak, which he was cutting into large pieces and chewing deliberately. His jaw wound down, as he finished each bite, then swallowed with a gulp of cold beer.

"According to DuRoy, the boy lives on the family estate of a prominent cartel boss, here in San José. Apparently, the boy is companion to a son, who is about the same age—eight or nine, DuRoy thought."

"Does the boy appear to be treated well? In good health?"

"We think so. The local authorities have observed the boy leaving the grounds, always trailing the family core. If there had been any signs of abuse, they probably would have stepped in."

Diane knew that "stepping in" would be dangerous, in the face of a ruthless cartel. Williams was trying to protect her, to allay her concern. "Why Costa Rica?"

"The cartel boss wants to avoid the front lines, to keep his family a safe distance from Colombia."

"Steve, what if we do find Chris, right on the estate? I know he'll recognize me, his own mother. He'll run to me or cry out or react in some way. What then?"

"A good point, Diane. I plan to go over several different scenarios after dinner." Williams returned his attention, with obvious relish, to his food and drink.

"But what if something happens to Chris?" Feeling distraught and helpless, she fired questions at Williams. "We can't let him get hurt. What will we do?"

Williams held up his hands in self-defense, as if she were raining blows, not questions, upon him. "Hold on, Diane. I'll tell you," he said, shaking her shoulder and pointing discreetly to a nearby table where a dark-skinned woman with gray hair had lowered her glasses to stare at them, a schoolmarm's stern disapproval at commotion in her classroom. "You're asking for it, you know. I'll brief you till it's running out your ears. You'll beg for mercy. But calm down, and I'll tell you the plan."

He leaned close to her ear. "If we are successful in finding Chris, you must stay composed, speak to him softly. Try to get him away from other people; take his hand gently and walk away. Don't be disturbed, or surprised, if he doesn't recognize you at first, or if he shies away."

"Impossible."

"No, Diane, entirely possible, with a kidnap victim who has suffered from shock. But talk to him calmly, try to soothe him, tell him who you are, or that you know his real family in America, or that you want him to meet a new friend—whatever. Anything to draw him away from other people.

"If he recognizes you immediately or runs to hug you, shouts out 'Mom' or starts to cry, greet him affectionately and comment, as if he's confused, 'What a lovely, friendly child,' or some such, just to give me a few seconds to intervene. If he freaks, or gets close to you, hold him in your arms, just enfold him, and call for me loudly. I'll be right there. I'll take care of the rest."

"But you're only one person. And this is a cartel! They'll have guns."

"We'll have back-up. A local swat team will penetrate the grounds while we're there." He looked down at her fidgety hands, the cuticles red and swollen. One hand tore at the other, the thumb and forefinger nails tweezing and pinching and pulling away skin.

With his grandfatherly hands, he separated hers and chided, "Don't. Don't do that to yourself." His hands were gentle, despite the calluses, and his eyes looked deep into her soul. "You can do this, Diane. We'll get Chris home."

The next morning they drove to the briefing site—Poas, a towering volcano with a mile-wide crater, less than an hour outside San José. Diane lost herself in the beauty of the countryside—coffee plantations set in the rolling hills, undulating verdant rows, vibrant swirls of color, thick textures of green and gold. Although the temperature was comfortable, the roads were dry, and their rental car was not air-conditioned. They stopped at a lone grocery stand, a one-room lean-to beside the road with a bench outside, only a few feet from a field of coffee plants. The breeze was lovely, and Diane's curls tossed in the wind as she drank soda from a bottle, resting her feet beside her on the bench. She felt peaceful here. Perhaps a good omen, she thought.

The volume and size of the vegetation stupefied her, as the winding road led up to the volcano. Florida was wild and proliferous, but this garden of giant greenery was uncanny, almost frightening. Huge elephant-ear plants, which would dwarf their zoological counterpart, edged the road. Tree trunks entwined into thick masses, a dark jungle shadowed by the tall foliage. Shoulder-high ferns, heavy green fans, weighted their tall stalks to the ground.

They stepped out from the car into thick humidity. The mist dampened Diane's hair and face as if she'd freshly showered. Williams led her through a guest museum, past a counter of information pamphlets and a relief map, walls of glassed-in charts and photographs, into a back room.

A dark gentleman, dressed in a white ribbed overshirt and khaki pants, looked up from his newspaper as they entered. His thin lips curled into a smile, stark-white teeth flickering, as he rose to deliver a brisk greeting. "Detective Williams? I am Officer Medina. And this is Mrs. Rath, yes? Please sit down." He gestured to two wicker bucket chairs facing his desk.

Settling back behind the desk, Officer Medina busily folded his newspaper and set it aside. "We are quite safe here, and private. You can speak plainly." His speech was polished, and he spoke with little accent. Perhaps he learned English in a British school, Diane thought.

Medina fleshed out the *modus operandi*. Until this moment, Diane had been privy to only the skeletal details. Williams had bolstered her courage the night before, after dinner, as they sat in a park square opposite the hotel, role-playing different courses that the ultimate confrontation might take. She felt prepared, more confident, but her heart was racing.

"Because of the high price you are offering for a child—seventy-five thousand dollars is exorbitantly higher than the going rate—you will be treated as royalty. Customarily the cartel boss would not allow business on home base, but he has conceded because of the unusual adoption fee. We set up the contact through our most reliable stoolie, who will drive you to one of Costa Rica's grandest estates to meet a potential adoptee. The baby dealers— or 'adoption service,' as they prefer—have assured that they will produce the 'finest of their inventory'—an infant of Caucasian and Hispanic mix, of good intelligent stock. If you approve the 'merchandise,' the child is to be appropriated, and the transaction, consummated.

"My most trusted men will cover those grounds, like, how you say, a blanket. You will be most safe."

# Child of Joy

## Chapter 34

Diane nervously fingered a pearl button at the neckline of her silk dress, as she waited with Detective Williams in the hotel lobby. She watched his glossy black shoes as they clicked on the checkerboard tile floor, pacing back and forth, until she began to feel dizzy, as if she were a child again, hands held tight with a playmate, arms taut, head back, spinning until the world became a streak of colors, a single line of motion. Unlike the complex, threatening world she faced today. And her nervous knight seemed to have a chink in his armor.

"Come sit down, Steve. Rest your weary bones."

"They're not weary," he said, throwing a confident wink her way, still pacing. "I'm just warming them up."

The stoolie, in a chauffeur's uniform issued for the occasion, pulled up in a shiny sedan and greeted them with a great show of civility. "Good morning, Mr. and Mrs. Williams. I trust you have rested well in our humble country." He attended Diane like a fragile flower, as she climbed into the sedan, holding her arm gently so as not to break the stem, carefully smoothing her skirt so as not to crush the blossom. He drove only a few blocks before they entered a wealthy residential section with homes of estate dimension, most surrounded by walls or fences, camouflaged in thick shrubbery. The styles of the homes varied—some modern, others Spanish colonial—but the colors were compatible, all white or pastel. The landscaping was lush and trimmed to a fault, manicured meticulously by the groundskeepers at work in the gardens.

They drove through an impressive iron gate and down a long driveway lined with stands of bougainvillea. A concrete wall, five-feet tall, grandly defined the perimeter of the estate, although a barbed-wire extension around the crown turned it unfriendly, forbidding. It was painted white to match the two-story main house with stuccoed wings sprawling outward. A thick, tall hedge of Surinam cherry, cut flat as Formica across the top, encased the pool area protectively.

Three acres of impeccable grounds enveloped the stately San José mansion. The lawn was endless, punctuated with tiny gardens of intricate plantings, set into colorful flowered patterns, with large expanses of green between them.

"Guess I should have brought my putter," Williams cracked. "Looks like one giant green."

The car stopped under an imperious portico, its red barrel-tile roof protecting from the weather a vintage Rolls Royce of two tones, taupe and cream. Decorative iron gates with ornate grillwork led into the entry hall. The driver jumped out of the car solicitously to open Diane's door and to help her up the front steps, holding out his arm in a triangle to cushion her hand. A butler appeared to usher them in.

Diane felt completely vulnerable. Costa Rica was noted for its neutrality, a peaceful country with a reputed lack of crime, yet she was walking into the home of a ruthless criminal. Steve had instructed her to appear calm. Nervous eyes were giveaways to professionals, he said. She could exhibit excitement, which was to be expected, but not fear. A tall order.

The butler led them to a gracious open terrace, with a floor of coarse Mexican tile and decoratively molded terra-cotta planters, spaced evenly in an elegant border. He motioned that they should take a seat and walked away with a dignified carriage, holding his shoulders high. She heard the sound of children's voices, speaking in English and then Spanish, laughing, playing.

"Enrique, Enrique, *alto!*" She saw two boys playing in the pool, the darker pleading for mercy, begging his taller companion to stop a ferocious barrage of water. The taller boy's head was capped with curly blond hair. His hands skimmed the pool surface, spouting water against the face of the other.

"Then speak English, José, like I said." Enrique stopped but hunkered in the water, his hands held up flat to protect his face, in case his companion decided to retaliate.

Diane gasped, mesmerized.

"What is it?" Williams asked, searching her face. But she just stared at the boys in the distance and shushed him with a finger pointed to her lip.

"*Esta bien,*" José agreed, then ranted in Spanish, at the same time attacking his friend with a force of water into his face.

Enrique rared up high in the water and landed on his playmate, gripping his neck in a full nelson and dipping him into the pool. They burst through the water with a huge splash.

"I'll get you." José's threat came out garbled.

Enrique laughed, spitting out water. "Well, at least you're speaking English." He gave one last playful splash for good measure.

"Boys, boys," a young Hispanic lady, with a sheer apron of crisp lace at her waist, called from the terrace. "It's time for your English lesson." The tip of her forefingers rapped the palm of her other hand in short claps, tapping instructions. "Come along, hurry up, now." She was greeted with groans, as if the boys were about to be taken off and beaten.

Diane watched as they got out of the pool, dried off, and put on shirts. "Maybe I can go over and get a better look," she said, imploring with her eyes but speaking softly.

Williams placed his hand on her arm and nodded his head solemnly, up and down. "Just remember what I told you. If it's Chris, stay calm. I'll take care of everything."

She walked down the terrace steps to a bench beside a small garden, in clear sight of the children. Now they were on the lawn, jostling a ball, romping, reminding Diane of Chris and Matt together, so long ago. The light-complexioned boy was much taller. How tall would Chris be now? She couldn't see the boy's face, but she recognized the movement of his head, the way he pulled his tee shirt at the neck to wipe the water from his chin, his crouch to the ground, and quick feet when he kicked the ball. The boy laughed. The sound of Chris' joy, the music of his delight, transporting her to a world she'd lost.

Now the boy turned, and his smile blossomed. Her eyes caressed his pug nose, freckled cheeks, streaked blond hair, which was wet and dripping into his eyes. She moved closer.

His eyes twinkled in the sun, huge gray-green lagoons flecked with brown, large in proportion to his face, which had not lost its angelic roundness. She held her hand to her throat and closed her eyes to keep from bursting into tears.

She called out gently to the boys, walking slowly toward them. The blond boy looked her way, and his sparkling eyes locked into hers. He stood perfectly still, paralyzed.

"What is it?" his companion asked. "Come on, let's go to lessons."

"Go on ahead. I'll be right there." His eyes remained on Diane, his feet anchored, stock-still as a well-trained soldier, his face white, shaken. "Vamoose!" he yelled to his friend, who took off for the house, running.

He walked slowly, timidly, toward her, and their eyes embraced. So softly she could barely hear, he said, "Mommy? Is it Mommy?" and he burst into tears, falling to clutch her knees desperately.

She knelt and grabbed his shoulders, pulling him to her, holding him close. "Chris, you're safe."

"Mommy, they said you were dead." His sobs were uncontrollable, his small body shaking in her arms. "You're not dead, are you?"

"No, son, I'm here, I'm alive. We're all alive—Daddy and Matt and me—and you're coming home." She was crying too, in shock and disbelief and outlandish joy. She wiped her eyes on Chris' shoulder, smearing mascara on his shirt.

"Diane." A voice called out her name. She turned quickly in its direction, surveying a tall cherry hedge, just as Buck Stanley leapt out.

"So here you are. I didn't give your Boy Scout detective

enough credit."

She tightened her grip around Chris.

"Enrique!" The cry came from the terrace. She looked up and saw Williams at work on a Hispanic woman, elegant, with slick black hair swept into a bun. He wrapped her arms behind her, snapping handcuffs into place.

Time seemed to stand still.

Buck pulled a handgun from behind his back and pointed it at her, moving closer. "Don't make a sound, or your little boy's history."

She looked desperately toward Williams, but he was tackling a massive bodyguard to the floor of the terrace. Buck grabbed her hand and pointed toward the hedge, motioning with the barrel of his gun. "Come on, move. You too, kid."

She dragged her feet, glancing back desperately at the house, but he pushed her roughly behind the hedge. "Don't think I won't shoot you, and blow this kid away. *Move*, I said!"

When she tried to pull away, he slammed the butt of his gun into the back of her head, and she staggered, her legs weakening under her. Chris began to cry and put his arms under her shoulders, trying to support her weight. Buck pulled him away and kicked Diane, who moaned as she fell to the ground. He picked up Chris, kicking and screaming, squirming to get free. Buck stopped suddenly and slapped him hard with the back of his hand, then bolted for a car parked just beyond the pool.

Diane struggled to her feet and began to run after Buck, her legs wobbling as she looked back toward the house for help. "Steve! Steve!" she shouted, at the same moment spotting a shiny sedan speeding over the lawn, rutting the perfect green, past the pool toward Buck.

She yelled at the top of her lungs. "He's got Chris! Be careful!"

Williams screeched to a halt, almost hitting the front bumper of Buck's car. Buck held Chris in front of him like a shield, as he opened the door to the driver's seat. "Don't move, you idiot," he said, taunting Williams, "if you want to keep the kid alive."

Williams jumped out of his car, with his hands held high. "Whatever you say, Buck." The detective backed up slowly, his hands in clear view, as he spoke calmly, respectfully. "We'll let you get away. Just go easy on the child."

Buck shoved Chris roughly inside the car, holding his gun steady on Williams. He didn't see Officer Medina, dressed in the sooty black of his swat team, creep up from behind. As he slid backwards into the car, fighting Chris off with his elbow, a gunshot rang out. Buck's gun went off reactively, without direction. The bullet hit a tree limb above, which split off and fell with a crash.

Buck grabbed for his side, blood spurting through his fingers as he crumpled to the ground. Medina walked over and gestured toward the stone-still body, sprawled across the manicured lawn. Blood splotched the brilliant green, red streams trickling, seeping through the grass into the ground, like wine spilled on a plush carpet. "Is he dead?"

Williams knelt beside Buck to test his carotid artery. "Nope, but he's not feeling so good."

"Shouldn't we try to stop the bleeding?"

"If you insist," Williams agreed, searching his back pocket for a handkerchief to compress the wound. "Better call an ambulance."

Diane rushed to the open car door, high stepping over Buck's body like a drum major. She slid onto the seat, propping her legs against the ground. Her hair was matted with blood. She grasped Chris, holding him tightly as she wiped his tears.

The grounds stirred, as Medina's team swept the estate. A policeman jumped from behind a tall hedge to tackle the butler to the grass. Another pulled his revolver on two maids, running down the long driveway until he motioned them back toward the portico.

Diane felt Chris' body relax, and she returned his sweet smile. "Mommy, I'm really going home?"

She buried his face in her breast, cradling him, rocking back and forth. The years slipped back through time, to the freckled cheeks and laughing eyes of a five-year-old boy, stolen from her, so long ago—the face of her child of joy.

"Yes, love, we're going home."

# Part Five

# Epilogue

It was Chris' birthday. In Costa Rica he had celebrated with José, sharing his birthday, since he couldn't remember the date of his own. Matt and John promised not to pick on him all day, as a special present. "Fat chance," he said.

Diane baked a yellow layer cake, which came out lopsided. She tried to camouflage its shape with thick chocolate icing, but some of the edges tore off as she smeared.

Chris licked the spoon and left chocolate smudges on his freckled nose, grinning. "I can't believe I'm nine years old."

"Yep, you're getting tall, too. I'm afraid to blink; you'll be a teenager," she said, wiping the tip of his nose with the dishcloth. "Now, let's go out to the beach and wait for our special guest."

She sat down on the sand, and Chris romped with Hounder in the surf, splashing wildly, spattering milky sprays. Mel, who had waded out to a sand flat, cast out his line, freshly baited with a pilchard he had netted that morning. Matt and John lolled on plastic floats, their arms and legs sprawled out, looking like giant turtles overturned in the water.

Diane hadn't seen Steve Williams since they'd parted at the airport in San José. He had been forced to stay behind, to finish up paperwork with the local authorities. She remembered hugging him so hard that he had to squirm away, embarrassed.

"What's this?" she'd kidded him. "My husband's gone frigid?" He'd broken into a hearty laugh, dropping his stern demeanor, but only for a moment, then walked briskly away, looking back with a last grin and a hasty wave.

Williams was a professional puzzle-solver, but a bit of a mystery himself. He could ramble like a stranger or cut his words short as a reluctant apology. He could be circumspect, analyzing a clue *ad infinitum*, yet act impulsively on the most abstract lead. He percolated with ideas, but stewed in self-doubt. He was tough but flexible, rugged but sympathetic, agile-witted but absent-minded—a mixed bag of gentle and gruff, hard and soft, open and shut. By his very nature he produced friction, always rubbing, but seldom the wrong way. Somehow over the years, she had come to love him like a father.

Williams was retired now. He had called to give her a follow-up on the key players in the cartel. Buck Stanley had recovered from his gunshot wound, attended by the prison physician at Reidsville, where he and his half-brother Laffey sometimes played checkers in the yard. Donny had weaseled his way into a deal, landing in a minimum-security stockade, where he had kowtowed to the guards and now headed up the laundry staff.

Diane curled her toes into the sand, uncovering the dampness beneath, and picked up a snail-shaped gray shell, as glossy as the sun's glitter on a tin roof. "Chris, come here," she called. "A shark's eye."

Chris ran over, his head a tangle of blonde hair, streaked by the Florida sun. "Is it really from a shark?" His eyes grew in wonder.

"No, but it's called that."

He stared into the shaft of the shell, holding it close, looking for the tunneling mollusk. "It's not alive, is it?"

"No. That's why it's here on the beach rather than wallowing on the sand flats. When the animal dies, the shell drifts in from the deep water."

Chris plopped down on the sand beside her, shuffling to get comfortable, leaning on one hand to smooth the rough shells under him. He placed the shark's eye in his palm, fingering its spiral, a pinwheel spinning into a shiny eye. "Amazing. This could have floated in from José's country." His eyes searched the sea. "All the way from Costa Rica."

"Do you think about José much?"

"Not really."

She saw no sadness on his face, as he watched Matt

and John wade into shore, dragging their rafts and beaching them on the sand. Matt picked up a Frisbee and threw it to John in the brisk wind. The Frisbee flew high and skipped across the sand, like a flat rock skimming the water. Chris jumped up to tear after it, and Hounder joined the pursuit, biting into the Frisbee, tugging.

Matt yelled, "Dog fight," and he and John ran over, shouting like banshees. Hounder let loose and barked ferociously, yapping at the circle of boys, playfully nipping at one foot after another, as they hopped in retreat, laughing.

Diane cupped her hands over her ears, which were filled with the wonderful racket. At first she didn't hear Detective Williams call, "Hey, pretty lady." She turned, as he called again, and ran to him, her handshake progressing into a bear hug.

He took in the panorama slowly, his eyes scanning the gentle rolling surf, the endless sky, a pale blue blanket tufted with cottonball clouds, and her family at play. "So this is paradise," he said, smiling.

"Closest thing to," she answered, taking his hand and calling to her sons.

Hounder broke away from the ruckus to chase after a flock of sandpipers, their stick legs whirling as they left the ground, wings flapping and feathers plastered flat in the wind. Chris took off in the sand and ran toward Diane, almost tripping over his own legs.

Williams watched his tanned body fly down the beach. A real Florida boy, healthy and happy—and home. Home at last. He couldn't wait to tell his grandchildren.

Order *A Place to Go Someday*
also by Cleda Hedrich

Give the Gift of *Threat of a Stranger*
to Your Friends and Colleagues

*CHECK YOUR LEADING BOOKSTORE
OR ORDER HERE*

_____ **YES**, I want _____ copies of *A Place to Go Someday* at
$14.95 each, plus $3 shipping per book (Florida residents
please add $.90 sales tax per book).

_____ **YES**, I want _____ copies of *Threat of a Stranger* at
$22.95 each, plus $3 shipping per book (Florida residents
please add $1.38 sales tax per book).

My check or money order for $_____ is enclosed.
(Allow 15 days for delivery. Canadian orders must be
accompanied by a postal money order in U.S. funds.)

Name_____

Address_____

City/State/Zip_____

Phone_____

Please make your check payable and return to:
**NewSouth Books, Inc.**
10911 Bonita Beach Rd., #2073
Bonita Springs, FL 34135
Fax: 941.947.4531
E-mail: NewSouthBooks@yahoo.com